Someone Like Me

By Pam Francis

ISBN-978-0-9957698-0-9

Published by White Cat Books

Cover design by Jessica Bell

DEDICATION

For Mike, Holly, JC, Briana and Amelia

.

SOMEONE LIKE ME

SOMEONE LIKE ME

SOMEONE LIKE ME

ACKNOWLEDGEMENTS

A huge thank you to all those who have played a role in me writing this book. Friends Karen E Lee, Jean Gray, Judith Williams, Steph Evans-Jones, and Wendy Cooper for their encouragement. My friend and chef Alyson Featherstone who inspired Lottie. My daughter Holly and son JC for their love and support. Ann Jaloba (www.annjaloba.com) for her publishing skills. Jessica Bell for the gorgeous cover. Ken Sanders for the lovely garden I write in. Pippa Gearing and Dunstable Rock Choir for helping me sing my way through writer's block. Millie Smith, Julia Abel, Joanna Findlay, and Alyson Pengelly for their feedback. My dear friend June Walton who has never stopped believing in me. All the celebrities I've ever interviewed. And my other half Mike Johnson who has been with me, every step of the way.

1

It never ceases to amaze me how life can change in an instant. One minute you're trundling along thinking 'is this it?' And within a nano-second your destiny has altered beyond belief. This is what happened to me one mediocre Monday morning as I was about to dish up lunch for customers in The Loft.

Me. Charlotte Emily Gilbert, aged 39½, whose only claim to fame until then had been winning a baking competition which resulted in a picture of me and my lemon drizzle cake in the local paper.

The very same Charlotte Emily Gilbert, now shamed on the front page of every tabloid in the land, stalked by the paparazzi and threatened with the most gruesome forms of torture by Twitter trolls. I stood to lose everything I valued and held dear to me. But if you'd warned me on that damp chill September morning, where the fickle finger of fame might be pointing, I would still have ignored you and followed it.

'You will never guess who's just ordered a shepherd's pie,' announced Jess, as she skidded into the kitchen.

'A shepherd? I don't know. Give me a clue,' I said as I carried on stirring the cock-a-leekie soup.

She took a deep breath and whispered loudly: 'Daniel French!' I could feel Jess staring at me and glanced up to be met by dark brown eyes wide with disbelief. 'Daniel French. *The*

Daniel French. The superstar Daniel French. The Daniel French who had a hit with…' and she started to sing his last number one, "My Kind of Woman" very badly.

'Oh, *that* Daniel French,' I said peering out of the serving hatch at a guy in a denim jacket and plaid scarf sitting with his back to the kitchen.

'Why, is there another one?' asked Jess, looking bemused. 'Oh, you're making a joke, sorry. Yeah, he moved into Great Morton a couple of months ago. You know that posh village where footballers live? Morton Manor. Massive house with a swimming pool and tennis courts. And he's got the most gorgeous dark chocolate Labrador called Oscar,' said Jess, who, if she was ever on *Mastermind* would have celebrities as her specialised subject.

'What am I missing?' asked Pat, who had been sitting outside on the iron fire escape steps having a crafty cigarette. The last time a ripple like this went through our kitchen was when Jess spotted the local mayor with a young brunette who clearly wasn't his wife or daughter.

I re-joined Pat at the serving hatch where I could see that the man in the plaid scarf had been joined by another with a mop of curly hair wearing a very dodgy Norwegian-looking jumper.

'What am I supposed to be looking at?' asked Pat, cleaning her glasses on her apron.

'It's Daniel French,' said Jess, squealing with excitement.

'What? *The* Daniel French?' asked Pat, who was leaning so far out of the serving hatch, I had to yank her back in. 'How do you know it's him? It might be one of those lookalikes.'

'He's got the same cool hairstyle,' said Ryan, who had deserted the little musical world he lived in courtesy of his permanent earphones, and joined us.

As if sensing four pairs of eyes on him, the man in question turned round momentarily. Moving as one, we drew back into the kitchen so that he couldn't see us. Not being a huge fan, I'd never spent much time studying Daniel French. Not even when he was in the boy band Three to One. I was much more a Take

That girl. So, I couldn't be a hundred percent sure it was him.

Pat sounded more certain. 'Judging by those yummy mummies gawping on the next table, it's either him or his twin brother.'

Jess looked puzzled. 'I didn't know he had a twin brother. Oh,' she said, checking our faces for clues, 'is that another joke?'

Pat was busily texting. 'My Frank is never going to believe this. Do you think he'll do a selfie with me?'

I opened the oven and slid out the freshly cooked shepherd's pie. 'Look we all need to calm down and get these meals dished up. Even if it is him, he's only a customer like anyone else.'

Jess's voice rose an octave in protest. 'No he's not. He's a megastar. I've just checked and he's got four and a half million followers,' she said, showing me his Twitter profile.

The next thing I knew, Pat had disappeared out of the kitchen and was wiping down the table next to the two men, engaging them in conversation. A few seconds later and she was back.

'It's him! I knew it was. And he says yes he'll do a selfie with me,' she said fishing around in her bag for her mobile phone.

So, Daniel French. What was he doing in my vintage café, of all places? Okay, so The Loft wasn't exactly mine. It belonged to Marsha who owned the antiques emporium, Pandora's Box downstairs. On my way in this morning, she'd stopped me.

'Charlotte, could you re-do the blackboard menu outside when you get a moment?' she'd asked, sounding more annoyed than usual. 'Some smart Alec with a piece of chalk has drawn a rather unfortunate picture next to the cock-a-leekie soup.' I tried to swallow the giggle which was just about to burst forth and put on my serious face. 'Of course Marsha. I'll get onto it.'

'Make sure you do. Pornography gives a very bad impression.' That time I had to disguise my laugh as a cough. If I didn't love my job so much, I'd probably have been out of here months ago. But Pat, Jess, Ryan and me had become like a little family, which was just as well. If not, I don't think we could have coped in a kitchen the size of a cupboard and as hot as a sauna.

'My hands have gone all shaky,' said Pat, giving a little giggle as she hurried out of the kitchen. 'Maybe his friend will take the photo.'

As Daniel French stood up to pose with Pat, I couldn't resist spying through the serving hatch. When he looked straight at me, my stomach did a somersault. What was I feeling so excited about? He was only a guy who had popped in for a bit of lunch. Within seconds the three yummy mummies were on their feet and clamouring for photos.

'Would it be okay to get his autograph for my mum?' asked Ryan, slipping a pad and pen into his pocket.

'I don't see why not,' I said, checking my celebrity customer wasn't being hassled too much by his mini fan club. 'But maybe wait until he's finished eating.'

For the next ten minutes there was frantic activity in the kitchen while we dished up shepherd's pie and peas fit for showbiz royalty. Normally I wouldn't mind if I spotted a splodge or two of gravy on the rim of the plate. But Jess meticulously wiped it clean as she prepared to deliver it to the man himself. His friend – he didn't look like a minder, he was too skinny – had ordered steak and kidney pie and chips which Jess dished up as carefully as if it were caviar. Nothing like a celeb to spice up a dull Monday morning at The Loft. And I must admit, listening to the excited hum of the chat from the café, I was feeling a bit of a buzz myself. It wasn't everyday a superstar walked in to taste my food.

Jess hurried back into the kitchen. 'He wants to see you.'

'Why? Is there something wrong?'

'No, he just said he'd like to meet the chef.'

'You can't go out like that,' said Pat, unknotting the scarf at the back of my neck and releasing my curls which immediately sprung up out of control. With my sleeve, I wiped the steamed-up mirror hanging on a nail. 'I look as if I'm having a hot flush – not that I've ever had one.'

'He probably wants to praise your food, not propose,' said

Pat, sorting me out a clean apron.

'Quick. He'll be gone otherwise,' said Jess virtually pushing me out of the door. Daniel's friend was watching me closely as I tried to sashay nonchalantly across to their table, tripping over a chair leg. He muttered something under his breath, at which point the star himself turned round. The sight of him so close up took my breath away.

There is something about being near to someone who is so famous. Someone you've seen so often on TV or read about in magazines, that you feel you know them, except they don't have a clue you exist. It was probably my imagination, but he seemed to have some sort of aura around him, mixed with intense familiarity.

'Hi, it's Daniel, isn't it?' I said, hearing my voice going all wobbly. What a stupid thing to say. 'I'm Charlotte Gilbert, the chef.'

'Great to meet you Charlotte,' said Daniel holding out his hand. He was certainly a bit gorgeous. Short spiky fair hair and mesmerising green eyes, which gazed at my face, and a three-day beard that gave him that rugged look. It was as if some sort of celebrity spell had been cast over me making me go all gooey. For Heaven's sake, it wasn't as if he was George Clooney. Then I really *would* have been a gibbering wreck. I should have stopped talking there and then but I couldn't. It was as if I had a mission to explain everything I ever said.

'You can call me Lottie. All my friends do. That is, I know we're not friends, but if you'd like to. Lots of people do. Especially the customers, unless they have a complaint, then I'm Charlotte, so...'

'No complaints, so Lottie it is,' he said, gently freeing his hand from my nervous grip.

'So what made you call in at our modest little caff?' Caff? What was wrong with me? I never called it a caff. I was making it sound like a greasy spoon instead of the beautiful old café that it was, with food served on bone china plates. Very boho chic with distressed pine furniture, and rich red brickwork walls decorated with framed Hollywood movie posters.

'I think it was the interesting art work on the blackboard outside,' he said with a totally straight face. Oh heck the rude drawing next to the cock-a-leekie! I'd forgotten to rub it off. Marsha would kill me.

He laughed in a sort of husky sexy way. What a great laugh. A great everything really. He was so relaxed, with a smile that lit up the room and those amazing white teeth that don't come cheap. I loved his Yorkshire accent too. Of course I'd heard him talk before, but in person his Northern pronunciations sounded stronger.

'It was the thought of a home-cooked meal,' he said. 'The sort I wish my mum had cooked me.' His mum? I hoped I didn't remind him of his mum. I wasn't *that* ancient. I was pretty sure he was a bit older than me.

I managed to tear my gaze away from him long enough to be introduced to his personal manager Kevan O'Brien. 'That's Kevan with an A. He's from Dublin,' he said as his friend nodded at me with a bored look.

'We were driving back from London and Kev decided he was hungry. But then he's always hungry,' he said giving his manager a friendly punch on the arm.

'Come on master, we need to be leaving,' said Kevan whose deep voice had an Irish lilt. Hidden behind nerdy black glasses, he had serious blue eyes, an expression which gave nothing away, mad curls which were even wilder than mine if that was possible, and a terrible taste in sweaters.

'I'm sure you'll see us again Lottie,' said Daniel, his eyes smiling into mine as he flung his scarf around his neck.

'Oh gosh, that would be…thank you for…it's been…I'm so pleased you…' I gushed, as he waved to the yummy mummies and blew a kiss to a couple of old ladies who were beaming with delight. There was a flutter of excitement as the celebrity party left the building.

Back in the kitchen Jess was madly texting her friends, and Ryan was on the phone to his mum, while Pat was chuckling to herself as she wiped down the work surfaces.

'Okay. Fun over,' I said trying to sound stern. 'There are

other customers waiting to be served and we need some fresh coffee.'

Jess appeared to be ignoring me as she slid open the serving hatch and looked out. Everything had gone strangely quiet.

'He's back,' she said.

2

'Daniel has a question for you,' said Kevan with an 'A', casting his eyes around our teeny stainless steel kitchen as he spoke. Well in that case, why can't he come back to ask it himself, I thought. But then I suppose when you're that famous you have minions to do everything for you.

'He wants to know if you do catering. You know for parties,' he said, turning to Jess as she let out a victorious 'Yee-ess!' under her breath.

'Well that would depend,' I said, trying to sound as if I got asked to cook for a world-famous star every day of the week.

'On what?' asked Kevan, as though he wasn't used to being met with any sort of resistance.

'On the date, the time, what sort of thing he's looking for, and the cost,' I said, realising that money probably doesn't come into it for a superstar who has sold zillions of albums worldwide.

'Saturday, Sept 24 at 7 p.m. for his housewarming party at Morton Manor. Around seventy guests who need feeding. Just let us know the cost and what other help you might need.'

Before I had the chance to speak, Jess beat me to it: 'Who's going to be there?' she asked, presumably hoping for a run-down of the star-studded guest list.

'Daniel's friends,' is all he would say, turning back to me with a raised eyebrow.

'Er, let me check my diary,' I said, knowing full well that like most Saturday nights these days, the evening would be achingly empty.

Sometimes Helen would grace me with her presence, and we'd spend a girly night catching up, mainly on her life, as mine wasn't that interesting. She'd tell me about how much money her husband Ben was earning as a divorce lawyer, and what she was spending it on. Then she would moan and boast about her four children in equal measure.

'Tell you what, call me back later this afternoon when you've checked your diary,' said Kevan, handing me a business card. And with that he was gone.

'Come on. Quick,' said Jess dragging out my bag from the cubby hole in the corner. And before I could get there first, she'd spotted the slim plastic red diary I got free with a women's magazine, and flicked through the pages.

'There's nothing in it for the next few weeks, apart from the chiropodist next month, a dentist appointment and Colin's birthday. Who's Colin?'

'Someone I know,' I mumbled, almost snatching the diary from her.

'It's her cat,' said Pat, roaring with deep throaty laughter.

Jess's eyes widened with curiosity. 'I didn't know cats had birthdays. That's so sweet. Do they get nine a year because of all their lives?'

That sent Pat off again. Her laugh was infectious. It was all I could do not to join in. So I said: 'Well no, cats don't have birthdays. Not really. But Colin's date of birth was on the certificate when I got him from the rescue centre. I just thought I'd take him home a piece of chicken.'

'We're going to have to find you a bloke soon, lady,' said Pat, who by this time was wiping tears off her glasses with the corner of a tea towel.

Jess was almost hyperventilating with excitement. 'So you can do it then? Daniel's party? Can I waitress? Ryan could help out too. You'd like that wouldn't you?' she said giving him a dig with her elbow. 'And what about you Pat?'

'No, I'll leave it to you young 'uns. I'd scare all those glossy young things off. Anyway, it's my granddaughter's birthday and we're having a bit of a do,' she said, as she carried on polishing her glasses. I could tell she was disappointed, but nothing came in the way of Pat and her family. Married young, her whole life revolved around her grown-up daughters and five grandchildren, who kept her busy when she wasn't working in the kitchen.

I poured a black coffee into my favourite chipped red mug. It was one thing preparing sandwiches and stews for the customers who drifted in and out of the café daily. Cooking up a menu for seventy celebrities who were used to five-star treatment was as far out of my comfort zone as whipping up a State Banquet at Buckingham Palace.

'I need to think about it,' I said, noticing that one or two customers were looking impatiently at their watches.

'Right then, let's think,' said Ryan taking a piece of chalk out of his pocket to write on our staff blackboard. 'Okay, you could do chilli con carne. That would be good. And some mini meat pies.'

'Lots of celebs don't eat meat,' said Jess, grabbing the chalk from his hand, and adding vegetable curry.

Inside I could feel the panic taking over. The biggest event I'd ever catered for was a scouts' Christmas party with fifty hungry boys whose only real interest was in throwing the food rather than eating it.

Pat had finally calmed down, and was looking up something on her phone. 'You could make him a house-warming cake. Here, look at these. Love this one with the yellow marzipan house and chocolate roof.'

I stuffed my diary bag into my bag. 'No. It's not going to work.'

Pat flicked through a few more cake photographs on her phone. 'Okay, so you could do a chocolate house with a marzipan roof. Would that work? Or there's this gorgeous gingerbread cottage and...'

I turned my back so I didn't have to look at their faces and wiped the chalk off the board. 'None of it works. I don't care how famous he is. It's a big fat no. Daniel French will have to find someone else.'

3

'You had twelve days to do it. We could all have helped you. And I would have made the cake,' Pat grumbled as we locked up. 'Opportunity doesn't always knock a second time, lady. You never know, it could have led to something else. Someone there could say, that Lottie Gilbert's grub is a bit of alright, she could do *my* party. But no. You'd prefer to stay home and watch *The X Factor*. You're a silly moo.' Maybe I was a silly moo, but I wasn't a very confident moo. I got stressed enough planning menus, cooking ahead for the café, and making sure we got food out of the kitchen on time, and that was just with customers wandering upstairs in twos and threes. Seventy hungry celebrities? Well, I just didn't want to think.

I decided to soak away all memories of Daniel French and his posh party in a bubble bath. A couple of candles, and a glass of chilled white wine balancing on the edge, and I was already starting to feel better.

I could hear my phone on silent, buzzing angrily from somewhere under a towel, but I couldn't find it. When I did, it was a withheld number. Probably Mark. He knew I wouldn't answer it otherwise. I picked it up with a soapy hand and put on my bored, slightly cross voice. 'What!'

'That's not very friendly,' said the male caller.

'I'm sorry, I thought you were someone else. Who am I speaking to?'

'It's Daniel French here. Sorry if I've caught you at a bad time. It sounds as though you're in the bath. Are you naked?'

I sat bolt upright causing a tidal wave over the side of the bath, followed by my glass of wine which smashed on the floor.

'No, no. Of course not,' I said, trying to work out a way of getting out of the bath without dropping the phone and shredding my feet on the broken glass. There was a pause, and another laugh. 'You mean you wear clothes in the bath?'

'I'm not in the bath,' I said trying to sit still so that the water didn't make sloshing sounds. He probably knew I was lying. You can tell when someone's in the bath by the echoey sound, can't you?

'Er, can I call you back in a few minutes?' I asked, wondering how I was going to write down his number. Anyway he probably wouldn't want to give it to me in case I turned out to be some sort of mad celebrity stalker.

'Lottie, one simple question, that's all. Please will you cater for my party?'

'But I've already...'

'I know. Kevan told me you'd said no. But Lottie, I love your food. I mean, I *love* your food. I've already told my friends about your cooking. It will make such a change from all the tasteless buffets we usually have. A bit of home-cooked comfort food. It's in short supply these days. Come on, what do you say? Whatever it takes. We can lay on waiters, washer-uppers, whatever help you need. And...I wasn't going to mention it, but it's my birthday. It would be the best present. Please?'

'How old are you? Oh my God, that's so rude. I just wondered if it was a special one.'

'No, I'm forty-two. The only special thing about it is that it's my wife's idea, Lottie. She says she can't fly back from the States for both the housewarming and my birthday. So we thought we'd roll it into one.'

According to Jess, Daniel's wife, the American actress Beth Blackshaw who played a ditzy teacher in the US sitcom *School*

Daze spent most of her time at their house in the Hollywood Hills. He must miss her dreadfully.

'Look, I don't want to pressure you, Lottie, but if you change your mind you'd make my day.' I just loved the way he kept saying my name in his warm rich Northern accent. Lottie this and Lottie that. As though I mattered, as though I was important in his life for just that moment. Someone like me.

4

'You're doing what?' shrieked Helen, spitting out a mouthful of wine as we tried to keep warm under the furry throw I kept on the sofa.

'I called to tell you, but you never answer your phone,' I said, topping up her glass, knowing that my attempts to make contact often got ignored in her frantic life.

For once she had a night off from her four children. Harry, who at sixteen had already decided he was going to be a Formula One racing driver. My goddaughter Rose, fourteen, who unlike most of the other princesses in her class at private school, was intent on earning her own money. She had already started her own little business empire in crafts, making necklaces to sell to her friends. George was twelve, and appeared to have no life apart from the virtual one on his tablet, which was rather worrying. And Freddy, who at ten was always kicking footballs which flattened Helen's flowers, and was probably the healthiest of the lot, both in body, mind and spirit. All of them delightful, but in small doses.

No wonder I rarely saw my best friend. Every hour of the week had to be micro-managed to make sure that her children were ferried to and from their various activities, ranging from gymnastics to gymkhanas. Rose, like her mother before her had her own pony, and a collection of show-jumping rosettes in every colour of the rainbow.

The last time Helen had been over to see me, she was so exhausted that she virtually fell asleep into the fish pie I'd rustled up after work. A few times I'd offered to babysit so that she and Ben could go out on a date night, but she seemed reluctant. 'He's as exhausted as I am after swimming lessons and Freddy's football coaching. All he wants to do is collapse on the sofa, or take the dogs for a walk to the pub.'

Tonight, however, her husband had been the one to offer his babysitting services. He could probably see how frazzled she was after a week of juggling five lives including her own, while he enjoyed eight hours a day in his ultra-modern solicitor's office, lending a shoulder to husbands and wives as they ranted and sobbed over their broken marriages.

Straight away, Helen was trying to work out how she could come with me to Daniel's house. 'I could wear that sexy maid's outfit that Ben likes,' she said, checking her diary on her phone.

I tried to think of a tactful way of letting her down gently so as not to upset her too much. Helen had the sensitivity of a block of ice when it came to other people's feelings, but you only had to say boo in the wrong way, and her cornflower-blue eyes would well up with tears. Helen was not someone I would readily let loose as a waitress. Within minutes, she would forget she was supposed to be serving people, start sipping one of the drinks and swan around the room networking.

The first day we met aged five, at Albury Infants, she put me in my place with her sense of entitlement. She was the girl with the pretty brown curls and perfect pearly teeth, who only had to breathe a wish and it came true courtesy of her parents. They must have inherited a pile of money, because I never heard the word 'work' mentioned in the five-bedroom Victorian house where she'd been cosseted as an only child. It was only half a mile away from the grey council estate where I lived with my dad and my nan, but it could have been on another planet. She was the little girl with the midnight-black pony called Ebony kept in a field at the back of her house, and whose bedroom was like something out of a Disney movie. Cute and pink, with fairylights around her dressing table, all the latest toys and gadgets, and a wardrobe stuffed with clothes which made mine look as though they came from a charity shop, which they probably did.

'I've already asked Jess and Ryan to help. But I promise to give you the low-down on the entire evening.'

She pouted just like she always did when her life didn't fall into place like some magical jigsaw. 'Just the juicy bits, ok? My life is so dull compared to yours.'

Both she and I knew that this was not the case, but I let it drop. There was so much to think about in the run-up to the big day.

'Is your boss, Miserable Marsha, okay with you doing this?'

'Of course she is. Why wouldn't she be?'

'Because of this text on your phone,' said Helen, who frequently infuriated me by reading my messages before I could get to them.

And there it was: ***Keep Saturday September 24 evening free. I need you to cater for my godson's 30$^{th.}$ Marsha.***

5

I spent the next couple of days dreaming up reasons why I wasn't free on the twenty-fourth of September ranging from previous engagements to hot dates. The problem was that none of them would wash with Marsha. Not even that I had a prior booking to cater for Daniel French. First thing she would ask is why hadn't I run it past her? Then she would insist that her godson was more important.

When it came to my job, a bit of outside catering for Marsha was part of the deal, and unless I was dying, I would have to find a way of doing both. Maybe that was it. Not exactly spreading rumours of my demise, but being struck down with 'food poisoning'. That being the case, she wouldn't want me anywhere near the kitchen on Saturday. I'd make a miraculous recovery from what turned out to be a dicky tummy and back at work Sunday morning. Perfect. Tricky part number one was that because I needed to work late in the kitchen Friday night to prep Daniel's food, I wouldn't be able to let Marsha know I was going to be off sick until first thing Saturday morning. And tricky part number two was that Ryan and Jess wouldn't be available to serve the food for Marsha's godson.

At an emergency conflab over coffee in The Loft the next day, Ryan had the answer. 'My mum used to be a waitress at weddings. She and her mate could pick up the food from here on Saturday afternoon and do the godson's party for you. It's only about thirty people.'

'Marsha's not even going. She said the thought all that loud music would give her a migraine,' said Jess. 'So she won't know that Ryan and me aren't there. Just that her godson is happy with the food.'

This dastardly plan was beginning to take shape. We all work our socks off into the night on Friday to prepare the food for both events. I call in sick on Saturday morning. Ryan's mum collects all Marsha's food late afternoon with the story that she is helping out her son by driving it to the venue. Then Ryan and Jess pack all Daniel's party food into cold boxes and transport it to Morton Manor, where I would meet them fresh from having a sneaky day off. Why should I feel guilty? I'd worked enough days for the old dragon feeling like death warmed up. Just one small sickie. Surely it wouldn't hurt.

On Friday evening it all worked like a dream. Once she had closed her shop, Marsha showed her face to check that her godson's food preparation was underway. At that point, we hadn't made a start on Daniel's menu of Thai vegetable curry, coq au vin, and enough shepherd's pie to feed an army. And we'd managed to keep my *pièce de résistance* under wraps. A birthday cake worthy of winning *The Great British Bake Off*, which Pat helped me design.

It was a three-tier sponge cake, each layer a different flavour – chocolate, strawberry and vanilla – decorated with white icing, and black musical notes, all of which had taken me an age to get looking right. Jess had insisted on taking dozens of pictures so that she could tweet them on the night.

'I'm not sure he'll want his cake all over Twitter,' I said, as I checked to make sure all the twiddly bits of icing were intact.

Jess shrugged, taking more pictures from every angle. 'He'll probably tweet it himself, or his guests will.'

'Cakes are for eating, not bloody tweeting,' said Pat, as she wiped down the kitchen surfaces in preparation for the next day. Five foot nothing of energy, she never stopped still for a moment, smoking and drinking far more than is supposed to be good for a woman in her early sixties.

I kept going through lists of everything in my mind, to make sure there was nothing I'd forgotten before I went off sick for the whole of Saturday. Kevan had reassured me there was nothing we needed to bring except the food. Daniel's kitchen, he said, was blessed with every gadget and mod con going. That was all very well but, like most chefs, I wanted to take my own set of knives, and my lucky saucepan which I'd had since dad first taught me to cook.

I barely slept that night and when I did, I dreamed that when I turned up at Morton Manor, Ryan and Jess had forgotten the food and I had to cook something on the spot, which was a problem, since all the food in the fridge was covered in fur. I woke in a panic, with Colin sitting on my head.

Throughout the day there were texts from Jess and Ryan with a running commentary of what was turning into a top secret military operation. I felt such a fraud calling in sick in the morning, that I was too guilty to enjoy my day off. It wasn't as if I could go into town for a shopping spree, Marsha might spot me. According to Ryan she had appeared upstairs in The Loft to inspect her godson's party food, just as they were packing my three-tier birthday cake for Daniel. Luckily Jess had the presence of mind to stop her peering into the boxes by telling Marsha it was a surprise cake for *her* birthday. Now I'd have to make her one too.

'Marsha's not happy with you,' said Jess in a text as I was getting ready for the evening.

'She's never happy with me,' I texted back. And if she were to discover that I'd let loose two women I didn't even know to waitress at her precious godson's special birthday party, she'd probably hate me forever.

I'd set my phone alarm to make sure I left for Morton Manor on time. But after scorching a hole in my white blouse with the iron, I wasted half an hour frantically looking for my spare.

Mark always teased me that I was born with a 'late' gene.

Time was a bit of a mystery to me. I'd get lost inside it thinking I had plenty of it to spare, and then it would creep up on me and say "Boo, you're late again!"

Finally I was ready to go and only half an hour late, which was good for me, when my phone rang. It was Kevan checking that we'd all be with him by seven.

'Of course,' I said in my sweetest voice. 'Ryan and Jess have all the food and will be with you any time now. And I'll be there soon after.' Fat chance I thought, as I tried to sound as businesslike as possible.

'Sooner the better. Looks like we're in for a storm,' he said and hung up.

6

Nerves were starting to build as I keyed the post code into my phone. As a precaution, I'd printed out Kevan's directions to drive seventeen miles to the prestigious village where Daniel was now lord and master of Morton Manor.

As I kissed Colin goodbye and told him to wish me luck, it was twilight and already starting to rain. I'd spotted an itchy-looking nerve rash coming up on my neck, and tried to disguise it with foundation, which had made it worse. Mentally, I ran through a final checklist of what I needed to do once I got there. Hopefully Jess and Ryan would arrive well ahead of me to start prepping the food. Just as I got in the car, a text alerted me that they were there, that the house was 'awesome' and that Daniel's housekeeper Meg was on hand to help.

I started to feel a ripple of excitement. It was Saturday night, and instead of sitting at home with Colin, trying to shrug off my loneliness, I was on my way out to a celebrity party. How cool was that? I started to wonder what other stars might be there. I had already briefed Jess not to ask for autographs or selfies as we needed to stay professional at all times, and I made it especially clear she was to resist flirting with any famous footballers.

'Will you fire me if I do?'

She looked totally serious. 'Possibly yes,' I said, wondering how on earth I'd ever manage without a waitress who could carry three plates up her arm without ever dropping one.

'In that case I might have to risk it,' she said. And I knew she meant it. She'd be willing to sacrifice her job for the chance to be a WAG, even a second division version.

To get in the party mood I changed the radio station to something which was playing thumping dance music and ramped up the volume. As I left the well-lit town roads for dark country lanes, the heavens turned almost instantly black and the rain fell as if God had just wrung out the clouds. But I didn't care. I was enjoying the drama of it, that is until I heard the noise. Although I know more about rocket science than cars, I knew it sounded serious. Breakdown-by-the-side-of-the road serious. Should I stop and call out the car rescue service, or risk causing serious damage and carry on? That was the question.

Surely a few more miles wouldn't hurt. And the closer I got to Great Morton, the better. I could then call Ryan to pick me up. Hammering down on the car roof the rain grew louder, as did the racket coming from my engine. My headlights, although on full beam, were barely making any impact on the darkness which felt like it was sucking me into it.

My plan was to carry on driving until Moaning Mini, who was making the most agonising noises, gave up the ghost and died on me. Twenty minutes later and I could see lights in the distance which had to be Great Morton. At last. Surely the house couldn't be too far away. Now was the time to call Ryan, but wouldn't you know it, there was no signal. By now Mini was positively screaming. Heaven knows what it was but it sounded terminal, and just as I was thinking about switching off the engine, it died on its own. With a sort of giant sigh.

Grabbing my coat from the back seat there was nothing for it. I'd have to walk. Maybe I'd be able to hitchhike the rest of the way, I thought as I slung my bag containing my knives, over my shoulder and grabbed my lucky saucepan.

In the boot, on my dad's advice, I'd always kept a large torch for emergencies, and what's more it still worked. He would have been proud of me. I scrabbled in my bag for a fold-up umbrella which once opened, lasted about five seconds before it blew inside out so violently there was no saving it. My hair was already plastered to my cheeks, and my coat was doing little to protect me from the sleet. The only thing that might save me from presenting myself at the front door like a totally drowned rat was putting my lucky saucepan on my head, like a sort of tin soldier helmet. Okay, so it might not be a good look, I said to myself as I hurried along in the rain towards the lights in the distance, but it did the trick. What I needed was a village pub where I could make a phone call, and someone would come and rescue me.

Before I reached any sign of civilisation I saw it. A battered wooden signpost which clearly pointed the way to Morton Manor.

It led me onto a long and winding road guarded by menacing giant oak trees. I could definitely see what looked like a house in the distance, but quite how far away was difficult to tell in the lashing rain.

Ten minutes later and the lights seemed as distant as they'd done earlier. Like some sort of mirage of an oasis in a desert. I felt like I was inside one of those dreams where, however hard you try to get somewhere, you never arrive. This was insane. Checking my phone again, there was one bar of signal, but it disappeared before I could make a call. The rain was now almost horizontal and apart from under my saucepan there was nowhere to shelter. One thing is for sure, black high heels were not the footwear of choice for such an occasion. My tights were covered with mud splatters giving my legs the Dalmatian look, and my face was so chilled, any tears of frustration froze before they trickled down my cheeks.

Behind me I could hear a car approaching. Hopefully it was a guest who would ferry me up to the house. Frantically, I waved my arms about, hoping I wouldn't get splashed to death if the car didn't slow down. It did, and out of the large black four-by-four climbed the biggest man I've ever seen. At about six feet seven inches, he was as wide as he was tall with long hair tied back into a pony tail and dark glasses, although why anyone needed them in this weather was beyond me.

Without saying a word, he grabbed my arm, opened the back door and virtually threw me onto the seat, before striding round to the driver's seat and getting back in.

A familiar Irish voice from the passenger seat spoke: 'Chas, go gently with her. Sorry Lottie. I didn't recognise you with the saucepan on your head. You could have been one of Daniel's nutty fans,' said Kevan. He turned round, and when he saw the state of me, had the decency to look concerned. 'What happened? Are you okay?'

My teeth were chattering so much, either through nerves or cold, I'm not sure which. 'My car broke down, and there's no phone signal, so I had to walk from the village.'

'What's wrong with your car?'

Typical man, more interested in the car than me possibly dying of pneumonia. All I knew was that my ancient Mini was dead.

'She was making a screaming noise and then the engine stopped.'

'Sounds like...don't worry I'll get your car picked up and towed to a garage. Meg our housekeeper will look after you and get you dried out. You must be freezing. Ramp up the heater in the back Chas. Chas, Lottie, Lottie, Chas. He's in charge of security around here.' Daniel's bodyguard, more like, I thought taking another look at the man mountain in the front who gave me a nod in the rear-view mirror.

Dripping all over the back seat, I tried to look for the positive side to all this. Nope. There was no positive side. I'd turned up late for my first ever celebrity catering gig looking as though I'd just swum the channel and been slung in the back of a car by Daniel's bodyguard who thought the mad woman with a saucepan on her head was a deranged fan.

I looked at the well-worn stainless steel pan in which many a warming winter dish had been created and thought of its original owner, my dad who taught me everything I knew about cooking, mainly from the busy kitchen of his small cafe in an unfashionable part of town. I suppose you could call it a greasy spoon, but in Ron's Caff, he did more than fry-ups, teaching me to make good home-cooked basics like stews and steak and kidney puddings. Without a mum, it was just him and me in the flat above the café. My bedroom looked out onto the main road, the scruffy houses and the rubbish bins. Rather than keeping me awake, the constant drone of the traffic became a reassuring lullaby. That and the sound of my dad singing out of tune in the kitchen as he prepared food for the next day's customers. Happy times. If only he was here now.

As we came to a halt in front of huge black gates, Chas keyed numbers into some sort of security device after which they opened slowly.

'Welcome to Morton Manor,' said Kevan as we drove towards what looked like a floodlit mini Downton Abbey.

As the four-by-four crunched slowly along the gravel drive and over a bridge which spanned a small river, I listened as he gave what sounded like a well-rehearsed speech about Daniel's new home. A seventeenth century Jacobean manor house set in about twenty acres of gardens and grounds. The original part of the house, he said, dated back to the mid 1600's and had partly been rebuilt in Victorian times after a fire. Its last owners, he added, were descendants of some earl or other, but they could no longer afford the upkeep of the property and were forced to sell.

'How many rooms does it have?'

'Ten bedrooms and six bathrooms. So, there's quite a lot of re-decorating still to do,' said Kevan, jumping out of the car to open the door for me. My shoes were so full of rain, I made this embarrassing squelching noise as I jumped down.

'Daniel's wife must be really excited to get it finished.'

'Not sure that's the word she'd use. But yes the house was her idea. You know Americans. They love anything with history seeing as they've so little,' he said as we approached the ancient-looking arched wooden front door with a huge iron knocker. There was a dog barking somewhere from deep within the house and the sound of music and laughter as though the party had already started

Don't tell me I was that late. 'Are people here already?'

Kevan took the saucepan from me: 'It's just a few mates who said they'd get here early to help, but probably meant help themselves, to the beer.'

The door swung open to reveal a woman, roughly the same age as me, with a harassed expression on her face. For a moment I did a double take. With the rich brown bob, full on make-up, diamanté jewellery and sparkly black dress, I thought I was face to face with Daniel's Hollywood star wife, Beth. Not that I'd seen many pictures of her. There was an eerie similarity, but unless all the actress's recent photos had been dramatically photo-shopped, this certainly wasn't her. For a start the hair was more fluffy than glossy and the make-up so heavily applied that she looked more like a drag queen than an A-lister. Taking my hand she virtually dragged me in through the front door.

'You must be Lottie. You poor poppet. Look at the state of you. Come with me, I'll get you dried out,' she said marching ahead of me towards the back of the house.

I just about had time to absorb the enormity of the entrance hall. There was a wonderful smell of logs burning and sounds of crackling in a huge open brick grate, its flames reflected in a crystal chandelier, and the sort of staircase you'd expect Fred Astaire to come tap dancing down.

'Better use the back staircase in case we bump into any of Daniel's guests. You look like something the cat dragged in.' Gee thanks, I thought. I was starting to feel as though we were in a scene from *Upstairs Downstairs*. She must have caught the look on my face because she looked aghast.

'Oh I'm sorry. Silly me. That didn't sound very kind, did it? Big soz,' she said speaking in an awful baby voice. I suspected her real voice was much lower. Since there had still been no introductions, I figured she must be Meg, although I have to admit was expecting a much older woman with a perm and a floral housecoat, not this over-made-up glamour puss. Sick of being treated like some inconvenience, I stood my ground. 'I take it you're Meg, Daniel's housekeeper?'

'And personal assistant. I'm in charge of every bitty little thing that goes on here in Morton Manor.'

'Good, well I need a quick word with my staff before I do anything else. Where are they?'

For a minute her tone of voice lowered and she sounded irritated. 'They're fine getting all their scrummy food ready in the kitchen. But we need to get you changed before the main guests start arriving.'

She had a nervousness about her, her dark button-brown eyes, darting around as if always on the look out, and a smile which didn't quite reach her eyes. The more I looked at her, the less glamorous she looked. Not quite mutton dressed as lamb but more like someone wearing a very bad fancy dress costume. It was obvious she was as uncomfortable with my stare as I was with hers.

There were good smells coming from what I guessed must be the kitchen, and as I trotted upstairs behind Meg, I thought I could hear Jess laughing, which was a good sign.

'Follow me,' she said, maybe in case I had other ideas and was about to nose into the various rooms we passed.

We seemed to be walking miles. I just hoped she wouldn't abandon me anywhere as I'd need a map to find my way back.

'I don't have anything to change into.'

'That's fine. Mrs French has a closet full of clothes she never wears. There's bound to be something you can borrow while I get yours washed and dried. What size are you?'

'A twelve,' I said, which was a mini-lie because I'm between a twelve and a fourteen, but they don't make clothes in a thirteen, which is a huge problem for curvy girls like me. 'Won't she mind?' I asked as Meg opened double doors and led me into a vast bedroom complete with four-poster under a black chandelier big enough to swing on, should one have the urge. On the walls were beautiful black and white photographs of Daniel and his wife, one or two from their wedding day, and a couple of them cuddling up on a bed and a sofa. A glossy elfin bob – which Meg had presumably tried to emulate -- framed her heart-shaped face and huge Bambi eyes. Beth Blackshaw was stunning. There was no other word for her.

'Mrs French's filming schedule has changed, so she's had to postpone her flight. But she's such a sweetie poppet, she wouldn't mind a bit, that's if we can find something to fit you,' she said, talking to me as if I was about five as she opened the doors to a closet which was bigger than my bedroom. I could see the problem. The rails of clothes were obviously made for a woman the size of a small child.

Meg handed me a white towelling dressing gown.

'Get yourself out of your clothes and I'll start looking. Maybe there are some black trousers with a stretch waist,' she said leading me into the en-suite bathroom so huge it could house an entire family. There was an area which boasted a large mirror surrounded by bare light bulbs, like an old-fashioned theatre dressing room.

'Hairdryer, and help yourself to make-up,' she said pointing to what looked like the cosmetics counter in Harrods. 'And if you'd like to take a shower and wash your hair, feel free,' she said, sliding open the shower door.

As soon as she'd gone, I checked to see if there was a signal, and called Jess. Answer, answer. 'Lottie, we've been worried sick. Where are you?'

'Long story, but I'll be with you in about twenty minutes. You didn't warn me the housekeeper was like some dotty Mrs Danvers. How's it going?'

She sounded breathless with excitement. 'I've just seen Marco Richie, can you believe it? The footballer. He's so gorgeous.'

'I was thinking more of the food, Jess.'

'Oh. All good. It's heating up, and the guests will serve themselves. You ought to see the kitchen Lottie. It's to die for with an Aga and a fridge which is big as our kitchen at The Loft. There's even a tap with boiling water so you can make instant tea and coffee. Where are you?'

'Having some sort of mad *Alice in Wonderland* adventure upstairs. Changing out of wet things. So Jess, keep your mind on the job.'

'Oh my God, I've just seen Bosco.'

'Who the hell is he when he's at home?'

'The rapper. And he just winked at me.' I'd better hurry downstairs before Jess started flirting with the entire guest list. That's if I had something dry to wear.

It was only when I studied myself in the mirror I realised what a state I was in. My hair looked as if it had been super-glued to my cheeks, and there were rivulets of mascara down my face. In super fast time I'd showered, washed my hair with some exotic shampoo I'd never heard of and was back in my slightly damp underwear waiting for Meg to reappear.

Although she had given me free rein to do so, I felt guilty using things belonging to Daniel's wife. This was her private space. I wasn't sure how I'd feel about someone rifling through my make-up bag if I wasn't there.

'It's okay. Daniel is aware of the situation. And he has given full permission for you to be here,' said Meg who seemed to have appeared out of nowhere. She handed me a black shift dress which on Beth would have floated around her miniscule figure like a tent, but on me, hugged every ounce of flesh. Still it did the job, and after a last minute check, I was pleased. Whether it was the top of the range foundation I'd used or the gorgeous silky golden brown sparkly eye shadow, I wasn't sure, but I liked the result. All applied in five minutes flat. Even my hair was behaving itself for a change, my curls positively bouncing on my shoulders.

When Meg re-appeared, her smile of approval was more like a grimace. As I tried to keep up with her down long corridors and the winding stairs, she spoke in a high voice like an excitable squirrel about how Daniel liked things done in the kitchen – which I suspected was how *she* liked things done – and instructed me not to speak to guests unless spoken to. Really? I just nodded while trying to take in everything around me. A couple of immaculately turned out waiters and a waitress bearing silver trays of champagne glided out of the kitchen as we arrived, much to the delight of Jess who squealed when she caught sight of me. Meg shot her a disapproving look.

'Here's your boss. I'll be back in the shake of a little lamby's tail,' said Meg, as she turned on her heels and walked out. No wonder she was so thin, she must cover several miles a day looking after a house this size. For a couple of minutes it was hugs all round while I explained to Jess and Ryan where I'd been. They appeared to have everything under control. Food was bubbling gently on the stove, and they had set out a counter with plates, cutlery and napkins for guests to serve themselves. I took a moment to soak it all in. Silver spotlights over the glittering white marble work station complete with additional sinks and taps, the white Aga. In fact everything was cool, silver and white as if designed by Elsa for her palace in *Frozen*.

From the way Jess was making eyes at me, I figured that someone else must have walked into the room. But his voice still made me jump as he spoke. I didn't expect him to appear in the kitchen. 'Lottie, how are you? I heard all about your car. Did Meg look after you okay?' As I turned, I could see Daniel casting an eye over his wife's dress which was tight across my hips, his eyes lingering on the neckline which was showing far more of my cleavage than I would have liked. The sleeves were just about long enough to cover the scars at the top of my arm.

'She did, thank you. I borrowed a dress. I'll change as soon as my clothes are dry.'

He nodded. 'Stay as you are. You look great. And if you give me your car keys, Chas will get your Mini to a garage.'

'Really, there's no need.'

'It's no trouble Lottie. We'll get you a car home.' There he was, saying my name again. For some reason it sent a little shiver of delight down my spine. Daniel French knew who I was. What a bizarre thing to think. He was just an ordinary person. Except that he wasn't, was he? He was someone who millions of fans would die to meet. And here I was standing inches away from him. If I wanted to, I could reach out and touch him. I could even grab him and kiss him firmly on the lips. I wonder what he'd do.

While he wandered round the kitchen, inspecting and tasting the food with Jess and Ryan, I had a chance to look at him properly. He was taller than I remembered and dressed in black trousers, a dark grey shirt, the sleeves slightly rolled up revealing strong and slightly hairy tanned arms, and hands with long artistic looking fingers, one of them wearing a gold wedding band.

I was slightly disappointed not to be meeting his wife. For some reason I had this urge to see them together, to see how they acted as a couple. I was fascinated by other people's relationships, probably because my own had always been so disappointing. If I was honest, which I rarely was, not even with myself, I'd never been in love. Not really. Not even with Mark although I tried to convince myself I was.

When I first bumped into Mark, literally, knocking a tray of drinks out of his hand, he was a cheeky twenty-six-year-old with fantasies of expanding his struggling painting and decorating business into an empire, and I was a bored thirty-three-year-old chef working for a local businessman's restaurant, who dreamed of finding 'The One' and settling down. No one thought we were a good match except us. And the fact he pursued me as though I was the most dazzling creature in the world was a new experience. Even when I initially tried to finish with him, just in case throwing in my lot with a toy boy was a bad idea, he refused to let go. In his own flashy style, he wined and dined me, swearing undying love, and two months later, used the excuse that the lease on his flat was up, to move in with me and almost immediately we were talking marriage. Except that it never happened. Oh, he proposed, with a one carat diamond ring which I later discovered was a fake when I found the receipt for fifty pounds.

'It's a good fake though, doll,' Mark often said when I complained that I wanted a real one.

Daniel's voice brought me out of my reverie, as he dipped a spoon into the Thai curry, tasted it and closed his eyes. 'Lottie, I don't know how you do it. You cook like an angel.' He was talking to me. Me! Charlotte Emily Gilbert. I looked over at Jess who gave me a thumbs up, and Ryan who clenched his fist in a victory salute.

'If you need any help throughout the evening, just ask Meg or Kevan. And make sure you help yourself to drinks, or whatever you need.' He smiled, and touched my arm. He touched my arm. Daniel French touched my arm, and it felt like some kind of orgasmic electrical current. Now how was that possible? Maybe it was like reflexology where the person treating you presses an area of your foot and you feel it in your back. Or else I was being seduced into becoming a fan. Before I had a chance to reply, he'd gone.

7

Star spotting became fascinating as we handed round the canapés. Every time she walked past me with a tray, Jess mumbled another name under her breath. 'Cat Tyson,' she said nodding towards the beautiful mixed race singer who was married to gorgeous black actor Brandon Webb. Shaking her head as I offered her a selection of mini appetizers, CT as she was normally known to her fans, looked as though she'd rather be somewhere else. I felt sorry for her.

Every other week there was a new story in the press that her husband had been seen with another woman, leaving her to explain to their two young children that daddy had gone away for a couple of days while they worked things out.

There were also three Premier League footballers according to Jess, although I would never have recognised them, and a couple of reality TV show presenters. As well as the rapper Bosco, Ryan informed us that three members of his favourite band A Dog Named Phred were in the house with their chattering wives all of whom waved me away when I walked past with my trays of food. What was the matter with these women? Didn't they ever eat? Probably not judging by the size of them.

In amongst the sea of familiar faces, I spotted at least two West End stars I'd seen in some musical. And working the room with a huge smile on her face was one of my favourite TV actresses, Naomi Lincoln. Not a week went by when I didn't tune into the medical drama *City Hospital* in which she starred as a doctor who was secretly in love with a married surgeon.

She smiled at me as she helped herself to a couple of mini sausages, and I had to stop myself from asking her if she thought her character would ever get together with her handsome boss.

I was just beginning to relax when I heard the front door slam and a loud female voice shouting and cursing about the weather and a taxi driver who'd turned up late. Unable to resist checking out the source of this drama in the hall, I nearly collided with a tall, well-built woman with sharply cut jet black hair, who stared at me as if I was something on the bottom of her bright red Jimmy Choos.

'Oh God, you're ginger!' she said, handing one of the waiters her dripping umbrella.

'I'm a redhead, yes,' I said as politely as I could in case she was someone important. Personally I preferred to think of my hair as a kind of dark copper. People had always commented on my red hair and freckles, but not in a good way. At school I had to tolerate the name-calling. But since the popularity of Prince Harry, it was slightly more cool to be red, so I stopped trying to dye it blonde, which always turned out orange. On a bad hair day, my curls went wild and took on a life of their own, corkscrewing outwards at every conceivable angle.

Jess was forever offering to set up a Twitter account for my hair. 'It would deffo get followers,' she'd say. Hopefully more than I did. The last time I checked, I only had fourteen and they included the window cleaner and the paper boy. But back to this loud woman who was tossing her wet raincoat at the waiter.

'So Lottie, Queen of the kitchen. At last we meet.'

'How do you know my name?'

'I know everything,' she said, 'He's been going on about discovering the next Nigella, although that might take a bit of work,' she said looking me up and down.

'These aren't my normal clothes. I got wet and...'

'Wasn't looking at your clothes hun.'

'I'm sorry I don't know who...'

The waiter returned with a glass of champagne which she took from him. The contents barely touched the side as she glugged it down, and handed back the empty glass.

'I'm Stella Smith-Brewer, Danny boy's agent, hun. Talking of which, where is he?' she said striding off towards the other party-goers who parted like the Red Sea in her wake.

Good point, where was he?

I could see Meg by the doorway talking to one of the waiters while she was keeping an eye on what was happening in the room. But there was no sign of Daniel. Maybe he was waiting to make a grand entrance. After all it was his birthday.

Tucked away in the corner of the room I glimpsed Kevan, this time looking more presentable in a denim shirt, closeted with a much younger animated guy with bleached blonde spiky hair. I was just about to turn away in case he thought I was staring, when he leaned forward and kissed his young companion gently on the forehead before taking him into his arms for an extended hug. An odd couple to say the least. Ryan told me later that the young guy was Max Diamond, owner of a gay club in London called Chill.

As I continued to scour the room I spotted Jess talking to a fit looking guy in his twenties who I vaguely recognised as a footballer. He appeared to be putting a number into his mobile phone. That didn't take long, I thought, smiling to myself as I made my way to the kitchen to check on my birthday cake for Daniel. I'd bought sparklers to pop into the icing for some extra pizzazz.

Minutes later from inside the living room I could hear a burst of applause and the first notes of "Happy Birthday" from the guests. Hurrying back, I looked through the door and saw Meg standing next to a birthday cake which was not dissimilar to the one I'd spent hours creating. Hers was four layers, decorated in white icing, with a sparkling black ribbon. It featured a grand piano on the top, beautifully done with black and white keys. It was both bigger and better than mine to be honest. And unless Meg was telepathic, she'd almost certainly seen the photograph of the finished cake I'd sent to Kevan.

Unnoticed, I slid back into the room as all the guests burst into applause and Daniel hugged his housekeeper, posing with her for pictures by his cake. As well-wishers milled around him, I caught Jess looking at me, sharing my disappointment.

'Lottie, there you are. Could you fetch a cake knife?' Meg called out, speaking to me as though I was the hired help. Well, I suppose I was. On my way back from the kitchen clutching what could, in my imagination, be used as a deadly weapon, Kevan was approaching .

'I know where you'll be wanting to stick that!' he said as if he could read my mind. He held out his hand. 'Here I'll take it to her. You don't have to wait on the woman. And yes I know you thought you were making his majesty's cake, and so did she.'

'So why did she make another cake?'

'God only knows what goes on in that weird little head of hers. And she'd have paid fortunes for it no doubt. No way she could make a cake like that. I'll have a word with her later, but she'll swear it was all a terrible mix-up,' he said, before wandering back into the chatter of the room.

I wasn't sure whether this made me feel better or not. But it was fine. I'd take Daniel's cake back to the café and maybe re-ice it for Marsha's birthday. I reassured myself that after tonight I'd never have to deal with that awful woman again. As she hurried over to me, waving her arms around and shouting orders in her silly little-girl voice, I felt my stomach tighten. 'We need to get the main dishes ready to serve. Is everything set up in the kitchen before I make an announcement? The guests are getting hungry.' They didn't look hungry to me. They looked perfectly content, gossiping, as they sipped their champagne.

At this point, I'd lost sight of Ryan and Jess, and was beginning to wish I'd never agreed to feed this celebrity army. Even though I could have strangled Meg, I did what I always did. Put on my people-pleasing, happy, grovelly voice. 'Would you give me five minutes please?'

Meg looked at her watch. 'Do try to keep to that sweetie. There are lots of rumbly tums.'

Jess sidled up to me. 'You just want to slap her, don't you?'

'You don't know the half of it,' I said, thinking back to the cake in which I'd invested so much time and effort. As we headed back into the kitchen, Ryan appeared, his face flushed with excitement.

'I've been talking to Max Diamond who owns that club Chill, and he says he'll give me a trial, spinning some tunes. You know deejaying,' he added, probably because I looked so blank. While the three of us scurried around transferring the food across to the hot plates, he continued to chatter away about his new best friend and how he was determined to impress him.

'Hey I've just Googled him and he's minted,' said Jess, scrolling on her smartphone. 'He owns another couple of clubs in different parts of the country. How come he's so rich? Pity he's gay.'

'Pity who's gay?' asked Kevan, helping himself to a beer from the fridge. His presence began to make me feel slightly uneasy. I wasn't sure how much to trust him. I suspected that under that layer of low-key charm, could be an Irish temper ready to erupt. I didn't want him to think we'd been gossiping about his young boyfriend. So I changed the subject to ask if he would be kind enough to spread the word that the food was ready.

'Looks like the word has already been spread,' he said nodding towards the doorway as partygoers made an appearance. And before we knew it, we had quite a crowd around us, loading their plates. I wondered if I should hold back a portion of shepherd's pie for Daniel as it was disappearing faster than anything else. Maybe being so famous, you got someone else to dish up your food for you, I wasn't sure.

Naomi Lincoln helped herself to a huge portion of coq au vin and mashed potatoes. 'You have no idea how much I've been looking forward to this. I haven't eaten a proper meal for a week. My character is suffering from a broken heart and the director said she needed to look gaunt,' she laughed

'I usually eat like a pig when I'm upset,' I said, handing her a serviette and cutlery.

'Me too, but it wouldn't look good for Dr Reece to start looking porky when she is supposed to be seducing her boss.'

Maybe it was my imagination, but she seemed as if she wanted to hang around and talk. I was on the verge of telling her what a big fan I was of her show, when I thought better of it. She must get people saying that all the time. Anyway, I was here on a professional basis not as a *City Hospital* fan. After the mad rush, the kitchen cleared, and Jess and Ryan disappeared to collect abandoned plates for the dishwasher.

The music, which I'd been vaguely aware of coming from small overhead speakers, changed to a funky dance tempo and I looked for a way to turn up the volume. There it was, a small speaker tucked discreetly away. Within seconds, I was boogying around the kitchen trying out some sexy moves I'd seen on a music video. A bit of strutting to collect up the dirty plates, a few seconds of hip-thrusting while I scraped the left-overs into the bin, and some twerking as I loaded the dishwasher.

'Not bad,' said Daniel. How long he'd been standing in the doorway watching my performance, I had no idea. He was laughing. God knows what I must have looked like. 'I'm so sorry,' I said, my cheeks burning with embarrassment.

'Why? You ought to come and join us. Get the party started. No one else is dancing. They're all too busy gossiping.'

'Oh I couldn't.'

'No it's okay. I know you've got stuff to do out here. You've done a fantastic job tonight. Everyone is raving about your food. Promise me you'll stop and have a drink before you go.'

'That's really kind...' I said, not getting the chance to utter the word 'but'.

'Good,' he said. 'I'll look forward to it.

8

By 11.30 p.m. all the guests had gone, including Stella, whose voice had become progressively louder throughout the evening.

'Gorge food, Lottie hun,' she said, kissing me on both cheeks, as she headed out into the night. I'd assumed everyone would be partying until dawn, but Kevan explained that it had been kept short and sweet as his boss was in the recording studios the next day.

'A lot of hard work goes into being a superstar,' he said, helping me to load the final bits and pieces into Ryan's van. Chas had given me a note with the details of where my car had been towed, and a number for a car to drive me home, all on Daniel's account. When I offered to pay, at least for my car, he just shook his head. Not once had I heard him utter a word.

Towards the end of the evening, as Meg presented me with my dried clothes, a smug grin washed over her face: 'Kevan's just told me about the cake mix-up. What a silly I am. I completely forgot you were bringing one with you. Can you ever forgive me?'

Before I had a chance to answer, Jess hugged me. 'It was such a great evening. Are you sure you don't want a lift home? We can go your way, can't we Ryan?'

'I've got a taxi coming. But thanks guys you've been great. I'll see you tomorrow.'

Ryan gave me a high five which was more his style. 'We can hang out with you until your car arrives.'

'Go go go,' I said, pushing them out of the front door.

Kevan rattled his car keys at Meg who seemed reluctant to leave with me still there. 'Come on. I'll run you back to your cottage.'

'I'll stay with Lottie until her car gets here,' she said, taking off her coat.

'What about that boyfriend you're always going on about? Won't he be waiting for you?' asked Kevan.

'Oh, er no,' she paused. 'Not tonight. He's out with friends. So it's not a problem me staying on. There's still clearing up to do.' Her self-righteous look turned to surprise as she realised Daniel was standing behind her.

'There's plenty of time for all that tomorrow Meg. You all get off home. I can look after Lottie.' An expression of shock mixed with disappointment crossed her face to be instantly replaced by such a genuine smile that I wondered if she was a bit of an actress in her own right. Or maybe I'd misjudged her. After all it can't have been easy having a stranger in the house cooking for Daniel and his friends, when she was used to reigning over her little kitchen kingdom.

As the front door finally shut I stood awkwardly in the hallway wondering quite where to wait.

Daniel knelt in front of the fireplace, loading logs, and trying to poke the embers back into life. Exhausted, I looked longingly at the small sofa beckoning me into its soft cushions.

'Okay, so how about that drink?' he said turning to look up at me.

'That's really kind, thank you. But it's late. I ought to go. I'm working tomorrow, although not 'til ten. A lie-in, phew,' I said wishing that just for once in my life, I could laze in bed with Colin until noon with the papers and endless coffee and croissants.

'Okay, but could I tempt you with a quick glass of champagne, just as a thank you?'

Looking around, it was as if I needed to seek approval from someone. I wasn't quite sure how to feel. Surprised? Flattered? Why would he want to have a drink with me? Maybe he was going to ask me to cater for another function. What was I thinking, turning him down? How jealous his fans would be if they knew I was alone with Daniel French in his mansion about to partake of a glass of posh bubbles. Ooh, get me! At that moment a huge grandfather clock which I hadn't even noticed in this vast hallway, began to chime midnight. Maybe like Cinderella if I had the chance, I should hotfoot it out of here, but there seemed to be some invisible force making me stay. Oh come on. Who was I kidding? I was desperate to wring every moment possible out of being in his company. When, in the rest of my life, was that ever likely to happen again?

'Thanks, that would be lovely.'

'Your wish is my command,' he said, heading towards the kitchen. 'Make yourself at home.'

I couldn't imagine somewhere as grand as this ever being home. But I suppose it's what you're used to. Home for me had only ever been a cramped council house with my dad Ron and my nan, then a flat over dad's cafe, and now a rented terraced house around which I could barely swing Colin. There was a sense that Morton Manor had been styled by someone trying to make it feel like home. That it wasn't lived in that much.

Looking around, I noticed more photos of Daniel and Beth. Most of them in ornate silver frames, scattered about the room. Daniel and Beth toasting each other with champagne, Daniel and Beth in matching swimwear on a paradise beach somewhere. Daniel and Beth wrapped up against the cold in cuddly scarves and bobble hats, posing as they built a snowman. And, hanging over the fireplace, a huge framed photo, the size of a painting, of Mr and Mrs French, their arms wrapped around a dog I assumed to be Oscar. The perfect couple. But for me it was almost as though she didn't exist apart from in those photos. She wasn't here with him, and I was.

Someone had lit the candelabra on top of the black baby grand. Bathed in the light of the log fire and candles, I was beginning to feel as if I was part of some surreal movie in which I was about to become part of a glittering new world. A world where celebrities lived and partied as though they were an entirely different species. I couldn't wait to tell Helen. She'd never believe it.

I sank down into the sofa and sighed. Okay, so it hadn't been the easiest evening, but I felt a sense of achievement. Maybe this could be another string to my bow. Charlotte Gilbert, caterer to the stars. Moments later Daniel returned with a bottle of fizz and two glasses, followed by the patter of large feet, belonging to his dark chocolate Labrador who nuzzled up to me.

'Oscar doesn't often do that with strangers. He must like you,' said Daniel, pouring us both a drink.

'He can probably smell Colin,' I said, as he passed me a large glass of champagne. Smell Colin? Oh God, that did sound weird!

'Colin? Is he your boyfriend?'

'God no, I know he sounds like an accountant, but he's my cat.'

'Great name, I love it.'

Walking over to the baby grand, he sat on the piano stool, and started to softly play a few melodic chords as he spoke.

'Lottie, tell me something about you. How did you get to be such a great cook?'

Immediately my mind froze and I couldn't think of anything interesting about me to say, apart from the fact that I wasn't a cook. I was a trained chef.

'Originally my dad taught me. Well, Ron wasn't my real dad. But he brought me up,' I said, wondering how much I should give away about my private stuff. 'Anyway it's just good home-cooked food, nothing special.'

'When you grow up with boarding school dinners and a mother who can't even boil a kettle, it's special.' He stopped playing and looked lost in thought.

Whenever there's a silence I always sense the need to fill it, so I thought I should ask him a question back. 'How old were you when you went to boarding school?'

'Too young. Eight.'

'Did you like it?'

'Hated it. I'd never been away from my parents before or

experienced home-sickness. But it was real. I felt physically sick for my home and my mum and dad – even though they weren't up to much as parents – and most of all for my dog.' For a moment it was easy to imagine him as a little boy, so vulnerable and sad and lost. When he started to speak again, his voice was strangely flat. It sounded like a story he'd told before, probably to journalists, although I didn't recall reading it.

'You could never show your emotions or the bigger boys would make fun of you, or beat you up. I couldn't understand why everyone else in my class seemed to be having such a great time, while I just wanted to go home, be in my own bedroom, hang out with my mates and be with my dog. Not that there was much to go home to. My parents started travelling a lot with my father's job and my dog had to go. They gave him away to the guy who did their odd jobs for them, and I never got to see him again,' he said, rubbing Oscar's ears.

'That's awful.'

'I was so angry I refused to go home for the summer holidays. In some ways I think it suited my parents not to have a little kid hanging around. I used to go to Ireland to stay with Kevan's family. They lived on a farm with five dogs – still do – and we rode horses and ate real food, which helped make up for it.'

'Your manager Kevan? He was at school with you?'

'Thank God he was. I'm not sure I would have survived, a weedy little kid like me. Kev was a tough farm kid who knew how to take care of himself, and taught me. And his mum was more of a mother to me than mine ever was.'

It was hard to know how to respond. This was not the sort of situation in which to be swapping childhood tales, but I felt I ought to offer a few titbits back about me, as you often do when others share something about themselves.

'What about you Lottie?'

Why on earth he'd be interested in my childhood I wasn't sure. 'I never really knew my mum. She left when I was three.'

'That must have been tough. What happened to you?'

I stroked Oscar as I spoke, wishing I could change the

subject. 'She had me when she was really young. A teenager. My dad didn't talk much about her. He married her a few months after I was born and brought me up as his own. His mum, my nan, looked after me while he worked. He had a café.'

'What happened to your mum?'

'She left dad when I was about six months old for a guy she met in the pub where she worked. He sang in a band, and she'd go on the road with him. Nan says my mother was a waste of space. Always drunk or on drugs. But sometimes, until I was about three, she took me on the bus to see her.' Daniel's eyes were riveted on me. I wished I'd never started this.

'What happened then?'

I should stop. This was too much. Too personal. But I so rarely talked about it that when I did, the floodgates seemed to open and I couldn't slow down. You'd think by now I'd be so used to telling my story that it wouldn't hurt anymore. And quite often it didn't. But every now and again, the feelings would sneak up on me. And this was one of them.

Sometimes it was a piece of music which sent me back in a time travel machine to be that little three-year-old girl who felt so alone and abandoned in the world. Tonight I don't know what it was. The candlelight, the fire, the unfamiliarity of my surroundings, the soft chords he was playing on the piano like a soundtrack to my life. Maybe it was just being with a man who also suffered as a little boy. Two kids in the same boat. Both of us lonely.

'Something happened at the flat where my mum was staying with her boyfriend. An accident. I got burned,' I said, pushing up my sleeve to give him a quick glimpse of the deep red scarred tissue which had become part of me.

'Lottie, that must have been...'

'I remember being in hospital where apparently I had two skin grafts. The nurses were so kind.'

'Do you remember the accident?'

'Not really. But afterwards, my nan didn't want me to see my mum anymore. She said it was her fault. And soon after that my mother moved to Liverpool with her boyfriend.'

Wiping the tears away with my sleeve, I looked in my bag for a tissue. Get a grip Gilbert. This had to stop. 'I'm really sorry.'

Before I knew it, Daniel was beside me on the sofa with his arm around me. His touch was so warm and comforting, I wanted to cuddle back into him but resisted.

'Hey Lottie. I'm the one who should be apologising. It was me who started all this. I had no right to pry. Can I get you anything, a glass of water, tissues?'

I couldn't resist piping up: 'A new mum?' He laughed, and then so did I. The spell of the past was broken, for now.

'Okay, let's change the subject,' he said, bounding back over to the piano, where he started playing and singing an upbeat song. 'This is from the new album we're recording tomorrow. What do you think?'

I didn't really know what to think, except that I shouldn't be sitting here alone with a married man, who I clearly fancied judging by the way my insides were acting.

When he'd finished he looked at me, waiting for a reaction. I should have been concentrating so I could give him feedback. Instead of which all I could think about was the feeling of his arm around my shoulder. And the way he'd looked into my eyes as if he understood my pain. What I had to remember was that this guy was a showman, a performer, and a star who was used to having women fall at his feet, which I was determined not to do.

'It's really good. I'll definitely buy the album when it comes out.'

'You can hear a couple of the tracks live. We're recording our TV show, *The French Connection* next Saturday. Why don't you come? Bring someone.'

Yes, no, maybe. I didn't know what to say. He was just being polite. It probably wouldn't happen. All I did know was that I needed to go home because I was in danger of doing something stupid. Like walking slowly over to the piano, taking his face in my hands and kissing him on the lips. Not that I would really. It was probably just one of those urges I was always fighting. Like the one I used to have as a kid in church when I wanted to shout out rude words.

Standing up, I walked over to the window. 'I thought I heard the car.'

'That's strange because we haven't called your taxi yet,' he said, walking over to join me.

At that moment, the front door opened and Kevan burst in followed by a heavy gust of wind and rain. There was a rumbling of thunder in the distance. 'That storm's getting worse, I'll drive you home,' he said.

9

The rain was coming down so hard it felt as though we were driving through one of those car washes. You know. Where the water and giant brushes attack the windows like monsters as they scrub them clean.

'It's very kind of you to drive me. I could have waited for the taxi.'

'Sure it's no problem. I was doing nothing else.'

For the next few moments there was silence as I tried to think of something to chat about. He certainly didn't seem in the mood for exchanging pleasantries.

'Daniel was telling me you were at school together.'

'Oh he was?'

'Did he always want to be a singer?'

'He wanted to be a footballer, but he didn't have what it took. I don't think the singing came into it until he formed a band in the last year of school.'

'Were you in it?'

'For five minutes. But we could never agree on the type of music to play. So I was promoted to manager, which I quite enjoyed since I was able to boss everyone around.'

'Have you always worked with him?'

This time there was a slight look of irritation. 'What is this? *Twenty Questions*?' There was an uncomfortable pause and then he started to talk. 'No. I helped run my parents' farm in Ireland for a while. But we kept in touch, and as soon as his first single as a solo artist reached number one, he called and asked if I'd look after him.'

Instead of leaving well enough alone, and listening to the beat of the windscreen wipers, I felt the need to make conversation. 'It must be a fun job.'

'It has its moments.'

'Sorry for the all the questions, I've never met anyone famous before, and it's a whole different world.'

'That it is, and if you want my opinion, you're best off out of it,' he said, and then switched on the radio presumably to drown me out. On reflection it was a bit of an odd thing for him to say, but I didn't think anything of it, except that maybe *he* was a bit odd. Or maybe it was a warning. Maybe he wanted to put me off catering for any more celebrity events.

Outside my house, he kept the engine running and turned up the speed of the windscreen wipers to cope with the downpour. A loud clap of thunder made me jump and the lightening lit us up like a spotlight. Okay it was time to make a run for it. I opened the passenger door and was immediately soaked as a gust blew the rain in. He glanced down at my feet where everything was stored in a large carrier bag.

'You can always put your saucepan on your head,' he said without as much as a smile and pulled away into the night.

At three o'clock I was still awake, running through the events of the evening. But most of all I couldn't stop thinking about my reaction to Daniel French. Every time I re-lived the feeling of his arm round me, my stomach did a treble flip. I tried to convince myself I was just enjoying a fantasy, that was all. I mean, whose stomach wouldn't flip in similar circumstances? But it felt more than that. It was as though we had some kind of emotional connection. Or at least our childhood selves did. Even though he didn't know all the details of my sad life, it was as if he didn't need to.

The loneliness of the night closed in on me like a fog. Maybe I should let Colin out of the kitchen and let him sleep on my bed except that he would probably wake me at some unearthly hour. What I needed most of all was a cuddle. That's what I missed the most about Mark. He was a great cuddler. In many ways our physical closeness was the best bit about our relationship. He used to drive me mad with his crazy career dreams which never came true, basically because of his laziness. Then there was his flirting. But on a dark night, he could comfort me like nobody else could, just by holding me. I wrapped my arms around myself, trying to recall how it felt. I thought back to the last hour of the party where couples slow-danced, lost in each other, and for a moment, imagined what it might be like smooching with Daniel.

That is enough. I sat up, and flicked on the light, reminding myself that I was fantasising about a married man. And one that, until this evening, I had never even remotely fancied.

Twenty minutes later Colin was curled up on the pillow beside me, and I was checking Facebook on my phone, wishing I could show off and post something about my touch with fame, when realised I had a text message.

'Can't thank you enough for tonight. Sleep well. D x' Oh my God, he'd texted me with a kiss. What did that mean? Nothing much probably. I mean everyone puts kisses on texts these days. Even the window cleaner when he lets me know the date of his next visit. By the time I'd finished agonising over how to reply I was wide awake.

Have you ever had one of those nights when you think you'll never sleep again, ever? Well, that! I went down to the kitchen to make hot milk much to the excitement of Colin who thought it was morning. Back in bed I waited for it to cool a little, then took a massive sip, swallowing half of the skin which had formed on the top, making myself feel sick.

Through my headphones I played an app on my phone which is supposed help you sleep. A woman's robotic voice told me to start concentrating on my breath in and out, which I did, while in the background was the sound of heavy rain on leaves. All it did was make me need to go for a wee. I went downstairs again, this time to make a hot water bottle which was quite comforting to cuddle in its white furry cover.

When that didn't work, I started Googling Daniel French, discovering that his Virgo-Libra cusp birth date made him sensual, meticulous and charming. That his favourite place in the world was Tuscany and that his top colour was royal blue. Mine too. Who would have known? I bet he wasn't lying in bed wide awake thinking about me. Or maybe he was. Why else would a text come through so late? I checked. It was one o'clock when he sent it. Maybe I should send one back, or just a kiss to acknowledge I'd received it. No that might wake him up.

I decided to reply in the morning. Just something nice and polite, like "you're welcome". Imagine, I had Daniel French's number. I could text him like a friend. Yes that was it, maybe we could be friends, and I'd cater for all his dinner parties. And he'd confide in me with all his showbiz gossip.

By the time I'd worked out what menus I'd cook at the Tuscan villa I'd persuade him to buy, I'd drifted off into a dream. Daniel was on stage singing to a crowd of thousands, and I was waiting in the wings for him. But it was as if he couldn't see me. I was invisible and...the rest of my fantasy was drowned by the sound of my phone ringing. I needed to change that ring tone. A duck quacking seemed like a fun idea once upon a time. Now it was embarrassing. Supposing my bag had started to quack when I was with Daniel.

The quacking continued until I found the phone which was underneath Colin. How he could stay asleep on top of a vibrating quacking duck, I have no idea.

'Charlotte where the hell are you? Your text last night said that you'd be well enough to come in today. If that's not the case I need to know.' It was Marsha in her very cross voice. Alarm. Forgot. Help. I should have been in work twenty minutes ago. 'I'm fine, I really am. Just a twenty-four hour bug. I'm sorry. It's my car. It's broken down with me in it. I'll be there as soon as I can.'

'If you're not here in half an hour...'

'I will be,' I said sliding off the bed, and landing on Colin who had jumped off ahead of me. He let out a dramatic wail.

'What is that?'

'It's the car. It's been making weird noises.'

Marsha sighed. 'You'll be making weird noises if you lie to me again,' she said and hung up.

10

For once I managed to catch the bus into town which gave me time to work out my story about why I was so late. I decided that honesty was the best policy, and that I'd grovel and apologise for oversleeping because I'd forgotten to set my alarm. On my phone was a text from Jess with a wealth of hearts and smileys to say that one of the famous footballers at the party had been in touch with her already. And one from Pat warning me that Marsha was on the warpath.

Looking dreamily out of the window as we chugged down the mile-long main road, it was clear that the storm had blown itself into oblivion, and given way to an Indian summer day. I kept drifting into a mellow floaty place, remembering the touch of Daniel's arm around me. All I wanted to do was curl up on the sofa with Colin and savour those moments. I kept replaying our conversation on a loop in my head, trying to read different meanings into everything he said. I still hadn't replied to his text message. What did he mean he couldn't thank me enough for last night? The cooking, the chat, the cuddle?

Okay so it wasn't actually a cuddle. It was him trying to comfort me. But it was quite an intimate moment between two strangers. I've always read that you should never text back immediately in case you come across as too keen. Keen? What was I thinking? He was a married superstar, I was just someone who did catering for his birthday party. What did it matter if I added a kiss or not? If I had a pound for every minute I'd wasted on text messaging, debating whether or not to add one kiss or two or agonising over what emojis to use, I'd be a rich woman. So I typed in: "You're welcome" with a kiss and then immediately deleted the kiss and added a smiley face. There. Sent. I looked round the bus at the other passengers most of whom looked as though they were in some sort of stupor, except for two women who were clearly gossiping about a friend. I bet they'd be impressed if they knew who I was texting.

I could try to convince myself that my feelings for Daniel French were totally professional. But there was no denying the butterfly effect in my stomach. The last time I'd felt like this, I was fifteen and had fallen madly in love with a new boy in the sixth form at school whose family had moved into the area.

The day he first appeared on the stage where the sixth form sat peering piously down on us fourth formers he sent our female hormones into a frenzy. He was the most gorgeous boy I had ever seen, all six feet two inches of him, with his Scandinavian blond hair and knowing dark blue eyes. He looked like some sort of Nordic god who only chose to take notice of certain people. And one of them was Helen. I'm not sure he ever so much as glanced at me, except once when I tripped over my schoolbag and fell at his feet. But as he held out a hand to help me, Helen got there first and yanked me up, smiling at him: 'Excuse my friend Lottie. She can't help being clumsy.' And I couldn't. My friends, mainly led by Helen, used to call me Dotty Lottie since I was always falling over, hurting myself, or dropping things. What chance would someone like me stand in the eyes of Ben Hart?

From the day he arrived in Abbey Cross, Helen decided he would be hers, no matter what. Even when he started dating the head girl, Susie who was equally blonde and as stunning as he was. They made a golden couple. But Helen was having none of it. By recruiting the services of her mean little group of Hellenettes, she started rumours that 'slutty Susie' had slept with nearly every boy in the sixth form, until even I started to believe they might be true. And sure enough, her dirty work was enough to smear Susie in shame, and entice the gorgeous Ben into her pretty web where she set about making sure he could never escape.

And he never did. Making sure she got a place at the same university, she became pregnant with Harry almost as soon as they graduated, at which point they married and went on to have Rose, Freddy and George in quick succession. Helen had always wanted to be an events organiser, but the only events she ever organised were her own extravagant wedding, subsequent baby showers and her children's birthday parties.

The bus stopped to let passengers on right outside Ben's office, Hart and Son Solicitors. He was desperately hoping that he could persuade Harry into the business one day, but unless he could offer him a racing car as a company vehicle, it seemed unlikely. Although it was Sunday, Ben was there, sitting on the corner of the desk in reception.

I rubbed the steamed up bus windows with my sleeve to get a better look. He was talking to a blonde woman and judging by the body language, there was an argument in progress.

Just as we pulled away, I noticed the family's two golden retrievers, milling around the office. He must have taken them out for a walk, and called in to catch up with some business. In which case, who was the woman? It was unlikely he would be seeing a client on a Sunday morning, especially with his dogs in tow. Unless? No, surely not. He would never risk his perfect marriage to Helen and his perfect family and perfect life for what? Who?

I was intrigued now. Should I mention to Helen what I'd seen? Maybe not. I got up to ring the bell, deciding that I'd walk the last block of shops so that I had time to think. Perhaps I should head back and catch Ben off guard. Then I really would be late.

My text alert made its dingle dangle noise. It was Ryan letting me know that Marsha's godson had been happy with the food and service and that his mum and her friend wanted to know if there was any more work in the offing. I'd already decided to up Daniel's bill in order to pay their fee for helping out.

When I arrived at The Loft, Marsha was out having brunch with an old friend, so I was excused her wrath, at least temporarily, for calling in sick on Saturday.

I stood for a moment at the top of the stairs and looked round. Every table was occupied, mainly by our yummy mummy regulars with their husbands and kids who, if they weren't yelling, were crying. Normally the noise wouldn't bother me, but today it set me on edge. If only I could turn the volume down. Out of the corner of my eye I spotted Pat clearing plates from a nearby table. She beckoned me over.

'Come on then. I want to hear everything about Daniel French's party. What was he like?'

'Surely Jess has already told you.'

'Yes, but only up until she and Ryan left. Have you had any feedback from his nibs?'

For some reason, I wanted to keep Daniel's text message private, so that it was our little secret. 'No, but everyone seemed happy with what we did.'

'Apart from the dopey housekeeper, so I'm told. I'd have given her what for,' she said.

I didn't doubt it. Pat wasn't afraid to stand up to anyone. I'd once seen her confront two youths who were trying to sneak out of The Loft without paying their bill. She blocked their exit at the top of the stairs, and when one of them tried to push past she grabbed a golf umbrella, which was leaning by the old-fashioned coat stand, and whacked him around the legs with it until his knees buckled and he fell onto the floor. She'd also taken on a tattooed biker who'd been making sexual remarks to Jess, tipping his glass of beer over his head, before grabbing him by the arm and escorting him to the top of the stairs.

'I know your mother Sonny Jim and I also know that you still live with her. At your age! She won't be too happy if she hears about this. So do one. And don't come back.' He never did.

Pat followed me into the kitchen where Jess and Ryan virtually leaped on me like excited puppies to hear my after-party news. I relayed an edited version of what happened after they left, and told them that Daniel had played me a song from his new album over a glass of champagne.

'You don't think he fancies you, do you?' asked Jess in a voice of disbelief. Thanks Jess. 'Of course he doesn't fancy me,' I said feeling a surge of disappointment. Why would someone who could have his pick fancy me?

'He might do,' said Pat. 'I mean look at her. That lovely red hair, and cute freckles, and all those curves. My Frank thinks she's gorgeous.'

'Yeh, no offence to your Frank,' said Jess, 'but superstars normally go for model types don't they. His wife's a size zero. Lottie's at least a fourteen.'

'Twelve, I'm a twelve. Okay, a thirteen,' I said, not that anyone was listening.

'I think he did,' said Ryan, handing me a mug of steaming coffee.

'Did what?' asked Pat.

'I think Daniel did fancy Lottie.'

'How do you work that one out?' asked Jess.

'Excuse me. I am here you know,' I said, intrigued at Ryan's observation. 'Yes, how do you work that one out?'

'The way he was watching you when you were stirring the curry. The way you lick your lips when you're concentrating. He was staring at you, and when you saw him, your face sort of lit up. And when we left, it was obvious he wanted to you to stay longer.'

I couldn't quite believe what I was hearing. If it was Jess, I would have dismissed her silliness. But Ryan? He was a great people watcher.

More. I wanted to talk about it more, but rustling noises from the café meant that customers needed attention. This would have to wait.

'Any rate, he's got a missus,' said Pat, as if reading my mind.

Jess held up her phone. 'Yeh, but she's in America, and Twitter's been going mad since someone leaked she didn't make it to his party last night.'

'Enough please. We are running a café here, and people need serving,' I said, taking Jess's phone out of her hand, while trying to surreptitiously read a couple of the tweets she was referring to. 'She's an actress, she's filming. There are pictures of them all over the house. She's gorgeous.'

'Yeh, but what's the point of having a gorgeous wife if you never see her?' asked Jess, taking back her phone, and putting it into her pocket. 'Anyway, he'd have been in touch by now, if he fancied you, like my footballer. He's champing at the bit to see me, but I'm making him wait.'

I took a deep breath and said rather smugly: 'As a matter of fact he has been in touch. I got a text in the middle of the night *and* he's asked me to his TV show.'

11

Helen was making one of her killer lasagnes, while Freddy prepared a salad. All was calm in her beautiful farmhouse kitchen as George sat engrossed on his phone, and Rose finished off making a necklace, while I could hear loud music coming from Harry's bedroom upstairs.

'Ben hopes to be home in time, but if not we might have to go ahead without him,' said Helen, passing me the olive oil to dress the salad.

Really? And what might be the cause of his delay, I thought, as I remembered back to the scene at his office on Sunday. I'd decided not to mention it to Helen. There was no point in upsetting her about something that might be totally innocent. But if I had the chance with Ben, I might hint at my sighting.

'So come on then, tell me more. What's Daniel French like?' asked Helen, as she poured us a glass of red and decluttered the table of family debris so we could sit there. 'Did you fancy him?'

'No, of course not. I didn't really think of it like that. It was just work.'

Helen guffawed. 'Oh come on, who are you trying to kid? He's once of the most fanciable guys in the world, and you were just thinking about your mushroom vol-au-vents?'

'Well no, yes. He is very attractive, and married of course.'

'And who else was there? Come on. Dish the goss. Did you do any selfies with them? Surely you did one with him.'

More than anything, I wanted to share what happened by the fire after everyone had gone, but I knew from experience that Helen would make it sound as though it was a superstar being kind to her emotionally disturbed friend, so I kept quiet.

I did however mention the invitation to the TV show which she immediately leaped on.

'Okay when's that? I'll check my diary.'

'This Saturday, but I've already asked Pat to come with me. She's a huge fan.'

'Thanks a lot,' said Helen pulling one of her pouty faces which made her look about ten-years-old. 'Anyway I couldn't come. We're been invited to a dinner party at the Ross's new house. One of those gorgeous new builds on the canal. Have you seen them?'

I hadn't, but it wouldn't have mattered what I'd said. She was too busy describing how much money her friends had made from the sale of their London flat and their plans to buy a cottage by the sea. The fact that I'd never even met these people didn't seem to stop her from imparting intimate knowledge of their relationship.

'She threw him out after he had an affair with the nanny, but forgave him, and he's back home now.'

I saw this as my chance to bring Ben into the conversation. 'So would you forgive your husband if you discovered he was having an affair?'

She laughed. 'He wouldn't dare. Why do you ask that?'

'No reason. I was just making conversation.'

She turned her back to me, and started vigorously chopping parsley. 'Could you round up the kids? I'm about to dish up.'

There was a bit of an atmosphere around the table, mainly because Helen was now officially in a mood, and the children seemed more interested in their mobiles than in their meals. Maybe I'd touched a nerve, or knowing Helen, she felt insulted that the idea had even occurred to me.

'Come on, you know the rules,' she said, holding out her hand for the offending phones. They groaned in unison. From outside I could hear a car pulling up on the gravel. Helen looked at her watch.

'Freddy could you get a warm plate from the oven and dish some up for daddy please?'

Ben did the rounds, kissing his children his wife and me, and within minutes any frostiness had melted as we entered into the spirit of the family meal.

It was hard to get a word in edgewise while Harry, Rose, George and Freddy battled to hold centre stage. I thought of entertaining them with the story of my star-studded evening with Daniel French, but it was doubtful they'd even know who he was, and I couldn't remember the name of the rap star Jess had been raving about.

'Fancy taking the dogs out while we clear up?' Helen asked her husband once he'd finished his dinner. Almost too eagerly he agreed and went to get their leads. Now was my moment.

'I'll come,' I said grabbing my scarf and coat which I'd slung over the bottom of the banisters.

'Whatever for? It's freezing out there. I'll only be about twenty minutes,' said Ben, checking his pocket, probably for his phone.

'No really, I could do with the fresh air. I've been stuck in a kitchen like a sauna all day,' I said determined to get time alone with him. It was probably nothing, but I was curious. Supposing the woman I'd seen him with was more than just a client. As I popped my head round the door to let Helen know what I was doing, she waved me off with a smile, while simultaneously taking a phone call, breaking up an argument between Freddy and Rose and uncorking another bottle of red.

For a few minutes we walked in silence before he started to make polite conversation.

'So Lottie, I hear you've been hobnobbing with the rich and famous. What's he like that Daniel French? Never been my cup of tea. Far too cheesy.'

'Well I didn't think he was mine, but when I stayed behind to have a drink, he played me one of his songs from the new album, and it's not at all bad.'

'Did he indeed? Your own private performance?' said Ben, shooting me a look as if to say, tell me more.

'Oh nothing like that. My car broke down and I was waiting for a taxi, and...'

'He is pretty hot, and I say that as a guy,' he said, laughing as he went on to chat about his love of real stars of their time like the Rolling Stones.

Determined to change the subject to work I asked him: 'Have you ever acted for anyone famous going through a divorce?'

'Only a local radio presenter and his wife. But I'd hardly call him famous.'

'Keeps you busy though, people having affairs?'

'Certainly does. I wouldn't be in business if husbands and wives didn't cheat.'

'You must be really hectic if you have to work Sundays as well.'

'I don't. Well, very rarely.'

Here goes, I thought, clearing my throat. 'I was on the bus and saw you in your office yesterday talking to a client. A blonde woman.' He stopped in his tracks.

'You're right. I called in to get some paper work I needed to bring home and she saw me in reception and knocked on the window.'

'So she's a client?'

Ben smiled as he pointed in the direction of his home. 'Come on Lottie, you know I can't talk about things like that.' In his most charming of voices he added: 'And I'd rather you didn't tell Helen that we had this conversation. She has such a vivid imagination.'

12

The only time I'd ever been to the recording of a television show was when I was about eleven, and so excited about meeting a puppet called Gordon the Gopher that I couldn't sleep the night before.

It was much the same this time as I counted down the hours until I could get up and start trying on outfits for the day. I settled on tight black trousers with ankle boots, a floaty lilac top and a long silver mother of pearl necklace which Mark had got me for my last birthday. As usual he had told me to go out and choose something from him, which I did, and then paid for it because he was broke.

I was so excited at the prospect of seeing Daniel again to check if my feelings were real, or whether I was just having a giant star crush, that in the last few days I'd lost my appetite and about five pounds which meant my cheekbones had made a welcome reappearance for the first time in years.

Getting the whole of Saturday off had proved impossible, but when Marsha heard where we were going, she reluctantly agreed Pat and I could finish after the lunch rush. This meant we had about twenty minutes to change in the toilets and hurry downstairs where a mini cab was waiting to take us to the station.

'Ooh I say,' said Pat as she settled into the cracked leather seats. 'This is exciting. I've made sure that everybody records the show when it goes out. We might end up on the telly, especially if we're near the front. Imagine.'

I was. I was trying to imagine meeting Daniel again or more importantly if I *would* actually meet him. I'd had an email from the TV company to explain how the evening would work. We'd be given access after to the show to the green room for drinks and Daniel *might* join VIP guests if he didn't have a prior engagement.

Instead of queuing with the rest of the audience, a small elite gang of us were given our special gold wrist bands and ushered upstairs to a roped-off area where a selection of drinks and crisps awaited us. After an age of waiting, a bossy posh girl called Poppy who kept saying "Ok ya" all the time escorted us to our seats. I noticed that other audience members kept glancing rather enviously at our gold wristbands and back to their silver ones. 'I'm never taking mine off,' said Pat, making sure her sleeve was rolled up so that everyone could see her status.

We were two rows from the front with the most amazing view of the stage which was bathed in red spotlights. From watching the show, I remembered there were normally about three guests who sat on the red velvet sofa while Daniel sat opposite in a gold velvet matching chair, a bit like a throne. But then he was the King of Pop.

Over on the other side of the set, was a baby grand surrounded by speakers and discarded instruments which I imagined would later burst into life courtesy of Daniel's band. I wondered if he'd spot me sitting in the audience, which was ridiculous. He probably didn't even know I was coming unless Kevan had remembered to mention it when I called him about the tickets.

'Ooh look that's what's-her-face from that soap,' said Pat nudging me as she pointed to someone I'd never seen in my life. 'Oh and that woman over there, isn't she Lily Salmon from that awful cookery show?' The woman concerned shot us an evil look which made Pat bristle. 'Who does she think she is?'

'She probably thinks she's Lily Salmon,' I said, losing

interest in the celebrity spotting game. The only face I wanted to see was Daniel's, but before he made an entrance, we had to sit through thirty minutes of a warm-up comedian. And yes he was very funny, but I wasn't there to laugh. I was here to lose myself in Daniel and his music.

'Daniel's wife, isn't here,' said Pat, looking round at the audience.

I knew that because I'd been searching the Internet to find out more about Beth Blackshaw, and discovered she was still filming in LA. They seemed quite an unlikely couple, so I was curious how they met. Apparently it was on this very show when she was making a movie and declaring her love of all things British and Northern, including pork scratchings and, as it turned out, Daniel French.

After a three-month love affair there were engagement pictures of them looking cosy in a Swiss ski chalet, Beth showing off a diamond the size of an iceberg. Six months later came the wedding photos. They were married in an historic white church in a Spanish village against a backdrop of mountains and olive trees. A few days later this was followed by a blessing on the beach in the Maldives, and a honeymoon apartment on stilts with steps down to the sea.

To begin with they were rarely pictured apart until she landed the role in *School Daze* last year, which meant her spending less time at Morton Manor and much more time at their Californian home.

A wave of excitement washed around the room and Pat tapped me on the arm as a girl with a clipboard and headset held open a curtain. And there he was. The man who I had felt so close to last Saturday when we exchanged our childhood stories. Two lonely little kids who had grown up trying to hide their scars of sadness.

He looked amazing. Different somehow, as though he had a celebrity aura around him. His hair was spiked up and he was wearing a pale blue suit over a black T-shirt. Waiting for the cheers and flurry of screams to die down, he waved and smiled, blowing kisses to us all. I sat rigid in my seat wondering why on earth I'd come. What was I expecting might happen? That he'd spot me sitting in the second row like a frightened rabbit in the headlights and serenade me?

For another ten minutes, he disappeared again while the floor manager strutted around lecturing us about what to do in the case of an emergency or a fire, and then as the invisible orchestra struck up, I started to feel excited. The warm-up man appeared again and made us rehearse a standing ovation with yelps, claps and screams the moment that Daniel appeared. Then the stage exploded into life with what seemed like a million different coloured lights. Slowly, through the floor, in a cloud of red smoke, he appeared almost in slow motion as we clapped our hands sore. Pat kept whispering in my ear, but I was lost in a world of my own, lapping up every note Daniel sang as though it was just to me. At one point on the monitors either side of the stage I glimpsed myself on screen and did what you're not supposed to do because it looks so silly when you watch it back on the telly, which is stare at myself.

After a short break, during which Poppy and a male assistant came round with cartons of orange and chocolate bars, another cool-looking guy in black chinos and black shirt who introduced himself as the producer, informed us that Daniel would be coming into the audience to choose a couple of people to sing on stage with him.

'If there's any chance I'm going for it,' announced Pat in a very determined voice, checking her lipstick in her compact mirror. 'Imagine what my Frank would think if he saw me on the telly singing with Daniel French.'

'There might be loads of others who want to sing,' I said, worried she might be disappointed.

'Nothing wrong with giving it a go,' she said, running her hands through her white blonde hair to spike it up a bit. 'If I've got a chance of my fifteen minutes of fame, then I want it.'

Ten minutes later and Daniel was racing through the audience as we clapped to the rhythm of a dance track, and when he spotted Pat waving manically at him, he headed towards us. Without even a glance at me, he grabbed her by the hand and led her up to the stage, collecting en route a curvy brunette in a tight leopard skin top who pouted and giggled at him. And before you could say karaoke, Pat was belting out Daniel's evergreen hit single "Once in a Lifetime", in her powerful rock and roll voice, which had the audience on its feet dancing and clapping. My God, I'd never heard her sing quite like this. She was phenomenal. Our very own Pat on stage in a duet with Daniel French who looked delighted with his discovery. I wondered if he remembered her from the selfie they took.

The brunette who turned out to be a nurse of all things, delivered a wobbly rendition of the same song sounding like Minnie Mouse on speed, much to the amusement of the crowds who gave her just as much applause but for different reasons.

Pat drifted back to her seat as if on a cloud. 'Did you hear them all cheering? They weren't taking the mickey were they?'

'Of course not. You were brilliant. I didn't know you could sing like that.'

'Nor did I. Well that is, it's been a while. I used to sing in the pubs before I married Frank. Even got spotted by a producer who wanted me to make a record. But it never happened.'

This was all news to me. Amazing how little you know about someone you spend time with every day.

'Why didn't it happen?'

She patted her stomach. 'Fell pregnant at eighteen with my Julia. And she was followed by my Rita and then Carol. So...' her voice trailed off, as our attention was diverted by more lights and loud music as Daniel threw himself into an energetic dance routine accompanied by half a dozen women dressed in slinky black cat suits. All of them stunning. Surely if he ever decided to stray, he wouldn't have to go far. I wondered if his proximity to beautiful young dancers ever bothered his wife.

As he skidded to the front of the stage on his knees to thunderous applause, I could swear he looked straight into my eyes. Although when the elderly woman in the seat in front of mine screamed in ecstasy at the same second, I had my doubts it was actually me he was looking at. Anyway, what did it matter? Why was I behaving like such an idiot, believing there was some sort of spark between a god-like superstar like him and a mere mortal like me?

At sixteen when Daniel was the spiky-haired pin-up boy in the band Three to One, I'd hardly given him a second glance. Why, I have no idea. A lot of it was down to who your friends fancied. With Helen and her Helenettes you were nobody unless you pledged your undying love to Take That. So to make sure I was in with the popular girls I convinced myself I was totally in love with Robbie Williams, and would conjure up scenarios of how we could meet and fall in love at one of his shows. Now I was re-living the fantasy but at an age which surely made me look desperate.

It was about ten by the time the audience, hands stinging from clapping on demand, trickled out into the night, except for those of us with gold wristbands.

'What happens in this blue room?' asked Pat, as a little group of us stopped off at the ladies while Poppy waited for us outside in case we got lost. 'Green room. Don't know. Drinks and nibbles I suppose,' I said, wishing the harsh lighting wasn't so cruel on the bags under my eyes as I freshened up my lippy.

'I need more than flipping nibbles. I'm starving. How come we've been in there for hours? The show only lasts an hour on the telly.'

Her question was never answered as Poppy ushered us out like a mini herd of sheep, down two flights of stairs and along several corridors into a packed room where everyone appeared to be shouting to make themselves heard.

A small bar provided us with a welcome glass of ice cold white wine, and trays of tired-looking canapés were passed around by hot-looking waiters.

A young couple who I'd noticed sitting near us bounded over to Pat to congratulate her on her performance which gave me a chance to scour the room. I'd worked out that the people here were either friends of the crew, or of the guest artists on the show.

There was a gentle tap on my shoulder and when I turned

round it was TV actress Naomi Lincoln.

'Someone I know, thank goodness,' she said leading me over to the bar. 'I was here with my mum who's a huge fan of Daniel's, but she's taken a cab home, so I thought I ought to pop my head in here to say hi to the man himself,' she said, gesturing to the barman to re-fill her glass.

'Shouldn't really be doing this, I've got lines to learn when I get home,' she said, clinking her glass on mine.

'Don't tell me what happens to Dr Reece, I'm still two episodes behind.'

'No worries, I can't even remember what happens to her. I filmed those episodes that are running now weeks ago,' she said laughing.

Surprised that she'd even recognised me from the night of Daniel's party, I was even more amazed that we were chatting away like old friends.

Making polite conversation, I asked after her husband, the East End actor Jerry Thornton who had starred as many a villain in TV cop shows. He must be in his mid-sixties now, while Naomi could only be about forty, resulting in endless tabloid stories about the couple and their age gap. And I seemed to recall they had a daughter Scarlet who was about three.

'Oh Jerry hates these things. He's much happier at his local pub with a couple of mates and a beer watching the football,' said Naomi, looking over to the commotion at the doorway as a security man ousted a crying young woman who had clamped herself to Daniel's arm. 'Oh poor Danny. That happened the last time I came to one of his shows, and I think it was the same woman. God knows how she manages to get past security.'

Naomi led me through the clusters of guests towards him. He was talking to Pat, who looked entranced. 'Hey Lottie,' he said, holding open his arms for a hug and a kiss. Oh my God, was it one cheek or two? I couldn't remember. Or maybe it was three in London. He stopped at two, and stood back to look at me. I wanted to gush about how brilliant the show was, and how much I loved his new songs, but somehow I was stuck for words, because what I really wanted to say was that I hadn't stopped thinking about him since last Saturday night. So I said nothing at all, feeling myself tense up as I waited for him to speak.

'My favourite cook is looking a bit of a dish tonight.'

Chef, I wanted to say. I'm a chef. I've got the qualifications. But I didn't mind. He could call me anything at all, especially a dish, and I'd be happy.

Somehow I needed to see him again. Just to satisfy myself that any moment of magic last Saturday was purely in my imagination.

'If you want me to do any more cooking for you, just call me.'

He smiled. 'Now that would be a treat Lottie. But we're off on our travels for a few days.' Travelling? He was going away. Where to? For how long? Was he off to America to see his wife? I didn't want him to go anywhere. Not yet.

Before I had a chance to say more, I was distracted by a loud familiar voice.

'You wouldn't believe what an awful seat they put me in next to a woman from Broadstairs who spent the entire evening crunching sherbet lemons,' said Stella, as Daniel engulfed his agent in a bear hug. 'What's wrong with sherbet lemons?' he asked looking bemused.

'Nothing except the bitch didn't even offer me one,' said Stella shaking off his arms, and smoothing down her long black bob. 'Oh it's you Lottie. Didn't recognise you out of your maid's uniform.'

Daniel put his arm around my shoulder and gave me a squeeze. I jumped as if I'd had an electric shock, and he took it away. 'Stella be nice. You should be thinking about putting Lottie on your books. She could have her own TV cookery show. *Lottie at the Loft*.'

'Mmm, she's a pretty thing, but she's not exactly Nigella is she?'

'No, she's a gorgeous redhead. Much more exciting.'

'Oh come on Daniel. I'd rather be bald than ginger.'

Er, excuse me. How is it that people are always taking

about me as if I'm not here?

Daniel was laughing. He was obviously used to her bitchy repertoire. 'Don't take any notice Lottie. In between sticking those little barbs into people, she has a heart of gold. Isn't that right Stella?' But Stella had already recognised somebody far more interesting and left the group. From what I'd seen, I doubted she had a heart at all. I tried to catch Daniel's eye as I excused myself to wander back to the bar, but he'd been accosted by two women asking for selfies.

As Pat was holding court with her new fans, I was free to watch as the man of the hour continued to dish out hugs and kisses around the room in true showbiz fashion. Let's face it, Daniel was obviously a touchy feely kind of guy, which led me to question if there was ever a special moment between us in front of the fire that night, or whether he was just doing what came naturally to a superstar with an upset fan.

'Mine's a beer,' said a voice so close to my ear it made the hairs on my neck stand up. It was Kevan, who seemed to have appeared out of nowhere in a black jumper striped with yellow which gave him the appearance of a bumble bee.

'I didn't think you were here.'

'Where else would I be?' he asked sounding amused. Well, possibly with your cool boyfriend Max, I thought to myself, but daren't say.

He looked different. No glasses, that was it. He must be wearing contacts which showed off those intense blue eyes that didn't miss a thing as he looked past me around the room.

Maybe he'd fill me in a bit more about his boss's plans.

'Daniel says you're off on your travels.'

'Well it must be true then,' he said, without his face moving a muscle. It would become my mission to make this man smile if it killed me. Surely no one could go through life looking that grumpy.

'Where are you off to?'

'Oh you know, here, there and everywhere. You can look it up on his website.'

'Do you go on the road with him?'

'Aye, I do.'

'What's it like? Do you have to fight the fans off?' I said, trying hard to think of something to say.

'No we have Chas for that.'

'What about Max, does he mind you going on the road?'

'No he's happy to get rid of me for a while. Are we back to *Twenty Questions* again?' he said, with a slightly bored look on his face.

'No, I'm just interested. I'm sorry if I annoy you,' I said, trying to sound jokey.

'Oh believe me, you'd know if you did that,' he said.

After we'd said our goodbyes to a bunch of enthusiastic new friends we were never likely to see again, I scoured the room for Daniel, but he'd vanished as if in the smoke that he'd first appeared in on stage tonight.

'My Frank isn't going to believe it when I tell him about tonight,' said Pat as we waited on the windy platform for the train to pull in. As the doors opened then closed behind us, I felt a deep sense of disappointment. Nothing in my life had really changed.

13

For once I had Sunday off, but wasted the morning moping and feeling miserable about my life. Even Colin picked up on my mood and stayed under the bed. It comes to something when even your cat finds you bad company.

When Helen called, I brightened up for an instant. Maybe she was planning to invite me round for a roast dinner. Something I never ever cooked myself. A roast dinner for one just didn't do it somehow. You needed to be sitting around the table with your family, except I didn't have one. The best I could hope for was to borrow someone else's relatives and snuggle into their cosy nest like a cuckoo.

As soon as she started speaking, I gave up all hope of crunchy roast potatoes and Yorkshire puddings.

'Oh my God, you should see the Ross's new house by the canal. It's a dream. And there was this other couple I'd never met before, the Suttons. Fascinating. He works in the City, something to do with banking, so loaded. And she's got that small dress shop in the High Street called Lulu's. That's her name. Expensive. Italian stuff which she sources in Milan. Bags, jewellery too. We ought to go.'

'And how are the Ross couple after the affair? Is he still forgiven?'

'I think he's still at it. He kept glancing at his phone over dinner. Sure sign. Gorgeous food though. And champagne. Bottles of the stuff. Hangover from hell this morning.'

Maybe she'd remember to ask me about my evening, but no such luck as, at the sound of children arguing in the background, she said: 'Got to go,' and hung up.

There was only one thing to do now. Make myself a cup of coffee and do a bit of Facebook stalking to see what Mark was up to. Tara was forever tagging him into pictures of them together at some expensive restaurant or other. According to him, the only cooking she ever did was a ready meal in the microwave. Once, soon after our break up, when he was worse for wear after a night out with the lads, he'd texted me to say he'd missed my cooking. Oh thanks. Is that all I was good for?

As usual there were photos galore of them out with friends. We rarely went out with other couples when we were together, so I could only assume they were mainly hers. Come to think of it all the girls looked like clones of Tara with their fake tans, blonde hair extensions, white teeth and skin tight dresses to show off their breast implants. The guys were all tall fit-looking twenty-something hipsters with beards, apart from Mark who was shorter with the hint of a paunch from too much beer. And then I saw it. A beautifully manicured hand with a close-up of an engagement ring boasting a diamond twice as big as the one he bought me. When was the rat going to let me know? I sank into a pit of despondency.

It's one thing realising you've stuck with the wrong man for the past five years, but he was *my* wrong man. Maybe I could have improved him. Maybe we could have improved as a couple. I mean it wasn't all bad. He was lazy and annoyed me with his silly plans that never came to anything, and his dependency on me to sort out his life. But we laughed and snuggled in bed. He was there to come home to after a hard day's work at The Loft, like a happy dog wagging his tail. In fact he was always so cheerful, and that's what I missed the most.

I studied the photograph of him with Tara. Oh yes, he looked like the cat who had the cream, and not only the cream but the whole bloody dairy since her daddy was rich and had already bought her a house. I should try to be happy for him. Let's face it, he wasn't suited to living with a woman seven years older than him who basically wanted to tie him to the sofa to watch *Masterchef* every night. The way I was hurting right now, I'd have taken him back like a shot, just to be held close and loved.

The rest of the day passed slowly, with no contact from a soul apart from a text full of smileys from Pat who was still on a high after her debut performance on a prime time TV show. And who could blame her? I went on Daniel's website to check out where he was off to, and could see only a couple of imminent concerts in Manchester, with a world tour the following year.

It was three o'clock when I gave in and opened a bottle of wine, convincing myself that at weekends wine o'clock could be any time. After a couple of glasses, I was ravenous and resorted to ordering an Indian takeaway for one which is a soul-destroying thing to do. And when the man from The Curry Cottage arrived at the front door bearing my food, I detected a look of pity in his eyes.

After polishing off the wine, I decided it was time to take charge of my love life and sign up to the new dating app everyone was talking about. Within twenty minutes of being on there I'd been asked out by an eighteen-year-old with the user name of Cougar-lover, received a dubious looking selfie of a guy who looked as though he might well be on death row for murder, and a picture of an erect penis. Every ten minutes I checked my phone just in case someone out there in the world was trying to make contact.

By around ten I'd had three text messages. One informing me I had £1376.49 waiting in a bank account for a whiplash injury in a car accident I don't recall having; one from a make-up company offering me free delivery on their latest range and one from Marsha telling me not to be late on Monday morning as she had meat deliveries arriving early. Not a word from Mark letting me know that he was engaged. I wondered what the verb was for getting unengaged like we did. I still had the ring in its green padded box stuffed in my knicker drawer.

For the next two days I existed entirely in my head, with negative thoughts about me and my miserable life multiplying faster than I could cope with them. Wading through my library of self-help books, I tried mindfulness, which is supposed to help you live in the moment, but my mind was full of so much regret about the past, I decided to give up and just wallow there. Every now and again, someone would notice my deep sighs and look concerned.

'You're well rid of that Mark, pet. You'll meet someone new,' said Pat, as she joined me out on the fire escape overlooking the town. Cold though it was, I'd taken to sitting there and staring into the distance as if trying to look into the future.

Matters weren't helped by the fact that Jess and her new footballer boyfriend were so loved-up. He'd taken her to a London nightspot where she'd rubbed shoulders with other WAGs. And Ryan was in contact with Kevan's boyfriend Max Diamond who'd invited him to his club Chill in London's West End.

Pat was enjoying her new-found celebrity status as a performer on *The French Connection* and counting down the weeks until the show went out in December.

And me? I felt I had become the archetypal lonely singleton living with a cat called Colin. A spinster. That's what I was. What a horrible word to be labelled with.

On Tuesday night I caught the bus home and even wondered if I should settle for a date with the driver who wasn't bad looking and always had a new chat-up line.

As I walked down the hill from the bus stop, I could see a man in a baseball hat, black rimmed glasses, and a padded black coat ringing the bell. For a moment I wondered if it was Kevan. Hurrying towards my front door I called out. 'Hello, can I help you?'

When he turned, I stood rooted to the spot, my mouth hanging open, which is not a pretty sight. It was Daniel French.

14

My hands were shaking as I poured boiling water over a tea bag. I stood with my back to him, while Colin purred as if in heaven and wrapped his long black body round Daniel's legs.

'You offered to cook for me again, so here I am,' he said, laughing, ruffling up his hair and tossing the baseball cap onto the sofa. He shoved the glasses into his pocket. They were just plain lenses, he said. A disguise when he was out in public.

'How did you get here?' I asked, praying that he wasn't expecting me to conjure up some sort of cordon bleu meal from the tins of baked beans, spaghetti hoops and Pot Noodles which languished in my store cupboard.

'Chas drove me. He's parked round the corner.'

'Does he want to come in? It's cold out there.'

Daniel took off his coat and hung it on the back of the chair. 'I'm sure he's fine. Anyway I'm not expecting you to cook me dinner, I thought I'd let someone else do it. At a restaurant.'

'Really?'

'As a thank you for doing such an amazing job at the party.' He sat down on the wooden chair by the table and stroked Colin gently.

'I'm sorry, I should have called, but we were driving back through town, so I thought I'd surprise you.' Surprise? This was the type of shock which would register at least six points on the Richter scale. I tried to sound casual. 'Where do you have in mind?'

'Morton's. Near me. I think you'll love it. So? Are you up for it? Or do I have to eat alone?'

'What about Chas?'

'I want to take you to dinner, not Chas. He's on duty.'

'Are you sure? To Morton's?'

'Yes, if you'd like to. Or we can go to McDonalds?'

Conscious of the fact I was wearing a faded old bobbly wool cardigan, I excused myself and ran upstairs. I needed to think. Was this like a date, in recognition there was something between us, or simply a thank you?

If it was a thank you he could have sent flowers or chocolates, surely. But it couldn't be a date because he was so famous and famous people only dated famous people didn't they? Anyway he was married.

Dragging my best baby pink cashmere sweater out of the washing basket, I did the sniff test, and threw it back. *No to knitwear*. This was a five-star restaurant which demanded five-star clothes. The problem was that most of my clothes wouldn't have looked out of place in a charity shop. They were old and if not old, then cheap. A quick rummage and I found a silky blue blouse. I could wear that with a camisole underneath and my skinny black jeans, and oh yes, my soft grey woollen wrap. The last time I'd worn it was to keep warm watching TV. It had become my security blanket.

Downstairs I could hear Daniel's warm Northern accent on his phone. His voice was the evidence that I really did have an international superstar in my kitchen. The door opened and Colin sauntered in and jumped on my bed.

'You may not realise this Colin, but you have just been stroked by one of the most famous men in Britain,' I said, trying to tame my curls by brushing them into submission. If only I'd had time for a shower to make sure I washed off any scent of fried onions. Instead I doused myself with perfume and refreşhed my make-up with some green kohl to emphasise my hazel eyes. There that should do it. My eyes were definitely my best point. Large and expressive framed by dark eyebrows which men for some reason always found sexy, especially if I made them rise slightly, widening my eyes in a suggestive manner. I stood in front of my full length mirror. A hint of glamour was needed. The exotic long dangly diamante earrings Helen bought me for Christmas should do it. I'd never had an excuse to wear them before.

As we left the house, Chas pulled up in a silver Mercedes with blacked-out windows. Climbing into the back with Daniel, I started to shake. Was this really happening? Even if it wasn't a date, I could pretend, couldn't I? I was already rehearsing how I'd tell the crew at work tomorrow, Marsha included. And Helen. How jealous would *she* be?

I was so lost in my own dream world for a second that I jumped at the sound of Daniel's voice. 'Did you mind me calling round?'

'Of course not. But doesn't your wife mind you picking up strange women and taking them out for dinner?'

'You're not that strange,' he laughed, 'Anyway my wife's not here,' he said, rather abruptly. I'd obviously strayed onto sensitive territory, so decided to change the subject.

'I'm really excited to try some of the dishes at Mortons. I might pick up a few tips for our menu,' I said, and as we started talking about our favourite foods, I felt the atmosphere lighten. Even Chas joined in, informing us that fish finger sandwiches would probably be his last meal on death row.

Mine, I volunteered, would be a chicken korma and Daniel was torn between shepherd's pie and steak and kidney pudding. By the time we reached Mortons, I had made a decision to enjoy every moment so I could write about it in my journal. Since that night when I'd physically pushed Mark out of the front door, hurling his mobile phone at him after discovering texts from Tara, it had been too painful to record my thoughts and feelings. But this was different. It was time to start scribbling again in the book which had become my constant companion, long before Bridget Jones ever made it fashionable to have a diary.

Daniel, with his baseball cap pulled down over his face, took my hand as we hurried through the restaurant. He was probably just dragging me along so that I didn't dawdle, but his grasp was so strong and warm, I never wanted him to let me go. The restaurant was only half full, and no one really noticed us, which was a shame. I wanted at least someone to clock that I was holding hands with Daniel French.

He was obviously a regular, judging by the reaction of the head waiter who showed us through to a private room at the back.

'Mr Daniel, always a pleasure. Champagne to start? Two glasses?' he asked in what sounded like a fake French accent. Daniel looked at me, and I nodded, wondering how many other women had sat in this chair.

Within minutes Daniel had excused himself to go to the men's room. He seemed to be gone such a long time. Maybe he was on the phone to his wife. Maybe he was realising he'd made a dreadful mistake and had driven off with Chas. Well, it had happened once before on a first date I'd had weeks after Mark and I split. An experience like that is enough to scar a girl for life.

While he was gone I studied the menu which had me salivating after the first line. This promised to be an experience and a half, and had me making mental notes of how to re-write our menu at The Loft to make it sound more appetising.

Along with all the exotic sounding dishes were one or two staples like battered cod and chips, which I guessed that Daniel might go for. I didn't realise he was back until I felt his hand on my shoulder. A shiver ran through me. 'Sorry to be so long. A work call from the States. A producer I'm in talks with. He might be calling back.'

'Of course.' Why would he even apologise? His life must be full of important people.

'So what takes your fancy?' he asked, his shoulders visibly relaxing as he ran through the treats on offer. I was used to going for the cheapest thing on the menu, so I was thrown by the fact there were no prices.

'Would you order for me?' I asked, interested to see what he might choose.

As he studied the menu I couldn't take my eyes off him. If you'd told me a week ago, I'd be sitting opposite Daniel French across a restaurant table, I would have asked what you were on.

'Okay for starters, I'll have French onion soup. And for you let's have the carpaccio of Maldivian long line caught yellow fin tuna with avocado, crème fraiche and sprinkled with toasted organic sesame seeds.'

He might as well have said orgasmic sesame seeds, because that's the way I was feeling. At one point he glanced up at me and winked. I was so excited and nervous that I noticed my hands were trembling. So much so that when I started fiddling nervously, peeling blobs of wax off from the candle, I set fire to the wine list. Dotty Lottie is at it again, I thought, harking back to those painful schooldays.

With the quick actions of Daniel and the waiter, and much laughter, there was no need to evacuate the restaurant, and once my red face had returned to its normal colour I tried to make conversation.

'When is your wife due back? I'd love to meet her.'

His smile disappeared and he looked tense. 'Not for a while. She's got at least three weeks more filming, and then? I'm not sure.' He stopped and looked at me, locking eyes in a way that virtually hypnotised me.

When he finally spoke there was emotion in his voice. 'Lottie you have no idea.'

'About what?'

'How beautiful you are, and funny and talented. All of those things. Ever since my birthday, I've been trying to work out ways to see you again.'

As he spoke, I felt like laughing and crying simultaneously. So there had been a spark. I wasn't imagining it like some loony fan. He really did like me. Me, me, me.

He leaned forward and tucked a stray curl behind my ear. Oh my God, I'd seen scenes like these in the movies.

This didn't make sense. I needed to know more. Why if he wanted to see me, did he turn down my offer to cook when I came to his show, and disappear without saying goodbye?

He held up his empty champagne glass to the waiter and looked at me. I nodded. More alcohol was needed here. I drained the rest of my glass in one gulp.

'So Lottie what do you think?' What do I think? I think I'm dreaming this and in a minute I'm going to wake up with Colin asleep on my head.

'Thank you so much for the compliments, but I'm not sure I understand what you are saying.'

His face took on a sheepish expression. 'Nor do I, except that I really like you. Not just because you are a gorgeous redhead and a great cook, but because in that short time we spent together by the fire, I felt so relaxed. As though I could tell you anything and you'd understand and wouldn't be shocked.'

I nodded. I wanted to tell him that I felt the same, but I couldn't trust myself for the words to come out right.

'Will you let me see you? Call you?'

'But you're...'

'Married, I know. I am married, but I don't have a marriage or a wife. We rarely see each other. She always has an excuse not to come home. And, I might be wrong but...' He shrugged and held up his hands.

'You think she's seeing someone?'

'I have my suspicions. But that's not why I want to get to know you Lottie. Could we just see each other? Maybe as friends to start with?'

He laid his hand across mine, and I felt volts of desire run up my arm. I wasn't sure about the friends bit. At this very moment, if we'd been somewhere private I think I would have dragged him off to the nearest bedroom. I had never in my life felt lust in such a raw form. And that's probably what it was. A physical attraction which would probably last a while and then fizzle. After all how would someone as unglamorous as me fit into the life of the hottest looking superstar on the planet?

'Your food is on its way,' said the waiter who had crept in with our champagne without us noticing.

Daniel's hand leapt off mine as if on a spring. 'Perfect, thank you.'

While we waited for our food we swapped more notes about our childhood. Daniel said his parents were still together, existing in a cold loveless marriage and living in Cheshire, but that he always felt more comfortable with Kevan's folks over in Ireland. 'I'd love you to meet them. They are a fantastic family.'

Once the subject of Kevan was raised I was curious to find out more about him and the flamboyant Max Diamond. They certainly made an unlikely couple.

'So are Kevan's parents okay with him and Max?'

He paused for a second and smiled. 'Max? Oh yes, he's treated like one of the family.'

By the time our starter arrived, I was onto my third glass of champagne, and the bubbles were clearly having an impact on my confidence. Instead of dithering over what I said, I could feel myself starting to flirt with him. And that's a phrase I never thought I'd use. Me flirting with Daniel French. Me flirting with any man, come to that. I knew that if I half-closed my eyes in a certain way, it looked sexy. I'd been told that by Mark, so had practised it in the mirror, along with pouting which unfortunately made me look like a rather smug fish.

Two forkfuls into our meal, and Chas appeared in the doorway looking serious. 'We need to go. And just you Dan,' he said, waiting as his boss stood up. 'Couple of the regulars outside. They must have got wind you were here with someone,' he added.

This was obviously my cue to leave. Did I have enough money for a taxi home? Daniel looked unfazed as if this was normal for him, which it probably was. He leaned forward and kissed me on the cheek. 'Sorry honey. Someone from the restaurant must have spotted us earlier and tipped off the paparazzi. We need to leave separately. Order what you like. The bill is sorted. Chas will send another car to pick you up at the back door. Call me?' I nodded. And with that he was gone.

So that was it. A couple of mouthfuls and no chance to savour my main course which was braised lamb shank with garlic mash and red wine sauce. Let alone salivate over the dessert menu. 'Can I get madam anything else,' asked the waiter who was looking down his nose at the still full plates. As if I wanted to sit there eating alone. I'd done enough of that in my life.

'Yes you can get me a man who doesn't have to sneak out and leave me behind feeling like a lemon,' was what I wanted to say.

When the taxi arrived I slunk out of the back door thinking that if I started seeing Daniel, even as a friend, then this would be my life.

15

Pale winter sunshine flooding through my bedroom window, I woke refreshed after the best night's sleep I'd had in months. Instead of feeling gloomy about the week ahead, I felt different as though I was an exciting new Lottie. Okay, so it could have ended better. "Last night I was wined and dined by a man who is a household name," I wrote in my journal as I sat up in bed with my early morning mug of tea. No, hang on, that made him sound like a packet of washing powder. I crossed it out. "Last night I was wined and dined by a superstar." There, that was better. Instead of my usual early morning moodiness, I virtually skipped around the house without tripping over Colin. I even got into work early, much to Marsha's surprise.

'Good morning Lottie,' she said jumping out on me from the doorway to the ground-floor antiques shop.

'We have two deliveries due today, and we need to change the menu. Possibly skip a couple of the salads and add more soup,' she said, rambling on about alternative dishes until I realised I hadn't heard a thing she'd said after the word soup.

'Lottie, come with me for a moment,' she said, ushering me into her shop and closing the door. 'What's going on? You're not yourself today.' She was right, I wasn't myself. I was a super confident version of myself. Even if I never saw Daniel again, the fact that he thought I was important enough to whisk me out for dinner was enough for me.

'By the faraway look in your eyes, there's a man involved.'

'No, well yes, sort of,' I said, realising I couldn't say a word about my adventure last night. Not even to Pat.

'Me and George Clooney, you know how it is,' I said, trying to make a joke of it.

'But he's married now,' said Marsha, clearly keen to carry on the fun. 'So you'll have to find someone else.'

Even though I knew the reality was that I shouldn't see Daniel again, I couldn't help enjoying the excitement of it all to take me through the day. It was as if my life was somehow effortless. Not one disaster in the kitchen, or complaint from a customer, or a moan from Marsha. I wasn't the only one who seemed to have undergone a personality transplant. Instead of being silent inside his world of music, Ryan had ditched the earphones and was chatting away about his new club owner friend Max Diamond, and how excited he was to get a second invitation to Chill in a week.

'I can't tell my step-dad though.'

'Why? Because it's a gay club?'

'He hates anything like that.'

I left the conversation there, but it did start me wondering if Ryan had been hiding the fact that he was gay. It made sense he was scared to say anything. His stepfather had once called into The Loft to deliver Ryan's phone which he'd left at home. I thought then how threatening he looked with his shaved head, knuckle duster rings and scowling face. I'd be frightened of him.

The only person in my world who hadn't caught my happiness bug was Jess who had already started complaining about her new footballer boyfriend because he didn't call her often enough and hadn't once taken her shopping.

I couldn't help but laugh, even though I knew she was deadly serious. 'What's shopping got to do with it?'

'I'm a footballer's girlfriend, that's one of the perks.'

'You make it sound like a job.'

'Well it is, kind of.'

'But do you even like him?'

'Yeh, he's alright,' she said in a tone of voice that clearly sounded as if he wasn't.

Nothing could deflate me. Okay, so I hadn't heard from Daniel. But who knew what might happen?

'You haven't taken that smile off your face since you walked in. Come on, spill the beans,' said Pat, who had finally come down from her high of being famous for fifteen minutes. But I wasn't sure I could trust her not to blab.

If nothing else, my adventure with a pop star had given me the incentive to throw myself back into the precarious world of love online. I spent the next two evenings reading through the profiles of a new and slightly more upmarket dating website, but none of the potential suitors jumped off the page at me. All I could think about was Daniel. Me and Daniel. Daniel and me. Us. When the doorbell went early on the third evening, it was the woman from next door but one with a giant bouquet of white roses and a package.

'These came for you earlier. I stood them in water so they should be okay. Someone's got an admirer,' she said, peering around my hallway as if looking for a clue to the man in my life. She stood patiently as if waiting for me to look at the card that came with the flowers.

I couldn't let her leave disappointed. 'They're probably from Mark. You remember Mark.'

'I heard he'd gone. You poor love, I hope you get him back.'

'I don't,' I muttered under my breath, and thanked her again for taking in the flowers.

As soon as she'd gone, I ripped open the small envelope nestling in the roses. The card read: "So sorry about Sunday. Can we try again?" Then I opened the package. It was a top of the range rose-gold coloured phone with a message waiting on the screen: 'Please call me on this number, Dx.' A kiss. Another kiss.

This was like something out of a spy movie. My own personal hotline to him. Should I do it? Should I call him? Of course I would. What girl could resist this kind of courtship?

Immediately I Googled the meaning of white roses to discover they are traditionally associated with marriages and new beginnings. And that a bouquet is the perfect way to say "I'm thinking of you."

I wanted to call him straight away, but resisted. That would seem too desperate. I knew deep down this was all wrong, but it didn't seem real. Plus, if Daniel's marriage really was on the rocks, maybe I wasn't doing such a bad thing. Right now, I needed to talk it through with someone.

Helen. She would be well impressed by my news which for once outshone any gossip she could dish up. It might even lead to one of her posh dinner party invites. As I started to call, I realised how ridiculous I was being.

There is no way that anybody could know just yet. Not Helen, not Jess, not Pat or Ryan. Nobody. For the time being this had to stay one big giant secret, but it wouldn't be easy. Over the years I'd tried so hard to keep things to myself, but the moment someone said: "You must never say a word about this," all I wanted to do was shout it from the rooftops. It was torture, like trying to sit on your hands when there was an open box of Maltesers on the table. It was too late to cancel the call, but when Helen answered, I barely recognised her voice.

'Do you have a cold?'

'No I have a fucking cheating husband,' she said with a giant sob.

'How do you know?'

'He used to do anything to get out of walking those dogs. Now as soon as he comes home, he is out the door even when it's pissing down with rain. So I checked his text messages.'

'And?'

'Nothing. But anyone having an affair would have a secret phone, right?'

'Er, right,' I said, sliding a cushion over the one sitting beside me.

I wasn't sure if I should say something about seeing him with the blonde woman in his office. But maybe that revelation should be for another time.

'So you've no evidence he's having an affair?'

'I just know. He's been acting odd.'

'Have you challenged him about it?'

Helen put her hand over the phone and I could hear her talking to one of the children, probably Rose, suggesting she went upstairs while she and daddy had a chat. Then I heard the click of a cigarette lighter. She hadn't smoked in years. 'I'm on the phone,' she called out. Ben must be back.

'What are you going to do?'

'God knows,' she said and hung up.

16

Every morning this week I'd woken with butterflies swarming around my stomach, and today was no different. Except today, I also had Helen to worry about. I'd planned to see her in The Loft for tea and sympathy during my afternoon break.

As I packed my bag for work, I slipped my new phone into the side pocket. It felt cool and smooth like a secret weapon. One that would make me forever happy, even if I didn't use it. Solid proof that someone like Daniel French found someone like me special enough to want to talk to. I wished my dad was around. He would love all this intrigue. Well, okay so he wasn't my real dad. It was never discussed who my real father might be. But when Ron was there to look after me, I didn't need another dad. All the way to work on the bus I found myself thinking about him and how proud he'd be if he knew I'd carried on cooking, *and* how my food had led to romance. He'd always joked with me that the way to a man's heart was through his stomach. How right he was.

When he died from cancer, my world fell apart. I was only twenty. I remember asking nan for clues to the whereabouts of my mother. Surely someone ought to let her know so she could at least come to the funeral.

'She went back to Liverpool where she came from all those years ago.'

'I didn't know my mum came from Liverpool.'

'Oh yes. Her dad brought his family down here to live when he got a job at the local car plant. She had a strong Scouse accent your mum.'

I tried hard, but couldn't remember her voice. Or much about her to be honest. I once found an old photo album with a few pictures of her. Tina Gilbert. Shoulder-length bleached blonde hair, and a cigarette and wine glass in almost every photo. There were no pictures of her with me. My nan never mentioned her. And if I ever said her name, she would wrinkle her nose as if there was a bad smell in the room. She always made it clear she thought her son was mad to take on a woman with another man's baby.

'Your mum never loved my Ron. She was just using him. But he didn't care. He loved you like you was his own,' she'd tell me every Christmas over a couple of glasses of sherry.

When dad died, I offered to move in with nan to keep her company. But she insisted I got a place of my own. Dad had made a few bob from Ron's Caff which he'd invested into a savings account for me. It helped me buy a car, and put down a deposit on a small flat to rent round the corner from nan.

Unlike most other girls my age who'd moved in with friends from uni, I'd always lived alone. At one point Helen suggested we found a place together, but before it ever had the chance to happen, she'd moved in with Ben. So there I was, Lottie no mates, or that's how it felt. Though nan never showed me much affection, I was sure she loved me in her own way. She was the only family I had in the world. She had been on her own since her husband died when she was in her forties and raised her son Ron single-handed. There was a hard edge to her, but she was totally comfortable in her own skin, and so certain of her husband's love even from beyond the grave, that she never seemed lonely. Just alone.

I was the opposite. Often surrounded by others at college doing my chef's exams, and in the chaos of kitchen life, I was lonely. Always.

Even when I met Mark, the feeling that there was

something missing inside of me. That 'hole in the soul' as they call it, never totally faded, but it became much better, especially if we were going through a period of feeling loved-up. Now and again that lost feeling would disappear, usually when I was giggly on champagne or cocktails. But it never totally went. It was always there lurking in the background and ready to leap out when I was at my lowest. When I finally threw Mark out, I immediately regretted it. I would have put up with anything just to have him back, filling the space in my life.

Since the flowers and phone had arrived from Daniel, the empty feeling had all but gone. I was full of excitement for what lay ahead.

Even Helen's woes couldn't faze me. In fact when she appeared at the top of the stairs in The Loft looking so sorry for herself, there was a bit of me that wanted to smile. Maybe it was all the years of having a best friend who led such a charmed life, while I had to make do with living in her shadow. Now she was having her own dramas instead of having to share one of mine.

As I carried over a tray of tea and biscuits to the round table by the window, she was looking down onto the High Street below.

She sighed, pulling a phone out of her pocket and slammed it down on the table.

'His work mobile. He's been calling me all day to see where he left it. I took it out of his brief case while he was asleep.'

'So he hasn't got a secret phone?'

'Well, no, I figured he didn't need one. He could just use his work mobile.'

'And?'

'There's a suspicious new name.'

'How do you know it's new?'

'Because I check both his phones every week for dodgy messages. The name is Simon and the last message was just a line of kisses.'

'So are you saying Ben is gay?'

Helen looked aghast at the idea. 'No, I've worked it out.

Simon is a surname. And the only person I know with that surname is Slutty Susie from school. She married a Tony Simon.

'It could be a coincidence.'

'Yes, except that their son who happens to be in George's class announced that his parents are getting a divorce. She's gone to Ben to get the divorce, I know it.'

'Are you sure? Have you asked him?'

'Not yet, I want to see him squirm.'

'He could just have a new friend called Simon.'

There was a long silence during which I passed her the shortbreads.

She shook her head. 'When did I ever eat fucking biscuits?'

'Always a good time to start when you're broken-hearted,' I said, immediately regretting my choice of words.

'Do I look broken-hearted? I'm just bloody furious,' she said, ignoring my empty cup while she poured herself another tea.

'The best thing is to sit down tonight and have a heart to heart. I'm sure he wouldn't cheat on you.'

'Really? Why are you so sure? You thought your Mark wasn't cheating on you with Tara. But I can tell you he was, because a friend of mine saw them together weeks before you two split up.'

Trust Helen to stick the knife into someone else, just to make sure she's not alone in her misery.

'Thanks, that's really good to know,' I said, pouring my own tea.

Why was she still my best friend? Probably because no one else would put up with her, and deep down, she needed me to be there for her, like some sort of long-suffering big sister.

'Sorry. What I mean is, men lie. Well, they do, don't they? My dad's a liar. He's been lying to my mum ever since they were married.'

'About what?'

'His affairs. She knows about them but pretends she doesn't. That's why they are still together.' For a moment I conjured up a picture of Helen's sophisticated mother who constantly had a large gin and tonic on the go, and her debonair father, who was a massive flirt. Of course. How could I not have noticed?

Over Helen's shoulder I could see Pat pointing to her watch, as she beckoned me back to the kitchen.

Helen sighed. 'I need to go out and get blitzed.'

'You need to sort out your marriage with Ben.'

'What marriage?' she said, grabbing a biscuit and eating it on her way out.

That night at home, I sat nursing the phone and a glass of wine for an hour working out what to say to my secret admirer and how to say it. "Hi Daniel." No, "Hey Daniel," like the Americans. "Hey Daniel, it's me." No he might have several 'me's' in his life. "Hey Daniel, it's Lottie. Thank you for the flowers." Always good to be polite. Then hopefully he would take up the conversation, and we'd make plans to meet.

'Okay Colin, no big noisy miaows while I do this,' I said stroking his back with my bare foot. Immediately he started yowling as he led me to the kitchen where I cut up a small piece of chicken from the fridge to keep him quiet. While he was busy eating, I disappeared up to my bedroom. I wondered if Daniel would ever be here? In my bed?

New bedding, that's what I needed, taking note of the faded lilac duvet cover stained with felt tip pen ink splots from where I'd written in my journal. I added Daniel as the only contact in my sparkly new phone, took a deep breath and called. It rang a few times and went to voicemail. It wasn't his voice. Just the regular recorded message. I hung up and tried again.

This time it answered in two rings, but it was a woman's voice. My heart flew up into my mouth. Maybe it was his wife.

'Hello Charlie, Daniel's phone. I'm sure he's hiding round here somewhere. I can go and get him for you. Or leave a message and I'll tell him to call you back. Oh I sound like an answerphone don't I?' said the voice, with a silly giggle. Who the hell was Charlie?

I knew who the voice belonged to. It was Meg, his housekeeper. I was just about to hang up again when I heard his voice.

'It's okay, Meg, I've got this, hang on a sec,' he said. It sounded as if he was taking the phone with him into another room. I could hear Oscar barking in the distance and tried to imagine where in the house Daniel was heading.

'Sorry about that. I've asked her not to answer my phones, but she thinks she is being helpful,' he said, sighing.

'Do you know who I am?'

'Of course I know who you are. I put you in the phone as Charlie, just in case. Do people ever call you that?'

'No. Just Lottie or Charlotte.'

There was a long silence, then we did that thing of both speaking at the same time as he said: 'I wondered if you...'

'Thank you so much for the...oh go ahead,' I said, waiting for him to talk.

'I'm off up North in a couple of days. Before I go, I wondered if you wanted to meet up in London? We could have dinner.'

'When?'

'Tomorrow evening. I'll send Chas for you at seven. Is that too early?'

'No that's cool,' I said, wishing I hadn't. I was too old to say 'cool'.

'We'll meet at the flat.'

'The flat?'

'I have an apartment in Chelsea overlooking the river. You'll love it.' Wow, that sounded super posh. The only thing I knew about Chelsea was the King's Road. Nan had taken me up there once when I was small, and told me she used to hang out there in the Sixties.

I could hear another mobile phone ringing. 'Sorry I have to take this,' he said. 'See you tomorrow. Text me.'

Text him? What would I say? What was I going to wear? Where was this going to end? Was it all a dream? What would my nan think if she knew what I was about to do? Sometimes I tried to imagine her voice from the great bingo hall in the sky.

I knew exactly what she would say: 'Girlie, you need to think it through. It doesn't matter how bleeding famous he is, he is still a married man, and you'll be his bit on the side. Is that what you really want for yourself?'

17

God knows how I got through the day without sustaining serious injury. I managed to burn a cake, as well as my hand on the grill, and forgot to turn on the oven to cook a casserole. Even Marsha noticed I was behaving oddly, in a manic fashion, she called it. I was high. High on life, high on love, or lust, or whatever it was.

'I don't know what you're on. But maybe this will help,' she said offering me a glass of wine at the end of the day.

'Sorry I have to dash. I've got a date.'

'Who with? George Clooney?'

'No, with Daniel French,' I said laughing. Ha, ha, if only you knew.

'Oh I see he's replaced Mr Clooney has he? Well, good luck with whoever it is you're going out with. Don't do anything I wouldn't.'

I wasn't actually sure what Marsha would or wouldn't do. I realised I didn't know the first thing about her, except that she had never been married or had children and had the most dreadful smoker's cough.

One day, I'd sit her down and find out. But for now, I needed to get home and transform myself into a woman fit for the star treatment. I'd already decided what to wear. My long black skirt, Victorian-style cream blouse, dark brown leather boots and the antique silver locket which dad had given me when he knew he wouldn't make it until my 21st. My lucky charm.

By the time Chas arrived to collect me, I was shaking either with fear or excitement, I couldn't decide. I don't remember ever feeling like this before a date. But then I'd never been on a date with someone who was the object of desire to hundreds of thousands, no, probably millions of women worldwide. Maybe it was some sort of cruel reality show. Secret cameras would be capturing my every expression as Daniel poured me champagne, and chatted me up. Meanwhile, the awful Meg would be sniggering behind the door, waiting to reveal that the joke was on me.

On the way over, Chas made polite conversation about the news of the day and the weather. He was surprisingly well-spoken and, it transpired, another of Daniel's old friends from boarding school. Over the years he must have done this dozens of times. Picked up girls for his boss and taken them home again. That's a point. What would I do if Daniel asked me to stay? Apart from a spare pair of knickers which I believe a girl should always carry, I hadn't brought a change of clothes. But then, why would I? I wouldn't be sleeping with him on a first date. Nan definitely wouldn't approve of that.

Unlike the last time Pat and I were in London to see Daniel's show, there was a chance to take in the sights and sounds around me. The streets were still full of late-night shoppers and office workers, smoking and enjoying a drink on the pavements outside the pubs, even though it was cold. Before I knew it, we were there, gliding into an underground car park, and heading up in a lift, arriving in a reception area where a concierge saluted Chas before walking us to a glass elevator. On the drive over I managed to find out that this had been Daniel's bachelor pad before he'd married Beth. It was very much still his bolt hole. She preferred staying somewhere like The Ritz if she was up in town shopping.

As the heels on my boots clicked along on the black marble flooring, I tried to take it all in. The giant palms in silver ceramic pots, bronze statues of lovers entwined, and the smell of luxury.

Chas spoke into the intercom at the heavy black door, and within seconds it opened. But instead of Daniel, I was met by Kevan who stood aside to let me enter. It was like walking into the sort of glass fish tank owned by James Bond. No walls as such, just giant windows looking out onto the fairy lights of the marina. The perfect setting for a seduction routine. Cream leather sofas on soft white rugs, a glass dining table with high backed red chairs, and an art deco style black and gold bar with what looked like a bottle of champagne on ice. There was a steel spiral staircase leading up to a gallery which overlooked the living room. And a white baby grand piano holding court nearby.

'Daniel's on the phone,' he said, helping me off with my coat. Oh, so this was going to be a romantic kind of date with him hanging around. What was he doing here?

'What can I get you to drink?'

'Oh no I'm fine. We're going out, I think,' I said, desperately hoping that he wasn't going to be joining us.

Kevan headed over to the gold fridge which was stacked with beers and wine and very little food.

'Are you sure?' he said holding up a bottle of Sauvignon Blanc.

'Just a small one then. Thank you.'

'And one for me,' said Daniel walking in from the balcony which ran the length of the apartment. He stopped when he saw me. 'Hey, you. You look totally gorgeous,' he said, holding me at arms length so he could study me.

Taking my glass from Kevan, he took my hand and led me back out into the cool of the night. 'I can't believe you're here.'

I couldn't believe I was here either. I'd never felt so out of place. Like I didn't belong. To say I was out of my comfort zone was an understatement. Helen would have known what to do. She would have been right at home.

'Come here,' said Daniel, guiding me to the edge of the balcony and standing close behind me so that our bodies touched. It was hard to concentrate on the view, but I tried.

Seven floors up gave us a bird's eye view of the yachts bobbing around on the black water. He pointed to one called *Paris* which he said was his. Next to it was a flashy-looking speedboat he described as his favourite toy. Was I just like another favourite toy, I wondered? I shivered. Daniel picked up a soft throw from one of the nearby chairs and gently laid it around my shoulders.

He used the chance to pull me nearer to him.

'I'm taking us out to my favourite restaurant, and then we'll come back here. Just you and me, and play some music. Does that sound okay? Chas can run you home or you can stay over and he'll take you early in the morning,' he said speaking slowly and so close to my face that I could feel his breath on my skin. It was like being in a trance. When his lips brushed mine, I almost swooned like some Jane Austen character. Where were the smelling salts when you needed them?

'Come on youse two, or we'll be late,' said Kevan from inside.

Daniel whispered, 'Later,' as he gave me one last look, and we walked inside where Kevan was waiting with our coats.

The sushi restaurant was made up of dimly lit discreet booths which made it more difficult to see the other diners. I felt sure that Daniel couldn't be the only famous face in the place. But even so, we caused a stir as we walked in, Kevan taking my hand, presumably so that any onlookers thought I was with him. I snatched it from his firm grip as soon as I could. There's no way I was holding hands with a man wearing yet another sweater which looked as though it had come from a Nordic drama costume department.

At the start of the meal it was me who felt like the gooseberry as the two old friends laughed and joked. Once or twice I caught Daniel looking at me, his eyes sparkling dangerously in the candlelight. All I wanted was for us to be alone, but I totally got it. It wasn't as if he could just whisk us out alone to a romantic restaurant without attracting attention and newspaper headlines about playing away from home when his wife was in America. We'd already tried that.

When people stared, I decided to play my part in not raising any suspicions. So I convinced myself that all we were doing was having a friendly meal out. We could be discussing menus for Daniel's next showbiz party, yes that's it. I was his catering consultant.

There was some showbiz talk about Daniel's tour dates the following year, and then the conversation turned to me as I talked about my time at The Loft, making them laugh with stories about some of our funny customers and our nicknames for them. It was the first time I'd seen Kevan looking anything other than grumpy. He even talked a little about his boyfriend Max and how he was thinking of opening another club in London. I asked if he ever went to Chill?

'I'm off there later to meet him for a drink. You're very welcome to come with,' he added with a raised eyebrow. 'Next time Kev,' said Daniel. 'Or you should get Max to come with us to dinner.'

Us? Did that mean him and me? That there was an us? Throughout the meal he gave very little clue as to whether this was an actual date. Apart from once or twice when I caught him looking at me, he was fairly cool and I wondered if I'd said something to make him go off me. But when Kevan disappeared to sort the bill, he whispered in a slow sexy voice. 'Your hair looks like gold in the candlelight,' and I was totally his. To someone who has grown up being called carrot tops or copper nob I had never thought of my wild red curls as being golden.

This lovely idea kept me smiling all the way back to Chiswick where we dropped Kevan off at a terraced Victorian house.

'I won't invite you guys in for coffee. I'm sure you have more pressing things to do,' he said as he walked up the path with a dismissive wave. Within minutes of being back at Eiffel Towers as Chas nicknamed Daniel's apartment complex, we were sipping champagne and warming our hands by the most impressive fake log fire I'd ever seen. Softly playing in the background was an album by an American artist I'd never heard of, who Daniel said was a friend of his wife's. Romantic and soulful it was the perfect sound for the way I was feeling. This time it didn't feel so odd sitting next to him on a sofa, it felt right. Just two people, attracted to each other, enjoying the closeness of being together. Locking my gaze into his, he leaned in to kiss me, I closed my eyes and...his phone rang. Well, that is, one of his phones rang. I'd noticed at least three on the nearby counter dividing the living room from the kitchen.

'It's my wife,' he said, before he'd even seen who was calling.

'How do you know?'

'She has her own ring tone. Sorry, give me a moment,' he said, disappearing off into what I assumed was a bedroom. I decided that when he reappeared, I'd make my excuses and leave. All this insistence that he had a wife, but not a marriage was not ringing true, especially as she seemed to be telepathic about what he was up to. I'd made him laugh earlier in the evening when I revealed how my nan still had a large input into my life by delivering advice from the great beyond. What would she say now? Probably, not to trust Daniel as far as I could throw him. The problem was, I did trust him. I felt safe with him. That he was telling me the truth.

I stayed perched on the edge of the sofa sipping my champagne. Even the bubbles had gone flat, and the atmosphere felt cold and empty. When he emerged, it was hard to read his face.

'I should go. It's late,' I said, standing up.

'Please don't,' he said holding me so close that I could barely breathe. 'I have no right to expect you to be here with me, I know that. I'm technically still a married man, with a wife who now says she's not coming home for another month because she needs her space to figure things out.'

Gently I eased myself away from him, and sat back down on the sofa. It would be so easy to go into my shell and let him do all the talking. That's how I'd lived most of my life, listening to others and doing whatever pleased them. It was as if their lives, their decisions, and their happiness was far more important than mine. And here I was again, about to play my part as some sort of favoured star groupie, because that's what I would be. But at what cost? Nothing was ever going to come of it. How could it? We might as well live on different planets.

'I'm not sure where I fit into all this,' I said, surprising myself.

'Lottie I'm not sure either, if I'm honest. But if you go now, I'm terrified I won't see you again.'

For a split second I could see the vulnerable face of the boy in the man, and he looked so lost, as though his cloak of fame had suddenly slipped off onto the floor. Without even thinking, I put my arms around the back of his neck and moved in for a kiss. Like some sort of uncertain teenager he slightly jerked his head back. 'Really?'

'Yes really,' I said. And then he kissed me. Oh my God I've had some lousy sloppy kisses over the years. In fact I'd started to wonder what all the fuss was about. Now at the age of thirty nine, I finally knew. His kiss was so tender, gentle and seductive. I didn't want it to end, and it didn't for some time. The longer it lasted, the more my body was screaming at me, take him to bed you mad woman! This might be the only chance you get!

'That was one of the best kisses I ever had,' I said, pulling him back for more.

'Only *one* of the best. Let's try to make it *the* best shall we?' And he did. That night we slept together, and that was it. Just the smallest amount of sleep in amongst the cuddles, talking and kissing. I told him more about my life with dad, and how I didn't really miss the mum I'd never had. And he admitted that he'd never miss the mum he *did* have.

The more we talked, the more relaxed I felt. As though I could ask him anything and he wouldn't mind. But it was the child in him that fascinated me. What is it in a little boy that means he will grow up to be so famous?

'God knows. To start with I was a pretty quiet insecure kid. Kevan was the noisy brave one. But as something I could do alone, I learned to play the guitar when I was fourteen which made me look cool and gave me more confidence.'

'Yes, but you became a star. Where did that come from?'

'It was an act. I acted as though I was a star because it was the only thing that kept me afloat when the waves of depression nearly drowned me, and gradually it happened. Deep down I was terrified I'd be found out. That someone would reveal me as an average singer writing average songs. I still feel that.'

'But you're not average. Your songs are amazing.'

'They got better over time,' he paused and as if deep in thought, and sighed. 'You know, sometimes it's such a relief to drop the act, and I can do that with you.'

'You can?'

'It's as though we can mess around like a couple of kids and invent our own private world.'

'I like the sound of that.'

'So, come on, what sort of a kid were you? Let me guess, feisty with all that red hair and freckles?'

'You must be joking. I hated my red hair. I tried to dye it blonde once and it turned green, and then another time I tried to cut it all off. I was a joke at school because of my clumsiness. I've got this friend Helen, whose mother collects all these expensive Swarovski crystal ornaments, and I picked one up. Mesmerised. It was this lovely swan that cost a couple of hundred pounds, and the way that the sun shone through it made rainbows on the ceiling. And then I dropped it onto the hearth and its head fell off. I always break things.'

He put his finger gently over my lips. 'The only things that matter if they're broken are hearts. Hey that's quite good. I might use that in a song,' he said, laughing.

I found myself opening up to him and telling him all my secrets. Like the fact I still read my childhood Winnie-the-Pooh books that my dad had bought me when I was little. While he confessed that the only Pooh Bear he'd ever seen was in the window of a Disney shop.

I didn't need any encouraging to talk about my favourite bear in the world. 'Oh you don't know what you're missing. Pooh says so many wise things about life.'

He was probably going to find this cheesy, but I didn't care.

I knew most of the famous AA Milne quotes off by heart. I'd written them down in my journal. So if I couldn't sleep at night, I'd read through them. The only person I'd ever shared this with before was Mark, who thought it was incredibly funny. 'Great, so my girlfriend is obsessed with Pooh, well that's not something I'd brag about,' he'd laugh.

Somehow I didn't think Daniel would mock. He was more the sensitive type.

'I think I should check out this Pooh Bear dude, he sounds cool.'

'Oh he is, the coolest bear.'

We started to swap silly jokes, except that he had loads, and I could only ever remember the one my dad told me about a banana who went to the doctors because he wasn't 'peeling' well. And, as the dawn rose, we played the most stupid game of I spy like kids, and I laughed until my stomach hurt. In between we just lay there looking at each other. And then he'd kiss me again.

When Daniel's alarm went off at six, I think I'd had about an hour's sleep. The problem was that every time I felt as if I was dozing off, I'd force open my eyes and look at him again, just to make sure I wasn't imagining it. He'd loaned me a cool looking white T-shirt with a giant D on it to sleep in, which he said I could take home with me, much to my delight.

Chas was due at six thirty a.m. to ferry me back to the house. I needed to feed Colin and get changed for work. As I stood in the shower, I kept re-living our night, and wondering how I was going to keep it to myself. We'd decided that we'd spend time together when we could. Get to know each other. Our own secret arrangement. It wasn't an affair was it? We'd been tempted, but nothing had happened. It was as if we were both holding back, because we realised how quickly it could turn into one.

By the time I was dressed back in last night's clothes, there was freshly brewed coffee and toast waiting for me. Luckily I'd found some products in the bathroom, so had managed to remove my make-up. It was odd that there were no signs of

Beth being here. It really felt like a bachelor pad. Maybe that was the idea. I didn't know how many other flings Daniel had enjoyed while his wife was halfway across the world.

Surely I wasn't the first. But somehow it didn't feel bad or wrong. No one was hurting anyone. She was thousands of miles away, and by the sound of things wanted to stay there. And if I was being realistic, our relationship probably wasn't going anywhere, but boy was I going enjoy it while it lasted. Not just because Daniel was famous. Actually that was one of the worst bits, because it meant we had to be extra careful. It was because he was gorgeous and kind and caring, and he made me feel like no one else ever had.

'We're off up North tomorrow for a few days. I've got two shows this weekend in Manchester, Friday and Saturday,' he said as he saw me out. 'Can you come?' Oh my God, this was getting more exciting by the minute. A weekend with Daniel instead of in front of the telly. I promised I'd try, even if I could only manage one day off work.

Chas left me languishing in my own little world on the way home. The battery on my phone had died so I couldn't check messages or Facebook. Instead I nodded off to sleep feeling as if life as I knew it couldn't get any better. That feeling lasted until I let myself into the house and something didn't feel right. There were no obvious signs that anything was wrong, but I felt tense and on edge as I climbed the stairs to look for Colin. Through my bedroom doorway I could see a figure fast asleep in his socks. One with a hole in the toe.

18

If there is anything worse than a man who has been dumped, it is a man who has been dumped *and* has a hangover!

Mark put his hands over his ears. 'Please don't shout at me.'

'You frightened the life out of me. What are you doing here?'

'She threw me out. I had nowhere else to go. I tried to call you.'

'My phone was dead. Why, what did you do?'

'It was the engagement ring. She thought it was a real diamond until she took it to a jewellers to get it valued for insurance.' And there was me being jealous about her fake diamond being bigger than my fake diamond.

He looked affronted. 'I don't know what all the fuss is about. It's just a glittery stone at the end of the day. Why waste all that money on the real thing?' His face which hadn't seen a razor in days, broke into a smile. I'd missed his smile and his dimples. 'Anyway that's enough of me, where have you been Lotts? Not like you to be a dirty stop out.'

'None of your business, and I need to get ready for work. So if you don't mind...' I held out my hand. 'Key please. I didn't even know you still had one.'

'Nor did I. Found it in a jacket pocket. Can I stay Lotts? Just for a few days until I find somewhere else to go?'

'Or she takes you back.'

He shrugged his shoulders and sighed. 'Yeh. She's a bit of a hot head, but she'll calm down. What have you been up to?'

Oh you know being wined and dined by a world famous superstar who's invited me to his show this weekend, is what I was dying to say. Instead of which I found myself agreeing to let him stay for a few days if he looked after the cat while I went to Manchester. He had strict instructions not to let Colin escape out of the front door because of the traffic. And would need to clear out the spare room which was full of junk and bags of clothes I kept meaning to take to a car boot sale.

'Thanks a lot Lotts,' he said, laughing at his little joke.

Once my mobile phone sprang into life, as well as the missed calls from Mark, there were more from Helen. She picked up after one ring.

'Where the hell have you been? I've been trying to call you forever.'

'On a hot date with Daniel French.'

'I'm in no mood for jokes Lottie. Ben is still denying there's an affair. I don't know what to think. I might need your spare room for a few days.'

'Mark's beaten you to it,' I said, trying not to smile. I think you can always tell on the phone when someone is smiling.

'Your ex?'

'The very same. He's had a bust-up with Tara.'

'So where am I supposed to go?'

'Your parents have a pretty huge house as far as I recall? Anyway you can't leave the children with Ben.'

'Why not? It's about time he looked after them for a change. He'll have to work from home.'

There was a call waiting beep in my ear and Daniel's name popped up on my screen.

'I'll ring you back,' I said and hung up. She would be furious. Tough! She was always terminating me if a more interesting name appeared on her screen.

Just hearing his voice turned me to jelly. I still couldn't believe it was him.

'Hey lovely Lottie, I can't stop thinking about you. How you doing?'

'I'm...' what was I? I couldn't think of a word that described the excitement that was coursing through my veins at the moment. '...on my way to work. Trying to find a way to come to the show both days.'

'Text me your email and I'll get Kevan to send you all the details and get you booked into our hotel for both nights. I'll also sort out a car to take you up there.'

'But I can get the train...' What was I thinking? He was offering a lift door to door. 'or a car would be...'

'Great. I have to go. Oh, and I have a surprise for you.'

I survived the countdown to Manchester by running little scenarios through in my head about who I'd sit with in the audience and how things would work once we were at the hotel. I mean, we would be in a public place together, so we'd have to be careful about being spotted. And the really big question, would we? Well, you know. Would Daniel French become my lover?

If only I could tell somebody. Anybody. Jess was oblivious to what was going on, apart from on her phone. And Ryan had once again blocked out the world with his earphones. Pat on the other hand would dine out on my news for weeks. Maybe the time would come when I could trust them enough to let them in on my secret new life.

'You know it's Marsha's birthday today, don't you?' said Pat as we were chopping vegetables for soup. 'I've re-iced Daniel's birthday cake for her. And I think she's expecting us to take her for a drink tonight.'

Marsha sat holding court at The Kings Head in the most comfortable leather armchair. Maybe it was the heat of the log fire, but her face was red from coughing and her breathing seemed more laboured than usual. The rest of us managed to squish onto the large sofa opposite, as we made polite chit-chat with our boss.

Earlier Jess had rushed out and bought her a card which we'd all signed, and was now propped up on the large oak coffee table nearby. Marsha, as usual, was dressed in brown which matched her nicotine-stained fingers. She was never seen without a piece from her vast amber jewellery collection. And had once showed me a fossilised fly thought to be sixty million years old in one of her necklaces. I'm not sure I'd want to wear anything with a dead fly trapped inside it, but there you go.

Jess kept looking at her watch, and whispered that she needed to get home for a date with a guy she'd met in the local wine bar a couple of nights earlier.

'What happened to your footballer?'

'There was a photo of him online with this other girl. They're all the same. I'm better off with this Eddie bloke. He hasn't got any money, so he's not like a babe magnet,' she said, speaking and texting simultaneously.

'What does Eddie do?' asked Pat.

'He's a Mortar Logistics Engineer'

'What's that?'

'A builder,' she laughed, and caught Marsha's eye.

'I can tell you're dying to leave, so off you go Jess,' she said, shooing her away. 'You too Ryan. I'm sure you've got other things to do.'

'And my Frank needs his dinner cooked,' said Pat, wrapping her home-knitted scarf around her neck, as she prepared to leave.

'And what about you Charlotte? Any hot dates tonight?'

'No, I'm all yours Marsha if you fancy a bite to eat. Their menu here isn't as good as mine, but it's not too bad,' I said, handing her a copy. I needed to sweet-talk her into giving me most of the weekend off.

'Well since you're offering,' she said, struggling to pull herself out of the armchair to wander through into the main restaurant as the others made their way out into the night.

I'd never spent longer than a coffee break or a quick drink after work with Marsha. So I was wondering what we'd talk about. With any luck, she would plump for just a main course, and we could be home by nine.

'So, what's going on with you?' she asked, once we'd

settled at our table by the window. Outside in the bustling high street, late shoppers were wending their way home, most of them to their families. I would be going home to Colin the cat and my ex, that's if he hadn't already returned to his girlfriend. I wondered what Marsha was going home to. I'd heard that she owned a sizeable house, and possibly had a lodger.

'Oh not much,' I said, determined not to open up about either of the men in my life.

'Oh come on, there's got to be a man on the scene, judging by the look of you. You've been glowing for the past couple of days.'

'Really?' I said, trying to catch my reflection in the window.

'Oh you don't have to say anything. I'm just a nosey old bitch who hasn't had a love life in years. So forgive me if I'm curious,' she said, pouring herself another generous glass of red wine.

I was bursting to talk about Daniel. To mention his name at every given opportunity, the way you do when you're falling in love.

'There is someone, but it's early days, so I don't want to say much in case I jinx it,' I said, trying to catch the waiter's eye for another bottle.

'Enjoy it while you can. It doesn't last,' said Marsha, looking at me as though she hoped I'd dish up some details. 'Is he The One, this mystery man?'

'I'm not sure there is such a thing,' I said, beginning to enjoy this conversation. Listen and learn Lottie, listen and learn. Older, wiser women had a lot of experience to draw upon, and now that my nan had gone, I didn't have anyone who fitted that bill any more.

'Oh believe me there is, and I had him in my life for twenty-five years,' she said, looking dreamily out of the window. 'Course he's gone now, so I'm on my own.'

'I'm sorry, that must be hard. When did you break up?'

'Oh he's dead dear, otherwise we'd still be together, and yes we did break up once. He was married, you understand.'

I wanted very much to understand. The waiter returned

with another bottle of red, and I waited impatiently while he made a palaver of uncorking the wine and topping up our glasses.

'Alan his name was. I met him when I was thirty. All my friends were married by then with a couple of kids. We got hitched young in those days, so I'd been on the shelf for some time. Oh there would be the odd boyfriend, very odd most of them. All the decent ones were snapped up by the time they were in their early twenties.'

I started to ask why she'd never been married herself, but she held up her hand.

'I know what you're wondering. How did I get to thirty without a husband? It was unheard of back in the day. My parents are to thank for that. My father ran the antique shop, except it wasn't called Pandora's Box then, and I worked there from the time I could reach the keys of the cash register. They had me late in life and always expected me to care for them, so I did.

'I was only twenty-three when my mother started to suffer with Alzheimer's. She was sixty-six, and father wasn't in good health either. Eventually he employed Alan to run the store for him. I could have done it, but he didn't trust a woman for those things.'

I could hear the waiter clearing his throat. 'Are you ready to order yet ladies?'

Go away, I wanted to shout at him, this is far more important than food. We both ordered the same, beef stroganoff and rice, and then Marsha carried on.

'I can still remember the day Alan arrived. I looked up from the counter and there he was. He wasn't even that good looking. Quite small in fact, but he had a strong face and a lovely deep brown voice. I thought he was a customer and said: "Is there anything I can do for you?" And he just looked at me and said: "I certainly hope so," in a suggestive manner,' she said her laugh turning into a rasping cough.

As she told her story I could imagine the young Marsha with her long dark curly hair and serious brown eyes. She looked past me as if I wasn't really here, as though she was back in a different time. Then she sat up and adjusted herself in her chair as if she'd returned to the present. 'Nothing more to say really. I just fell for him. Not surprising. We were together all day, every day working in the store, him teaching me everything there is to know about antiques, and love.'

'Did he stay married?'

'Yes, he had a ten-year-old daughter and a wife who he reckoned he didn't sleep with, but couldn't leave because of what she might do to herself. I didn't really care about her. Well, you don't care much about others when you're young, do you? He loved me and I loved him, and he'd come to my little flat above the shop – your kitchen in The Loft was my bedroom – and after making love, he'd go back home to her.

'At one point he said he'd leave when his daughter went to university, but it didn't happen. And still I stayed with him. There was this other chap who used to come into the store a lot, and I could have made do with him. He really liked me. But I only wanted Alan. He promised me that one day we'd be together, and I believed him, so I let it carry on.'

'Didn't you ever give him an ultimatum?'

Marsha laughed. 'Oh yes every couple of years I'd throw a hissy fit, and finish with him, but it only ever lasted a couple of weeks. I couldn't resist him. He had this way about him, this charm. I wasn't much to look at, but I had a good figure and a brain, and he liked that. We talked about everything.

'And then...' she paused and looked at me as if to make sure I was still interested. Interested? I was desperate for her to carry on.

'Alan's father died and left him enough money to buy his own business, so he gave in his notice and bought his own antiques shop a couple of miles away. He said we could still be together, but I wanted to punish him for leaving, so I finished it, certain he'd come running back. He didn't. Within weeks he was sleeping with a girl he'd employed to work in his shop. He said later that he couldn't resist her thirty-eight double D chest. She wanted a baby and a sugar daddy and he was taken in by her flattery. Silly old fool. I even went to their wedding, can you believe that? It was all I could do not to jump up out of my seat when the vicar asked if anyone had any objections.

'After she had the baby, she lost interest in him in the bedroom, so he left her to it and started coming to see me again. It stayed that way until five years ago. He was seventy, and retired, and would often spend the night with me. By that time I was in my house, and we'd changed my flat into The Loft.

'His wife didn't care if he didn't come home. I mean he was old and she was only about forty.'

'Did they stay together?'

'Yes, they had a young son to support, but they weren't together together, if you get my drift. Strange isn't it how people carry on with dead marriages because they haven't got the energy to start again.'

Marsha stopped talking, and drained the rest of her glass. Her eyes had glazed over with tears.

'One night he turned to me in bed and said: "I should have married you Marsha dear. I'm sorry". I said: "It's alright Alan." And the next day when I woke up I found him on the sofa, dead. Just like that. Gone. I think he'd popped downstairs to make some hot chocolate. Heart attack they reckon. The weird thing was being at the funeral, sharing tissues with his first wife and daughter who had a little one of her own by then, and his second wife and their fifteen-year-old son. I'm still in touch with his first wife. She reckons she knew all about me, and that there was no way she was suicidal, just relieved she didn't have to sleep with him. We sometimes have a laugh about it over a glass of wine.'

Who would have thought it? That Marsha was a mistress for twenty-five years, and never a bride. But she seemed happy with her lot.

'And before you ask, no I don't regret anything. I had a man in my life who loved me. But I had to accept that he'd never be with me during the holidays.'

'So you were always on your own then?'

'Yes, me and my bottle of wine and my King Charles spaniel

Henry who used to come to the shop with me every day. He died soon after Alan. So you might persuade me to have another dog in my life. But a man? No. Even with all the lonely times, and the Christmases I spent without him, it was still worth it.'

'Why though?'

'Because I'd rather have the love of my life part-time, than have someone I only half-loved full time.'

19

Finally, it was Friday. I woke up an hour before the alarm and forced myself to leave the warmth of my bed. There was no sign of Colin. He had taken to sleeping in the spare bedroom with Mark, who I could hear snoring through the wall. I checked through my weekend case to make sure I had everything ready. My clothes looked a bit cheap and cheerful for a five-star hotel. If only I'd had time to buy something new, maybe a bit more classy. We were bound to be going somewhere posh for drinks after tonight's concert. I bet Beth wouldn't be seen dead in a little black number she'd bought five years ago from a clothes catalogue, but if I dressed it up a bit with jewellery it would look fine.

After our heart-to-heart on Marsha's birthday, I seemed to have morphed into her new favourite and she had agreed to let me finish work two hours early *and* take the whole weekend off.

At three o'clock a car would be picking me up outside The Loft and whizzing me off up the motorway to Manchester. On my own special hotline mobile, Daniel had already sent me a couple of texts saying he couldn't wait to see me, so I was surprised when he called.

'I know it's early but I wanted to hear your voice,' he said when I answered.

'It turns me on, the funny way you talk, and I love your laugh.'

'I always thought I sounded like a donkey with hiccups.'

'You do. That's why I love it.'

The kitchen door opened: 'Hey babe have you got any of my old underpants? I've only got these shitty ones,' mumbled Mark looking bleary eyed in a vest top and track suit bottoms.

Daniel stopped talking 'Who's that?'

'Oh it's probably Colin,' I said gesturing for Mark to be quiet, and waving him out of the door.

'A talking cat eh? You ought to put him on *Britain's Got Talent.'*

'Oh it's the TV. Just a second, I'll turn it off,' I said, wishing I didn't have to lie. Well, I suppose I didn't. But I wasn't sure how well it would go down if I admitted that my ex-boyfriend was back sharing my house. Maybe I'd find a way to explain later. In the background I could hear someone calling for Daniel, so was saved any further embarrassment.

Every hour at The Loft felt like a day. The only thing which helped pass the time was reminding myself what Marsha had told me, that this was originally her flat above the shop, and this very kitchen her bedroom. The bedroom where for many years she made mad passionate love with Alan. I tried to imagine where her bed might have been. It must have been a single, there was no room for anything bigger. From now on, when I stood at the counter chopping onions, I wouldn't be able to get the image of Marsha and her lover out of my mind.

As the car pulled up outside Pandora's Box, I could see her at the window watching as I hopped in, so I threw her a cheery wave.

I'd had to make up a story about going to Manchester on a hen weekend. But Helen hadn't bought it for one moment.

'Who do you know who's having a hen weekend? You don't have any friends except me,' she said, sulkily, when I explained I couldn't see her to talk about Ben.

'You wouldn't actually believe the truth, so I made something up,' I said, promising I'd see her for drinks on my return and settling back to enjoy the ride. I'd sent Mark a reminder about feeding Colin, and hoped he wouldn't create too much mess before my return.

I'd forgotten how untidy he was when we were together. His dirty socks and damp towels seemed to be breeding. Maybe I was making him feel too much at home. I'd even made sure there was food in the fridge which would see him through the next couple of days.

Daniel messaged me during his rehearsals to make sure I was en route to the hotel, and said he would meet me in his dressing room at the stadium. Television cameras were following him for a documentary, so if anyone asked, he would introduce me as his chef.

'Oh and you'll have to wait for your surprise until we're back at the hotel,' he added. Normally I hated the idea of a surprise, either because I guessed what it was, or was disappointed. Mark was terrible at organising them. The biggest surprise he'd ever managed was turning up back in my bed when I arrived home from seeing Daniel. What was I thinking letting him back in the house?

'We're here, Miss,' said the driver Jay as we pulled up outside the grand Victorian hotel. A uniformed doorman ushered me into the foyer and handed my bag to a porter, and without even having to sign in, I was escorted upstairs to my room by someone from the hotel. I say room, it was a suite bigger than my house, with two sofas, elegant fixtures and a four-poster bed swathed in cream. Naturally, I took a couple of pictures on my phone including a selfie of me on the four-poster to show Helen where I was staying on my pretend hen weekend. Then I had about forty-five minutes to have a quick shower and change before Jay returned to take me to the stadium.

As he dropped me off at a special backstage entrance, Chas was there to meet me, an apologetic look on his face.

'Daniel says sorry but he is tied up with all sorts of last minute stuff. There's always something. So he told me to get you settled in your seat with a drink, and he'll meet you back at the hotel after the show.'

Of course he'd be busy backstage. I totally understood, but started to wish that I had someone to share this with, to chat to. Maybe I'd strike lucky with the person sitting next to me, but the seats both sides were empty. Production seats, Chas called them, in case someone important turned up. He gave me a VIP backstage pass to wear round my neck in case there was time to pop in and see Daniel during the interval, but he said it was unlikely.

'He likes to shower and change at half time. It's bloody chaos backstage. You're better off stopping here,' he said, squeezing my arm in a reassuring manner. Actually, I didn't mind too much. There was so much people-watching to do as the audience streamed in to take their seats and the buzz of anticipation grew. Daniel's fans came in all shapes and sizes, ages and class. There were dads with spotty teenage sons, groups of girls who seemed to be trying to outdo each other in breast size and the skimpy skirt department, women who would look more at home in the WI, and smart couples who looked as if they'd come straight from the office.

'Well if it's not Lottie of the lemon drizzle,' said a familiar voice as Stella wedged herself into the seat next to mine. It hadn't crossed my mind that I'd bump into anyone I knew, but then if these were guest seats, it made sense that she might be there.

'How do you know about my lemon drizzle?'

'That photo of you in the local rag? Googled you darling. You don't think I'd let just anyone loose on one of my clients? So what are you doing here?'

'Daniel invited me to see the show. I've never been to The Stadium before. It's pretty impressive.'

'Yep, 20,000 people. Nowhere as big as the O2, but Dan likes to do this as a warm up for his bigger shows. Where are you staying? Maybe we could have a drink after the show?'

'The Grand, but....'

'That's sorted then,' she said, turning away to take a call.

Looking around at the thousands of women who had paid

their hard-earned money to gaze from a distance at their idol, I felt like a fraud. I was kidding myself to think this could ever be anything serious. I was nothing but a glorified groupie with the bonus of being able to cook Daniel's favourite food. But just for now, I'd pretend. Pretend that I was his girlfriend, not his mistress. I hated that word. Pretend that he was falling in love with me, and that I meant something to him.

As the auditorium went dark there were screams and squeals as coloured flames exploded from the front of the stage, and a giant silhouette of Daniel appeared on a screen. Seconds later he burst through it on a motorbike, roaring up the centre stage extension as showers of gold stars rained down on us.

It was such a spectacular show, with its special effects and acrobatic dancers that I almost forgot that I wasn't just a normal member of the audience. But each time he sang a slow romantic song, I wondered if he might be thinking of me. If nothing else ever happened between us, I'd remember this concert for the rest of my life. He was a different person on stage. Even more so than when he was filming for TV. More confident, if that's possible, with a charismatic presence which was somehow diluted when we were together. Together, Daniel and me, in bed, in our own little cocoon.

'Would you ever fuck him?' said Stella loudly in my ear.

'I...I'm not sure how to answer that question,' I said, feeling my face flush.

'Think you just have honey.' God she had such a raucous laugh.

During the rest of the show, I tried to be polite to her, but not engage in conversation. And when she disappeared to make phone calls during the interval, I was relieved to say the least.

For some reason she didn't return for the second half, which left me to enjoy it in peace. And by the end I was almost breathless from the sheer energy and excitement of Daniel's performance. As he took encore after encore, the stadium erupted into a deafening feet-stomping frenzy. All I could think was that later I would be in his arms, or would I? I wasn't sure that would happen if Stella had anything to do with it. Maybe she had a crush on him herself. There had never been any mention of a Mr Stella.

I stayed put until a young security guy came to collect me and escort me to the entrance where Jay was waiting in the car.

'Good show, Miss?'

'Magical,' I said. 'Have you ever seen him?'

'No. I'm into heavy metal and my missus loves her Bollywood stuff. I hear it's good though, if you like that kind of thing,' he said pulling off onto a private road which led us out of the stadium complex without joining the other traffic.

By the time I arrived back at the hotel, there was a text message waiting on my phone from Daniel asking me to wait in my room. He said he'd be about an hour, and to order room service just for me. He'd already eaten far too much. 'Oh, and Stella's had to rush back to London,' he added with a smiley. Thank God, I thought as I lay down on the bed. Just a few minutes and I'd get up and change out of my jeans and into my dress and... the next thing I knew my phone was ringing. It was eleven thirty.

Daniel's voice sounded puzzled. 'It's me. You weren't answering! Everything okay? I've got a bottle of champagne on ice.' Help, how could I have fallen asleep? Somehow I managed to change in super quick time, put on my best lacy underwear, brush my hair and squirt on some perfume.

When he opened the door, I half expected to see some hangers-on in his room, but he was alone and smiling. There wasn't any time to dread how I might look with my clothes off, or remember to suck my tummy in. It just happened. He poured us each a glass of champagne and took me to bed as though it was the most natural thing in the world.

And it was. I haven't had that many lovers, ten if I'm honest, and he was just the best. Not because of any great technique on his part, but the way he made me feel. To start with I was shaking, literally. But as we talked and touched and kissed and laughed, I have never felt more relaxed, so much so that I drifted off into a place where I wanted to stay forever.

The magic was broken slightly when we woke again at around seven and I was hoping to carry on where we left off. Instead he explained he had a couple of early morning business calls to make, so it might be better if I returned to my room, and met him downstairs for breakfast. I tried hard to disguise my disappointment with a smile, as though, hey! Doesn't matter. But it *did* matter. It mattered because for the first time I realised that actually I was having an affair with a married man. We'd just made love, or maybe to him just had sex. But it mattered.

'Hang on a minute,' he said as I was about to leave, and handed me a beautifully gift-wrapped box festooned with ribbons. Inside nestling in tissue paper was a book. Oh My God! It was a Winnie-the-Pooh book. Not just any old Winnie-the-Pooh book, but by the look of the slightly faded brown cover, a very old copy.

'It's a first edition, 1926,' he said, beaming at my delight. 'Couldn't resist it. What do you think?'

Apart from thinking it must have cost him an absolute fortune, I was thinking this was the best present anyone had ever bought me. Ever.

Clutching the book, I drifted back to my room as if in a daze. And when it was time for breakfast, virtually floated downstairs. He and Kevan were already in the dining room, and deep in conversation about business. Daniel caught my eye as I sat down beside him and winked, which was enough to send my desire dial off the scale. Other diners – a selection of businessmen who were mainly preoccupied on their laptops and tablets – paid us only the minimal amount of attention.

'I gather you loved the book,' muttered Kevan quietly, while Daniel was ordering his breakfast. I was surprised he knew about it, until he volunteered that he was the one who tracked it down.

'He had me looking for Paddington Bear books to start with,' he said. 'Until he started going on about this cool bear dude, and I knew exactly who he meant. There's only one.' I felt slightly disappointed that Daniel hadn't chosen it himself, but I guess with presents it's the thought that counts. And he was obviously thinking about me.

When Kevan left the table for a few seconds to take a call Daniel's hand felt for mine under the table. 'I've got a couple of hours off. Let's try and get out for a walk in the city.'

'Are you able to do that without being bothered by fans?'

'Pretty much if I dress down in a baseball hat and my glasses. Chas will come with us, but he'll keep his distance.'

' If you're sure.'

'Sure I want to go out, or be with you? Both.' He gently squeezed my leg. 'How are you feeling after last night?'

'Yeh it was okay,' I said in a flat jokey fashion, not daring to elaborate just in case I made a fool of myself.

'Can we do it again?' he whispered, his lips touching my ear. Each time he did that I got another shot of horny hormones.

'I'll think about it,' I said with a perfectly serious look on my face.

20

As it was our first time out in public, I assumed there would be no physical contact in case someone spotted us. But it was as if we were drawn to each other like magnets. He'd grasp my hand for a few seconds, and then let it go. For a few glorious minutes no one bothered him, and we even managed to stop off for a coffee in a busy cake shop until the girl behind the counter started whispering to her friend. So we grabbed our takeaway cups and left.

Every now and then I'd check to see if Chas was behind us, and he'd give a little nod. But as we passed a narrow alleyway, Daniel pulled me from the pavement and into his arms for a kiss, and then straight back onto the street to continue our stroll. It was if I was a puppet, totally under his control. But I didn't care.

'That wasn't meant to happen,' he said. 'You'll get me into trouble.'

Keeping our distance all the way back to the hotel, I couldn't take my eyes off him. All I wanted was to be back in his room where we didn't have to worry about the world and what they thought. But for the rest of the morning I lost him to sound checks at the stadium, so I lounged in my room flicking through TV channels, eating chocolate out of the mini bar, and taking calls from Helen who was having a crisis at home.

'When are you coming back?' She kept asking.

Before I could answer, there was a loud thumping on the door making me jump. Strange. I didn't order room service. 'Got to go,' I said hanging up on Helen.

'It's me, Kevan, open up.' It sounded urgent. As I opened the door, he strode into the room holding out his phone.

'You're going to have to go.'

'Why? What's happened?'

'This is what's happened,' he said passing me the phone. It was open at a blurred photo of Daniel kissing me in the alleyway with the headline **DOES HIS WIFE KNOW?** And an online story questioning whether his marriage was on the rocks, and asking who I was. There was even a paragraph in bold print at the end with an email address and phone number for any information confirming my identity.

'It's hard to tell it's Daniel.'

'Not that hard. He even took his bloody glasses off to kiss you. You can tell it's him all right. It will be in every single tabloid tomorrow. Someone must have tipped off one of the paps.'

'Has Daniel seen this?'

'Not yet. But we need to get you out of here,' said Kevan. I'll meet you in the lobby in half an hour.'

As soon as he'd left, my secret phone rang. I was shaking as I answered it. So was my voice: 'I'm so sorry.'

'What for? I'm the one who's sorry for not being more careful when we were out. Anyway, it doesn't look like me. I'm going to deny it,' he said, sounding far more upbeat than I thought he would.

'But Kevan says it does, and that I need to leave. Now.'

'Okay, well maybe under the circumstances it might be better if we let things die down rather than risk us being seen together again, at least until we can be open about it.' Really? Did he just say that? If I was patient, could we be a proper couple?

'Sorry honey. I'll call you later.'

My emotions weren't used to being on quite such a roller

coaster, but at least I'd stopped shaking. Half an hour later, and I was downstairs following Kevan's text instructions to alter my appearance as much as possible. I changed into a fresh outfit, scrubbed off all my make-up and put my hair in a pony tail to make me look as different as possible

Outside a stray photographer was on his phone but barely glanced at me as I jumped into Jay's car which would take me home.

Chatting to him to take my mind off the disappointment of leaving, I checked my phone every five minutes in case Daniel tried to contact me. But there was nothing.

The last thing I wanted to do was spend the evening on my own, or even worse with my ex hanging around the place expecting me to cook for him. So during the drive home I texted Helen who leapt at the chance to meet me later for a drink.

Walking through the front door, the place was in such a mess my first thought was that I'd been burgled. But then Mark hadn't been expecting me home until later Sunday, so was probably making the most of my absence to live like some sort of lazy student, with newspapers and trainers strewn across the floor along with empty beer cans. Goodness knows how Tara put up with him. At least Colin had been fed and watered.

By now the blurred photo of us had turned up on a few more online newspapers. Kevan was right. It did look like Daniel, but apart from the fact I'd been described as a redhead, at least you couldn't tell it was me.

Helen was already on her first glass of wine when I arrived at the pub.

'You're up to something,' she said as soon as she saw me.

'What do you mean?'

'You sleeping with him?'

My heart missed about three beats and my breath caught at the back of my throat. 'Who?'

'Mark you silly cow? Who else would I be talking about? Unless you got lucky on your hen weekend. Anyway, why are you home early? I thought you'd still be there.'

'So did I. Long story.'

'Go on then.'

'You wouldn't believe it if I told you.'

By the end of her second glass she'd given up trying to pump me for information about my love life. She was more concerned with her own now that she'd established Ben was acting as a divorce lawyer for Susie Simon.

'Ben's still protesting there's nothing between them. Says the kisses were a joke to make her husband jealous.'

'Do you believe he's telling the truth?'

'Maybe, but now he's now being childish and saying that if I don't believe him then he might as well sleep with her. It's a complete mess, and the kids are beginning to pick up on it.'

For the rest of the evening we talked about Helen. But halfway through the second bottle of wine, I realised I'd forgotten to eat. I was drunk, which wasn't a great idea, especially if Daniel called me after the show. And what's more, I had this terrible urge to confess all to my best friend. I mean, why the hell not? Maybe no names, but I was desperate to tell Helen that I was in love. In love? Was I? Oh my God, it was the first time I'd admitted it to myself. Over the years I'd been in lust for a while until the desire faded, I'd had crushes on people. I'd experienced fondness for some of the men I'd slept with. But being in love. This was different.

When she returned to the table after a visit to the loo, I couldn't keep it in any longer. 'I'm in love.'

'With a man?'

'No, with a gorilla! Yes with a man, but I can't tell you who he is.'

'Why not?'

'Because he's...'

'Come on, you can tell me.'

'He's not available, yet. But he might be soon.'

'You mean he's married and you're having an affair.'

'Kind of.'

'Oh this is priceless, this is. Don't tell me. His name is Ben.'

'Oh God, no. I'm sorry, that was really insensitive.'

'Thanks a bunch, Lottie. It's really good to know that my best friend is screwing someone else's husband.'

'It's not like that.'

'Is he married or not?'

I lowered my head as if in shame.

'Yes. Yes he is.'

'Then it is like that,' she said, picking up her coat and bag to leave. 'It's just like that.'

I struggled getting the key in the lock which is always a sign that I'm much more inebriated than I thought, and it was only ten o'clock.

Mark was slouching in front of the TV drinking from a can of beer. Looking guilty he immediately leaped off the sofa and started scooping up the remains of his bachelor living.

'Hey, I wasn't expecting you home 'til tomorrow.'

'No, nor was I,' I said, trying not to sound slurred.

'Are you drunk?'

'No, of course not. Well maybe a bit.'

'Then I've got the perfect solution. I'll nip out and get us a curry.' I couldn't think of anything I lusted after more at that precise moment, not even Daniel.

'I know what you like so I'll order it. Only thing is...'

I handed him my purse with a 'take what you need,' and staggered upstairs where I threw myself on the bed which is the only place I wanted to be. By the time the curry arrived, I was in my pyjamas and dressing gown, and insisting in a loud voice that I wanted to eat my food in my room.

'Nah, nah you don't. If you get that awful orange sauce on your duvet cover, it will never come out. Come on down, you'll be pleased you did.'

I was pleased I did, and even quite enjoyed being with Mark who was a step up on Colin. Even if he was more annoying, at least he made me laugh.

He insisted I put the left-overs in the fridge for his breakfast, and then with a little twinkle in his eye added: 'I don't suppose you fancy a....?'

'You suppose right,' I said and headed up stairs.

21

By the time I staggered downstairs for coffee the next morning, Mark was already up, dressed and had been out to get the paper. It was never an intellectual broadsheet, but the tackiest tabloid he could find, and there I was on the front page. I snatched it out of his hand. This time the headline said, **FRENCH CONNECTION,** and there was a story, still maintaining that he was caught out with another woman, but with no comment from Daniel's PR machine or from his wife.

He snatched it back. 'Oy, I haven't read it yet.'

'Sorry, I just need to look at the picture.'

'What Daniel Whatisface being a naughty boy?'

'It's not him. it doesn't look anything like him.'

'His curly redhead bit of stuff looks a bit like you though,' he laughed.

'Thanks a lot,' I said, and boiled the kettle.

'You can finish my toast and Marmite if you like,' he said, nodding over to his plate. I immediately felt as if I was going to throw up, and my head started to pound.

I ferreted around in the drawer where I kept everything from painkillers to fuses, but couldn't find anything remotely helpful apart from a box of elastic bands and a sticky bottle of cough syrup dated 2004. Mark was trying to look sympathetic but I could tell he was trying not to laugh. 'There's some tablets in the bathroom cupboard. Shall I get them? Although maybe you should wait before you take them. You do look like you're going to be Moby Dick.'

'Oh do stop using that Cockney slang, you're not even an EastEnder. You're from Luton,' I said, realising how irritable I sounded.

Without even touching my coffee, I went straight back to sleep until a text on my phone woke me. It was three in the afternoon, how could I have slept so long? 'Hi, I'm outside. Let me in!' I sat bold upright. It was Daniel. I texted him back that I was in bed with a hangover. And he wrote back: 'Oh this I must see.'

From the window I could see Chas's four-by-four with the blacked out windows, the engine still running. I texted back. 'Down in five.' Rushing around, I washed my face, applied some blusher and perfume and a dab of lipstick, and changed into leggings and a sloppy jumper. I looked and felt like death, which would probably put him completely off me, and that would be that. I called out for Mark, but there was no answer. Thank God. He was probably at the pub with his mates or back at Tara's house.

As I opened the front door, Chas drove off and Daniel in baseball cap and black rimmed glasses hurried in. I kept expecting him to wear one of those plastic kid's disguises. You remember, the black glasses with the Groucho Marx eyebrows and the big nose. Thankfully Mark had fulfilled his promise of tidying up a bit, so the place wasn't too messy. I could feel the colour draining out of me and started to feel queasy again. For some reason my hangovers get progressively worse throughout the afternoon.

Daniel was clearly trying to keep a straight face. 'Right, so what happened? Is this because of the photo in the papers?'

'No, well yes, a bit. I went out with Helen and we demolished two bottles of wine without food. I look awful.'

'You don't look awful, well okay you do, but in a good way.'

'There's a good way of looking awful?'

'Maybe not. Come here you,' he said, holding me close and kissing my hair. 'You need to eat something. I do great toast,' he said, lowering me gently onto the sofa while he disappeared into the kitchen still talking. I dreaded what he'd find there courtesy of Mark who only had to heat up a curry to turn the place into a war zone.

Tea with toast and honey is obviously the perfect cure for hangovers, because after about five minutes, I could feel the colour returning to my cheeks. Or it could have been the fact that Daniel was gently rubbing my head as I rested it on his lap.

Although he looked tired, he seemed relaxed as he told me how well last night's show had gone, and how Kevan and Stella were fielding off press calls about the photo. There was no real proof it was him, other than the word of a Northern photographer, and he figured that the fuss was beginning to die down.

'Why don't you let me take you back home with me?'

Much as I loved the idea of being with him, the very thought of sitting in the back of a car was nearly enough to send me running to the bathroom to throw up. Plus after a whole weekend off, I needed to be fresh for work in the morning.

'Trust me, I don't do hangovers well. Why don't I cook you something special tomorrow and bring it over to yours?'

'I'll send Chas to collect you.'

'No, it's fine, I'll drive.'

I already knew what I was going to make him. I'd prepare it at work and take it over with me. Oh help, I must stop thinking about food. He looked at his watch. 'I've got to go, but I'll be in touch later,' he said. A sense of relief flooded over me. All I wanted to do was sleep off my hangover and wake refreshed, knowing that I was going to see him soon.

The sound of a key turning in the door made me feel sick again, as Mark strolled into the room.

'Hey mate, how you doing' said Mark in his normal chirpy manner, offering out his hand. Daniel smiled, but didn't take it. I could see the realisation dawn on Mark's face, and struggled not to giggle.

'Er, you're that bloke off the telly. Daniel French.'

'Lots of people tell me that,' said Daniel.

'No you are. Deffo. You're him.'

Daniel was pulling a quizzical face. 'You think so?'

'Yeh he is, isn't he Lotts? That's Daniel French.'

'Well if you say so,' said Daniel. 'And who are you?'

'I'm Mark.'

Daniel looked at me. 'Is this who I heard when I called you?'

'Yes. He's my ex. He's staying here because his girlfriend threw him out. I should have told you.'

As the penny dropped Mark tried to dig me out of a hole. 'Yeh mate, nothing's happened with Lottie. She wouldn't have it. This might seem a stupid question, but what are you doing here? Are you her new bloke?'

Daniel was still trying to look serious, and then a large smile spread over his face.

'Yeh I guess I am,' he said, then turning to me said: 'See you tomorrow.'

Mark stood scratching his head. 'I still think you look like that Daniel French guy. Mind you can't stand his music. You ought to be one of those celebrity doubles. They get paid a bundle for opening things.'

Daniel burst out laughing and lapsing into a strong Northern accent said: 'Aye, 'appen that's not a bad idea.'

For the rest of the evening, Mark couldn't stop talking about his encounter with the Daniel French lookalike.

'Should have taken a bloody selfie, that's what I should have done. Could have made out it was him.'

I couldn't stand it any longer.

'It was him, Mark. It was Daniel French.'

He stared at me as in disbelief. 'Nah, you're having me on. You are aren't you? You're having me on?'

22

Like a large percentage of the work force I hated Mondays. It was probably a left-over dread from school when we always started the day with double maths. But with the prospect of cooking for Daniel, it suddenly had a different feel to it. A pity the same couldn't be said for the rest of my little world. Marsha was at the doctors to get something for her persistent cough. Helen wasn't replying to my texts, and Pat was a bit huffy as she'd had to cover for me over the past two days. Plus there was a text from Ryan to say he was taking the day off sick.

Pat tutted as she reminded us that she had never had a day off sick in her life. 'You youngsters. Too many hangovers and no stamina. Mind you, Ryan hasn't been looking himself lately. Can't help having that man as his stepdad. Bit of a bully if you ask me.'

Jess, who had been sulky and quiet all morning because of man troubles, piped up: 'I think he's got a new boyfriend?'

I pretended that this was news to me. 'I didn't know he was into boys.'

'I'm not sure Ryan knew either until he met that gay club owner Max Diamond at Daniel's party. He's been hanging out a lot with him,' said Pat.

'But Max is Kevan's boyfriend. Kevan. Daniel's manager. They're still a couple aren't they?' Pat shrugged and Jess was busy texting, so I let it rest. This was all getting a bit complicated for my liking. I just hoped Ryan was okay and made a mental note to call him.

As soon as we had a lull in the kitchen, I started the pastry for the meat pie I was taking over to Morton Manor. Three of our regulars were in. We had nicknames for them.

There was Mr Meany, who always had Jess running around after him but had never once left a tip, Miss Cup Cake who as usual was making her Red Velvet last as long as possible, eating it crumb by crumb. And Selina, the slightly mad middle-aged woman who always sat opposite her fluffy bear back-pack which was her constant companion.

'She's not talking to her bear today, maybe they've had a row,' said Pat, laughing. I worried about Selina, or maybe it was more a concern that I'd turn into a Selina one day. A sad lonely middle-aged woman with a cat called Colin. But not anymore. Now I was a thirty-something (okay so thirty-nine is still a thirtysomething!) in an exciting secret love affair with a gorgeous superstar lusted over by millions of other women.

Even as I thought it, it sounded ridiculous. But the proof was in the lovely text messages I'd been getting all day from him. He wasn't in the least bothered about finding Mark at my house. In fact I think it amused him. I loved the fact that he wasn't really the jealous type. Unlike me. I wondered how I'd react if I saw Daniel with another woman, erm, like his wife?

As if reading my mind, Pat said: 'Did you see that photo of Daniel French kissing that woman? You can't tell me she doesn't know he's a married man.'

Trying to sound as matter of fact as I could, I answered: 'Yes, but we don't know much about his marriage. His wife virtually lives in the States, so maybe they're not together.'

But no-one was really listening. 'What a naughty boy he's turned out to be,' said Jess, bringing up the photo on her phone. 'And it won't be long before they find out who that woman is. The bitch. Pity you can only see the back of her head. Someone will find out and ring the papers. You can't keep something like that secret.' Marching over to the shutter which connected the kitchen to the café I yanked it down to give us total privacy.

'You have to.'

'What do you mean? We have to what?' asked Pat.

'Keep what I'm going to tell you a secret.'

From the look on Jess's face she knew exactly what I was talking about.

'It's you, isn't it? In the photo, with Daniel. You're the bitch. I knew he fancied you from that night at the party.'

'Oh my good gawd, I can see it now,' said Pat, studying Jess's phone. 'When was this taken?'

'Thank you Jess. I am not a bitch. It was taken at the weekend. I went up to Manchester to see him in his show, and a photographer must have followed us.'

'You crafty cow. So are you at it then?' asked Pat.

'You are, aren't you?' said Jess. 'I can see from your face. Oh my God, Lottie's having sex with Daniel French, Lottie's having...'

'Sshh. Stop. Please. No one can know about this. Not yet.'

'So you're his bit on the side then,' said Pat, echoing what I knew my nan would say if she was still here.

'Well no, not exactly. He's not really with his wife at the moment. I mean they aren't divorced, yet. But what we have, it's not just an affair. It's different.'

Pat laughed. 'That's what they all say, the women who have stolen other women's husbands. Face it pet. He's cheating on his wife, and you're going along with it.'

The door opened and Marsha marched in.

'And why may I ask is the shutter down and customers being ignored?'

Jess started giggling: 'Lottie's having...' Oh my God, there was no way that Marsha could know.

'I'm having...I'm having a bad day, and just needed a word with my staff to explain why. I'm sorry Marsha, it won't happen again.'

'Too right it won't,' she said, pulling up the shutter where a small queue had gathered. 'You've just had an entire weekend off lady. So get on with your work,' she said.

Before I left The Loft, I'd sworn Jess and Pat to secrecy. I had to trust them, what else could I do? They were the nearest I had to family. There was no way I could enlist any support from

Helen, now that she'd tagged me as a scarlet woman.

Back home, as I was changing, I heard Mark downstairs putting what sounded like tins of beer in the fridge.

He called up the stairs: 'Hallo babe, you alright?'

'Don't call me babe, and yes I am. I'm off to see Dan...Dave,' I said remembering to keep up the charade that the man in my living room was not who Mark thought he was.

'Oh yes, you said. When are you leaving?'

That's the question I wanted to ask him. He'd been here for far too long. I needed to give him a moving out date. Maybe that would motivate him into making it up with Tara.

'Ten minutes,' I said, just checking how I looked. I was fast running out of outfits to wear for Daniel, and the fake tan I'd applied after my shower was looking decidedly streaky.

'Okay, have a good time. My mate's outside. He's driving me to get an Indian.'

'You'll end up looking like an onion bhaaji,' I called back. He still made me laugh. But since getting more involved with Daniel, any feelings I had for Mark had changed. He was more like an annoying younger brother than an ex-lover. And to think that one day we might have been married. All those years ago when we first met, I was so desperate not to end up on a dusty old shelf, I was happy to settle for anyone who found me attractive.

As I loaded my overnight bag into the boot of my Mini, I thought back to the first time I'd driven to Morton Manor on that dreadful night. Now I was going as Lady of the Manor, ha ha. No not really. The Mistress of the Manor? That was more like it.

Part of me was hoping that the dreaded Meg wasn't going to be there. I could do without her peering over my shoulder in the kitchen as I prepared dinner. But I'd decided that even if she was I'd be gracious, and friendly and, well, I was only there to cook. She'd be gone by the time we went to bed. Not that I'd be spending the night in the actual house. Daniel said there was a guest suite which formed part of an outhouse in the grounds. Used to be the stables, I think. The fact that we wouldn't be sleeping in the house immediately helped me feel less guilty about being with him. I'd agreed to stay, so long as he got up early and made me coffee in the morning.

'What did your last slave die of?' he asked when I made the deal.

'I don't know. I've never had one.' And it was true. I don't think I'd ever had a man to wait on me, or spoil me. I used to envy friends who'd tell me how their boyfriends gave them foot rubs, or stroked their hair as they lay cuddled up on the sofa, or brought them breakfast in bed.

Daniel had texted me the security number I needed to open the gates and by the time I drove to the parking area just outside the front door, he was standing there with Oscar to greet me.

'Is our dinner in here?' he said, taking my bags from me.

'You just want me for my meat pie.'

'Yep!' he said as we headed for the kitchen. While Daniel went to sort out some music, he asked me to choose a chilled wine from the fridge and pour us each a glass. And for the next hour or so, as we prepared dinner together, we laughed, and kissed, and joked. Me in a state of the art kitchen cooking with my dream man to help me. My life was complete.

He laid the huge oak table in the dining room, with the most beautiful silver cutlery and cut glasses I'd ever seen. And by candlelight we ate our meat pie and mashed potatoes from delicate bone china plates which Daniel said had belonged to his grandmother.

After dinner, I sat in the same spot on the sofa by the crackling fire where Daniel had first put his arm around me.

'This is where it happened,' he said, as I lay my head back on his shoulder.

'Where what happened?'

'I knew that you were important.'

I sat up and turned to him. 'No one has ever used that word about me before. Important. I've never ever felt that important to anyone.'

'You are to me. And I don't know what's going to happen,

but I want you to be with me when it does.'

There was so much I wanted to say, but didn't dare, in case my tongue ran riot like it usually did, and I blurted out everything I'd been thinking since that first time by the fire. That all along I knew there was something between us, but hadn't trusted my instinct. That no one had ever made me feel like this. Ever. So I sat quietly.

I had drifted into the most magical place. Any minute I would wake up, and it wouldn't be real.

The sound of Oscar barking jolted me out of my hypnotic state and at the sound of the front door opening, Daniel leaped to his feet.

'Who the f...?'

Chas appeared as if from nowhere and gestured to us to stay where we were. And when he returned, he was followed by Meg.

'I'm so sorry, I left my phone here, silly me,' she said putting on what looked like a fake concerned face.

'Hello Lottie, fancy seeing you. I'm so sorry Daniel, I thought you were out tonight or I would never have come,' she said before excusing herself to the utility room where she'd apparently left her mobile. Yeh right, she wasn't fooling me. A minute later she returned with a phone in a luminous yellow case.

'Here it is. You wouldn't think I'd lose something this colour. I'll be off now and leave you to it,' she said, and wandered down the hall, letting herself out.

As she left, Chas made an appearance speaking quietly: 'I think it's your phone you need to be careful with boss.'

Daniel looked concerned. 'What do you mean?'

'I saw her scrolling through a phone a couple of days ago, and it certainly wasn't yellow. It could have been one of yours.'

I'd never heard Daniel so angry. 'She wouldn't do that. What sort of person goes through someone else's phone?'

Chas shook his head. 'Who knows? Maybe she's got a major crush on you and was doing a bit of phone stalking.'

'I thought she had a serious boyfriend.'

Chas shrugged. 'I've dropped her off home a lot, and never seen him. Always just the one car, her little old banger parked outside. Bit of a coincidence that she turns up to find her phone when you two are here.' The same thought occurred to me. Plus if she'd been checking Daniel's texts and messages to me, she had enough ammunition to make real trouble.

After Meg's ill-timed appearance, it was decided that I shouldn't stay, just as a precaution. Once again, I'd been deprived of my night of passion with Daniel. Thank you God, or fate, or whichever super power was wrecking my love life.

'If she has any suspicions about you two, then the last thing we need is for her to arrive early tomorrow and catch you still here Lottie,' said Chas, and I agreed.

Daniel locked me into his arms in a giant hug. He obviously didn't have any concerns about Chas knowing. 'Why don't I come back home with you?'

'Not with Mark there,' I shivered at the thought. 'But he'll be gone soon, so if you're happy to slum it...'

Chas disappeared to wherever he hung out in the house. I gathered from Daniel that he had his own rooms upstairs fitted with equipment so he could monitor the CCTV cameras outside the house. But once he had gone, so had the mood. While I wanted more than anything to experience a repeat of our night in the hotel, I knew it would have to wait until both the time and place were right. Daniel obviously didn't feel the same. As he started to kiss me and we sank down onto the sofa, I was almost tempted to abandon all my inhibitions and let him take me in front of the fire. But something stopped me.

And as I caught sight of Beth's face smiling down at me from the giant black and white photograph above the fireplace, it was as though she was watching.

23

It was one o'clock in the morning when I arrived home to a furry purry welcome from Colin and heavy snoring from the spare room. I checked to see if Helen had forgiven me yet, but all I could find was a posting on Facebook full of photos of her and Lulu the woman who owned the Italian fashion shop in the High Street and was probably now her new BFF.

I couldn't stop thinking about Meg and her arrival at Morton Manor. It gave me the creeps to think she might have been checking Daniel's phone. But then how would she know his security code? I suppose she could have been watching over his shoulder as he typed it in. She rarely seemed to take her eyes off him.

My imagination started running riot. If she had a crush on Daniel, or worse still, an obsession with him, then maybe her boyfriend didn't even exist. God, that was even more sinister. Despite the snoring soundtrack from Mark, I felt relieved to be back in my own bed.

When I woke I could hear Mark downstairs clattering around making tea. Maybe he'd even think to make me one. I was in luck. He appeared at the bedroom door with a mug and a bunch of newspapers.

'So it really was him,' he said, plonking the mug down on the bedside table so that the tea slopped over.

'What do you mean?'

'Front page,' he said, throwing one of the papers onto my

bed. And there it was, a photo of me, much sharper this time, emerging bag in hand from the house last night.

'How the hell did they get this picture?'

'How would I know? Here, you're famous.' He tossed three more newspapers at me, all of them with my picture on the front and details inside. The doorbell rang and Mark headed downstairs. I could hear talking but I was too engrossed in one of the papers to pay attention.

The headline read, **BIG STAR'S SMALL TOWN GIRL.** Small town girl? Flipping cheek. I turned to page six inside where they had printed the original blurry photo of us in Manchester and a story about how we'd met under the banner **CHEF CHARLOTTE GILBERT GETS SAUCY WITH SUPERSTAR.**

When I switched on my phone, there were a couple of missed calls from Helen, and a message from Daniel which said: 'Don't worry. We'll deal with it.' No kiss this time. Oh well. Colin was sitting on the clothes piled on my bedroom chair staring at me.

'What are you looking at?' I said out loud, slightly concerned that I was now falling out with my cat. I could hear a commotion outside the window, and the doorbell went again a few times.

Mark shouted up the stairs. 'There's half of Fleet Street outside.' I ran down to peek out of the living room window and it was like a scene out of the film *Notting Hill*, where the photographers are all waiting for Julia Roberts. Except that I wasn't Julia Roberts.

'That photo taken outside here. It wasn't anything to do with me, I swear,' said Mark. 'Although I did know all the time that geezer was Daniel French. You didn't really think you'd fooled me did you?' Well yes I did, but that wasn't important now.

I'd seen enough things like this on the telly to know that if I brazened it out, just got in my car and drove away without speaking, there was little they could do, except follow me I suppose. I'd need to put my foot down. I didn't want them knowing where I worked. My mobile rang. It was Chas asking if there was a back way out of my house.

'No, but the woman next door but one has a side gate out onto the street.' We agreed that I would hop over the neighbouring fences and into her garden, and ask if she would let me out. He would be in a car waiting for me.

Chas was keen to whisk me off somewhere secret where I could stay in hiding for a while, but I refused. Finally he agreed to drop me in town.

'I need to be at work. I can't just not turn up. I'll be okay there. I'm just going to carry on as normal,' I said, probably sounding more confident than I felt.

As I climbed the stairs to The Loft, I knew there was nothing remotely normal about my life anymore. Thankfully there was no press waiting for me outside, but how long would it take for them to find me? And then what?

Jess was hovering at the kitchen door looking worried. 'Oh Lottie, the press. They know it's you.'

And that's when I saw Ryan at the sink, and the remains of a black eye: 'Hey Lottie, what's going on?' I could well ask him the same thing.

'Ryan what happened to your eye?'

'Oh nothing. Got into a bit of a scrape with my stepdad. What's happening with Daniel French?'

'We're, I'm, the thing is...' The thing is, I didn't know what to say. What *was* going on? Were we having an affair or now that it had been exposed, was it over? When I'd tried to call him earlier, it had gone straight to voicemail. I sent him a text message asking for him to call me. Meanwhile, Helen had left a voicemail dumping me as her best friend now there was proof I was having an affair with a married man. 'You're no better than slutty Susie,' she said, adding: 'It doesn't matter how fucking famous he is. He's still a bastard.' There was also a text from Pat who was on her day off, and one from Marsha asking me to pop downstairs and see her as soon as I got in.

'Lottie, there were a few strange people with cameras outside when I arrived this morning asking if you worked here. I denied all knowledge of you. But I would like an explanation.'

She took me through to the little back room where she made me a cup of tea and listened while I tried to make sense of what had happened since that day when Daniel French came in for shepherd's pie.

'Well,' she said when I'd finished. 'So that's why you were so interested in my life as a mistress.'

'I don't see it like that though. His marriage is all but over.'

'Is that what he told you?'

'Yes and I believe him. His wife is in America all the time.'

Marsha nodded. 'And do you think she'll lie down and just accept it?'

I hadn't given it too much thought. It was as though Beth Blackshaw was just some sort of movie character who didn't really exist. At least not in my world where Daniel was fast becoming the most important thing.

'I don't know. She doesn't seem to care. She wants to stay out there longer, have some space.'

'But that was before you were on the scene. Trust me there is nothing like knowing another woman is in love with your husband to make him even more desirable.'

At lunchtime Jess rushed into the kitchen looked flustered.

'It's packed out there. I swear there's some dodgy looking paps at table seven waiting to snap you.'

Ryan wandered out to report back. 'She's right, there's at least half a dozen of them, ordering coffees and on their phones. And more outside on the pavement. You'd better stay hidden.'

When the kitchen door opened I froze until I saw it was Pat. 'Thought I'd better come in today and help you out. Marsha called to tell me what was happening. Take a break while I get stuck in. You look like you need it.'

The freezing cold iron fire escape steps penetrated through my jeans to my bones as I sat looking over the alley at the back of the shops, warming my hands round a steaming mug of coffee. A wintry fog had descended on the town making much of it disappear and I wished it would swallow me up too. If I snuck out this way after work, hopefully I'd be able to get home without being hassled.

There had been a missed call from Daniel who said he was stuck in the recording studios in London for the rest of the day and evening, but that he'd call me when he could. Three times I played it, trying to tell from his tone of voice whether he was angry, or just not convinced about us any more. I half expected to be dumped. *I'd* dump me.

Despite Mark protesting his innocence, I wasn't convinced. I remembered him asking me on Monday night how long it would be before I left. His friend could have been the one who snapped me from his car. Or maybe Meg had tipped off the press after checking Daniel's messages.

From inside I could hear raised voices and the next thing I knew Pat was throwing my bag and coat at me.

'There's a couple of TV crews just come in. Go,' she hissed at me. 'Scarper. Quick before they work out there's a bleeding fire escape.'

I'd never run down a spiral fire escape before, but I can tell you, it's not easy, which might explain why I tripped and toppled down the last four steps falling awkwardly on my ankle. I sat there for a moment not knowing whether to laugh or cry as my foot started to swell.

'Well that was quite an exit,' said a familiar voice. Kevan. What on earth was he doing here?

'Daniel asked me to look after you. I was just checking out the escape routes we could use to get you out of The Loft when you flew down all on your own. Here,' he said, helping me up. When I tried to put any weight on my left foot, I almost collapsed with the pain.

'Ok, there's only one way to do this,' he said, slinging my bag over one shoulder and me over the other like a sack of potatoes as he walked to his car parked nearby. Half an hour later and we were in a private hospital where after an X-ray I was bandaged up and sent home to rest with a nasty sprain.

'So what do you want to do? Daniel suggests you pack a few things and go to stay with friends or family.'

It suddenly occurred to me I didn't have one single friend

or any family members I could stay with. Mark was possibly my best bet. Surely he cared enough to keep an eye on me if I stayed at home. But Kevan thought it was a bad idea.

'You'll be pestered to death. It's better if you disappear for a while until things settle down.'

'But I don't want to disappear,' I said, hating the pathetic way I sounded. Kevan looked at me with a resigned smile. 'Then, you shouldn't have got involved with such a famous married celebrity.'

24

It wasn't that long until my fortieth birthday, and instead of planning any celebrations, here I was planning to run away and hide from my own life. I decided not to do anything until I'd sat down face to face with Daniel. As we approached my little rented house with its welcoming red wooden door and black iron knocker, it had never felt more like home.

There was no sign of photographers waiting for me outside, presumably because they thought I was still at work. But even as we went in, I noticed a motorbike pull up and park opposite. It wouldn't take them long to twig that I'd headed back home. One thing for sure was I wouldn't be welcome at Helen's house and I couldn't expect Pat to put me up. The one person I hadn't thought about asking for help was Marsha. But I was terrified to call her as I suspected she might be weighing up my future at The Loft seeing as I clearly couldn't be there for a while.

Since I had nowhere else to hide, the plan was that I'd go to Morton Manor and wait it out until Daniel returned home from the recording studios. Kevan made himself at home in the kitchen with Colin, chatting away to him like an old friend . So I wasn't the only one who talked to cats. Somehow I managed to get up the stairs on my bottom and pack some clothes. Mark had agreed to stay on and look after Colin, in return for temporary use of my car and the chance to live rent free. There was no sign of him returning to Tara, but for now, this suited me.

As I started to text Marsha to apologise for all the drama, she called me, and I tried to gain her sympathy by making my fall sound a bit more dramatic than it was.

'You don't need to lay it on Charlotte. I'll have to bring in a new chef for the time being, so I won't be able to pay you. You do realise that don't you? What you going to do?' I had no idea. For the first time in my life I didn't have a plan. All I could hope was that Daniel had one. That he'd look after me.

'Come on. We need to go,' said Kevan, zipping up my case. 'Word has got round that you're back home.'

'How long will I be at Morton Manor?' I asked, worried that I hadn't packed enough.

'Until the press find something more sleazy to write about,' said Kevan helping me down the stairs.

We were just leaving when an urgent text came in from Jess telling me to check my Twitter account which had risen from fourteen to two thousand followers. For a moment I was impressed by my new following until I read some of the comments which ranged from calling me "groupie trash" to "ginger minge" and other insults in between.

'Oh my God, I'm being trolled! Look at these.'

Kevan took the phone from me and turned it off. 'Come on they're just a lot of silly girls who are as jealous as hell. Ignore them.'

As the day went on, the comments got nastier and more threatening, most of them from fans of Beth Blackshaw who were unleashing their fury against me. There were at least two death threats, and a description from one of her male fans about how he'd like to mince me up, turn me into a spag bol, and eat me. Oh this was gross.

By the time we arrived at Morton Manor, Meg had obviously been briefed to be nice to me and she was trying her best.

'Oh you poor poppet. I've made up the guest room for you.

It's really pretty. Shall we get you up there? Daniel won't be home until late.'

With Kevan's help, I somehow managed to get up the stairs and hobble down a long corridor. And she was right, it was a delightful room. Various shades of lilac with lots of cream lace, white fur cushions and white carpets. This room had a woman's touch, probably Beth's.

Meg insisted that I rest and she'd bring me up afternoon tea and a snack to see me through until dinner. The fact she was being so nice to me was rather unnerving, but I was happy to lap up any kindness I could get. I couldn't help but think she'd be much prettier without all the heavy make-up. And the dyed brunette bob which she'd obviously copied from Beth just didn't suit her long thin face.

'I bet you've never known anything like this. What's it like being famous?' she asked, plumping up the pillows behind me, and giving me the remote control for the TV.

'Just as well you didn't fall any further than a few steps. You might have ended up splattered on the ground and that wouldn't be a good look, would it? I've put a lovely snugly white towelling robe in your bathroom, and various make-up goodies that Beth gets sent. She's got loads, she doesn't need them. Oh sorry, I'm not supposed to talk about Beth. But anyway, help yourself,' she said, before exiting backwards with a wave.

The next thing I was aware of was Daniel, sitting on my bed. It was nine o'clock and heaven knows how long I'd been asleep. I'd obviously slept through my tea and snack though.

'Hey gorgeous, how are you? Kevan didn't tell me about the fall, or I would have come straight home. Shall I get Meg to make us something and we'll eat it up here? Or do you want to come down?' Maybe it was the shock of the fall, but I was in no state to make any decisions. I just wanted to feel safe.

'What are we going to do?'

'I'm not sure yet. I need to talk to Beth, but I can't get hold of her. She turns her phone off on set. I can think of one thing we could do though…'

That night was even better than the one in The Grand,

except with a few 'ouch' noises from me when he happened to put too much weight on my sprained ankle. And we talked for hours about us and our feelings. He didn't say he loved me, and I didn't want him to, not yet. It was too soon. I don't believe in all that lightweight 'love you, love you' stuff that people say to each other every five minutes. And he said neither did he.

He told me about his eight years in the boy band Three to One, and how acrimonious it was when they split. I'd never been a fan, but I remembered it being headline news. All those girl fans declaring that their world had ended. Some even threatening suicide.

'Why did you split?'

'Well for a start most of us were just reaching thirty, so we weren't a boy band anymore. We were men with strong minds of our own, and in all cases, except me, wives and kids. But the main reason was that I always thought I deserved more say than the rest because I wrote most of the songs. And that I would be a much bigger star and take the credit I deserved by going it alone. I was an arrogant sod, wasn't I?'

'But it worked out didn't it?'

'Not exactly. I didn't write a song for years. I couldn't. Going it alone seemed like the worst idea I'd ever had. I was lonely and depressed. Those friendships that had been part of my life since I was twenty-two were over. The phone stopped ringing. Overnight I went from being part of a solid set of mates to total isolation. And what's more I think they hated me. None of the others made it on their own.'

'But you always had Kevan.'

'No, we fell out as well. He told me I was crazy to split the band, and that I'd grown too big for my boots. And it's true I had. They were a great bunch of guys and top musicians. But the most important thing is they were my friends. It can be a lonely life on the road.'

After a few seconds silence, he started to speak again. This time sounding more positive. 'By the time I was thirty-five, the songs had started coming, mainly sad ballads, but at least I was writing again. So I flew over to Ireland and begged Kev to manage me. And fortunately he said yes.'

It had to be asked. 'Did you have a girlfriend?'

'Yes, Naomi Lincoln, the actress from *City Hospital*. We were engaged. Don't you remember?' No I didn't. It must have passed me by. I was probably too pre-occupied with my own romantic dramas.

'We got together just after the band split up. So I guess I wasn't much fun to be with. But she stuck with me until she started filming *City Hospital* and fell in love with Jerry Thornton who was playing a cameo role. And they're now married.'

'Yes, I met her at your party, and at the TV show. She seems lovely.'

'She is. Just bad timing I guess.' Immediately, I felt that familiar twinge of unease in my gut. It was called jealousy. Maybe he still had a thing for her. Not that it would come to anything. After all she had a three-year-old daughter with her husband.

'But she's also about the only ex I've ever stayed friends with. Love her old man as well. Big drinker, but funny with it.'

That night we found out as much as we could about each other. He revealed how lonely life can get on the road, and that he was dying to have kids. He registered my disappointed expression.

'Thirty-nine's not too old.'

'I'm going to be forty on Valentine's Day. Not that I'll be celebrating.'

'Oh yes you will. We're not letting that birthday get away.'

'I'm not a big fan of birthdays.'

'Why's that,' he leaned up on his elbow and looked at me quizzically.

'Because I always hoped I'd get a card from my mum. But it never happened.'

'Really? Not even when you were twenty-one?'

'That was difficult. My dad had just died. He gave me this locket,' I said, picking it up from the bedside table. He opened it and smiled at the tiny photos inside of me and my dad.

'He looks like a great guy,' he said, laying the locket gently back down on the pine surface.

'My nan and Helen organised a surprise twenty-first party, but I knew all about it. I'm not good at those kind of things. I always get embarrassed. But they tried their best, all popping up from behind sofas when I got home from work. And I tried to be happy for a couple of hours. I even thought my mother might send me a card that day. Nan was still in the same house so she would have known the address. But nothing came. I felt like I was an orphan. It wasn't a happy time.'

Daniel spoke softly. 'Listen, we are going to change all that. On Valentine's Day, you are going to have the best and happiest birthday party ever.'

I could feel tears welling up, but they were a legacy from the three-year-old who still hurt inside.

'Promise?'

'Promise,' he said.

It was three in the morning by the time we turned off the bedside light. Through a crack in the curtains, his face was bathed in moonlight so that I could watch him in the darkened room. There was no doubt that I had strong feelings for him, but if he hadn't been in the spotlight and lusted over by so many other women would I have felt the same? If Daniel was, say, a cab driver or a painter and decorator like Mark, would I have felt so overwhelmed by what we had? The thing is, he would never have been either of those. He was born to sing, and create and write love songs and play music and make his audience fall in love with him. And so far it had worked on me.

25

The next day Daniel had to leave early to fly to Belfast for a chat show. But he promised he'd be in touch as often as he could throughout the day, and told me to rest.

Scrolling through various online newspapers it appeared journalists had managed to infiltrate my Facebook page to find photos of me pulling silly drunk faces with Helen on a girls' night out. Plus romantic shots of me with Mark which they'd used in stories about how I'd gone up in the world from dating a working-class painter and decorator to world-class performer.

The hours passed slowly. I took the bandage off my ankle and wished I hadn't. It was a morbid rainbow of browns, blues and purples, and still swollen.

'Ooh you poor little thing, that looks awful,' said Meg popping her head round the door. She had this habit of appearing silently like some sort of ghost. I rarely heard her coming.

'I'm about to clean downstairs, so if you need anything, just call,' she said, disappearing before I'd had a chance to answer.

With Daniel away, I felt uneasy. I needed to do something to distract me. While Meg was out of the way, I took the opportunity of hobbling around the first floor. There were a couple more beautifully decorated guest rooms similar to mine, and of course the master bedroom and en suite bathroom where I'd showered on that fateful night of the housewarming party.

The door was open, and the room looked different dappled in sunlight. I wandered over to the white wood dressing table and sat down on the fur covered stool. There were about a dozen different bottles of perfume, most of which I'd never heard of and definitely couldn't afford. I imagined that most of them had been sent to Beth by publicists who wanted her to tweet about them. Surely it wouldn't matter if I tried out a couple on my wrist. After a couple of sprays my attention was caught by a small mother-of-pearl box. Something told me not to open it. That it would be prying, but I didn't listen. Inside was the most beautiful pair of drop earrings I'd ever seen. Huge topaz blue stones surrounded by diamonds. Real ones, surely. I pulled back my hair and tried them on. No one would know would they? As I turned my head from side to side, they acted as a prism for the sunlight throwing rainbows on the cream walls. Why hadn't Beth taken them with her?

'They look cute. Anything else of mine you'd like to have?' said an American accent from the door. I looked into the mirror to see the reflection of an immaculately made-up woman with dark brown glossy hair and full lips staring back at me with a look of disdain on her face.

'Oh my God, I'm so sorry. I wasn't going to take anything.'

'What? Like my husband, you mean,' she said. The word 'husband' was like a little stab in the heart. But let's face it she was still his wife and I was still the mistress. A mistress in tracksuit bottoms, with no make-up, and hair which was obviously having as bad a day as I now was.

I spun round and stood up, forgetting for a moment about my ankle and nearly toppled over with the pain.

Beth Blackshaw, Hollywood A lister walked towards me and held out her perfectly manicured hand for the earrings. She can't have been much taller than five feet and so delicate and petite that I felt like an elephant beside her. Her hair was longer than in most recent photos which softened her face and emphasised her incredible amber eyes which reflected her emotions for all to see on the big screen.

'As you may have gathered, I am Beth, Daniel's wife,' she said smiling. 'And before you ask, my husband doesn't know I'm here.'

'He's in Belfast for a chat show.'

'Yes I know that. I have people who tell me things. Let's go downstairs and talk.'

Five minutes later and she was making us tea. 'You have no idea how much I've been longing to meet you Lottie,' she said, sounding quite friendly under the circumstances.

'Everything alright?' asked Meg, who had magically appeared in the kitchen clutching a pink feather duster. Beth smiled at her.

'It's okay honey. If you could give us a minute.'

'Of course,' she said, closing the door. I swear I could hear her chuckling to herself.

'Sit,' said Beth in the way you might talk to a dog, inviting me to the kitchen table.

'So when I saw the photos of you online, I got myself on a plane and landed at Heathrow this morning to find out what the fuck is going on,' she said, taking a chair opposite me.

This wasn't going well. 'Maybe we should wait for Daniel to get home, or we could call him?'

'I have a better idea honey,' she said, baring perfect white teeth as she spoke. She wasn't shouting, just speaking in the same calm measured voice as before, except that there was definitely nothing friendly about it. 'Meg is going to bring down your things and you are going to get the hell out of my house.'

'But Daniel said your marriage is virtually over, I would never have...'

'Men say a lot of things.'

'You mean it's not over?'

'Would I be sitting here if it was? And can I say one thing?'

'Of course.'

'I didn't expect you to look like that.'

'Like what?'

Oh perhaps she was going to play nice after all.

'Like some fucking freckle-faced carrot-topped scarecrow.'

I was so choked up with humiliation and tears, I couldn't even speak.

Outside, icy sleet was whipping through the air. As I dragged the case across the gravel to the taxi, my phone was vibrating with a call from Daniel. He must have heard that Beth was in town.

'Lottie what's going on?'

'I just met your wife who has thrown me out.'

'She's in the house? She told me she never wanted to set foot there again.'

'Women say a lot of things,' I said, repeating what Beth had said about men.

Silence. 'I'll sort it out. Can you wait there until I get home?'

'What do you expect us to do? Crochet? Discuss the weather until you get back?'

'Okay, of course. I understand. I'm sorry Lottie. My flight isn't until late afternoon. I'll call you.'

'It's okay. I'm okay.'

I wasn't okay. I felt so stupid, and worried about what I'd done to my life and the lives of others.

As the taxi pulled up outside my house, there was no sign of any photographers. The sleet had probably dispersed them, thank God. But the front door was open, and I could hear Mark shouting for Colin.

'What's happened?'

'The cat's done a runner.'

'You mean you let him out. He never goes out the front. You know that Mark. What happened?'

'I left the front door open for two seconds while I was dealing with a couple of reporters, and he escaped. He's only been gone a few minutes.'

'Is that a few minutes Mark time or real time?'

'About twenty minutes,' he said lifting out my case. 'Sorry Lotts.'

'All I asked you to do was keep the place tidy, and make sure Colin doesn't get out.'

'I know, I know,' he said looking so drenched and upset, that I realised I had to give him a break while we started a search.

By eleven we'd given up for the night. There is only so much time you can walk, or in my case, hobble round the streets shouting out 'Colin', before the neighbours think you are slightly mad or desperate to find a missing husband. So we were drowning our sorrows in a bottle of wine. There were a couple of messages from Daniel telling me to sit tight. I was certainly tight, but more through the effects of alcohol than sitting.

I still hadn't explained to Mark why I was back home and walking around as though there was a rain cloud over my head. He obviously knew all was not well, but took his time before he asked. 'What's happened Lotts?'

'Nothing, I'm fine,' I said, trying to force a smile. All I wanted to do was see Daniel and for him to hold me close and reassure me that everything was okay, which it clearly wasn't.

And Colin. I couldn't bear the thought of losing him. I'd made up my mind not to tell Mark anything, but after a few minutes he knew the whole story. I thought he might try to make a joke of it, which is what he usually did to deflect any dramas but he was acting with more sensitivity than I'd ever known.

So when he tried to give me a hug, after initial resistance, I let him. 'It'll all come out in the wash, you'll see.' That's what my nan used to say, but what the hell did it mean? Usually when I put things in to wash, like Mark's white underpants, they came out pink because I'd mixed them with something of mine.

Still, he was trying to be kind. 'I'll set the alarm early tomorrow and go out looking for Colin. He'll be back.' I wasn't so sure. He didn't have a lot of road sense, nor did he know his way around outside the front of the house.

That night I dreamed that I turned up at Morton Manor to find Daniel and Beth back together making mad passionate love in front of the fire. When I woke, my stomach was in knots and I felt sick with jealousy. She was obviously a woman on a mission. Mark brought me in a cup of tea waving a copy of *The Daily News*. This was becoming a habit.

'I didn't know Daniel French was married to Beth Blackshaw. I loved her in that film. What was it she played? A serial killer?'

I snatched it out of his hands. There was a front page banner, **HOLLYWOOD STAR BETH BLACKSHAW ATTACK ON CHEATING HUSBAND AND FLAME-HAIRED MISTRESS.**

Well, that was a slight improvement on being called an ugly scarecrow. Skimming through the story, she emerged as the loving wronged wife who had flown over to save her marriage, I was the harlot, and Daniel was the scumbag husband. She must have given that interview while she was still over in the States.

Just as I was about to call Daniel, a text arrived from Jess. 'Go onto your Twitter account. You've got 15,000 followers!' I had more on my plate than worrying about Twitter, but even though I was dreading checking the nasty comments that would come my way, it had to be done.

The trolls and Beth Blackshaw supporters were already out in force. "You bitch husband stealer" said one. And "Slapper. Whore. You deserve to be die."

"God will punish you in ways you never imagined," said another, and others too awful to repeat. I threw the phone down on the bed, hobbled into the bathroom and threw up.

I could hear Mark's voice outside. 'You alright Lotts?' No I wasn't. I'd never been less alright in my life. Where was Daniel? He must know what was going on. I looked at my watch. It was nearly ten, and not even a good morning text. God knows what he was dealing with.

I needed to do something. The press would soon be outside in force.

I tried calling Daniel, but it just kept going to his voicemail message. On the third attempt I left a message. I tried to sound at least a little upbeat. 'Hi Daniel. It's me, Lottie. Beth's given an interview to *The Daily News*. Have you seen it?'

I tried to hold it together, but my hands were shaking.

'Daniel, could we meet please, or speak. I don't know what to do. Please call me.'

After that I went upstairs to shower and dress. I needed to keep my wits about me. What's the worst that could happen? I'd lose Daniel. Forever be the victim of trolls on Twitter. Even worse be murdered by a Twitter troll? Lose my job? My home? My friends? What friends? My cat? Oh, he was already lost. My job was practically gone, and my best friend hated me. I needed some advice. Someone wise. What would nan say? Probably something like: *You've made your bed girl, now you've got to lie in it!* If only it wasn't Daniel French's super king sized bed. But then maybe I hadn't lost Daniel. Perhaps when he'd sorted the drama with Beth, we could be a proper couple.

My mobile phone rang from Daniel's old number. Why wasn't he using our secret phone? 'Daniel. Thank God. I've been worried. Where are you?'

There was a pause: 'Sorry Lottie, this isn't Daniel, it's Kevan. He's in a meeting with Stella deciding how to handle all of this. Are you still at home?' Why wasn't it Daniel? Surely he could find two minutes to call me. But then again, he must be busy. His wife's interview could affect his career.

'The master says he will be in touch as soon as he can. Call me if you need anything. This number's fine. I'm fielding all of his calls. Oh and you know that it's vital you say nothing to the press at this stage? Are you alright staying at your house for the moment? We could sort you a hotel.'

'No, I'd rather be here.' At least I felt relatively safe with Mark. I'm not sure he would be brave enough if a Twitter troll appeared at the front door with a knife. But then what would one look like? Who were these people who thought they had the right to judge you, abuse you and to frighten you? I couldn't help myself, I went back onto Twitter to see what else was being said. It was much of the same, with a couple of rape threats thrown in for good measure. Mark passed me a mug of coffee, but my hand was still shaking so much I couldn't hold it.

Outside I could hear voices as reporters and photographers

gathered on the pavement and in the road. It was at times like this I wished I had a front garden, any garden, so I could shut the gate on them, instead of the front door opening onto the street. When Mark went out to do some errands and carry on our hunt for Colin, they chased him down the road. I just hoped he would keep quiet and not be flattered by all the attention.

From the living room I peeped through a slat on the blind I had permanently pulled down to stop them peering in. Even though it was only mid-October, some cruel winds from Siberia were passing through. Who would want to be a reporter? What did they call this hanging about? Door stepping. A few of them were rubbing their hands, hopping from foot to foot to keep warm. Some were in their cars. Most of them constantly on their phones. I wasn't going to talk to them, but that didn't mean I had to ignore them stuck out there. They were only doing their job.

Searching through cupboards, I found about a dozen old mugs and a handful of cups, and made a selection of tea and coffee. When I opened the front door bearing a tray of steaming hot drinks, I was welcomed with a chorus of: "Hey thanks. Cool. You star." And various other compliments. An hour or so in the kitchen later when I reappeared with a huge plate of chocolate brownies, a cheer went up.

'These are well good,' said one photographer, helping himself to a couple more. Of course they tried to wheedle me into giving them a quote, but all I did was smile sweetly and wish them a good day. I was learning.

I decided that now was the time to make my escape. I needed to make my peace with Helen. Let's face it, she was the only real friend I had. I couldn't afford to lose her.

Now that they'd realised I wasn't going to comment, the reporters would surely start to drift away. Kevan had warned me that some photographers would probably give chase on motorbikes. But so what if they got a couple of pictures of me to add to those already in circulation? I still wasn't going to say anything. That didn't stop me from making sure I looked my best when I left the house. Mark had agreed to play taxi for me so as I waited for him to arrive outside the house, I turned to face them all: 'There is something I'd like to say.' Cameras started whirring and tape recorders virtually pushed into my face.

'Please could you help find my cat Colin? He's gone missing,' I said holding out my phone with a photo of him on the screen. Within seconds I'd sent the picture to as many of them as possible. There was some laughter and good-natured teasing about the "other man in my life" but I suspected I'd given them something to write about for the next day.

The one thing Mark is good at is driving like a maniac, so as he screeched up as planned, outside the house, I leaped in and he took off like a rocket. Hopefully this unexpected escape might foil any attempt to follow me.

There was a sadness about Helen's house. Usually she had radios in different rooms blaring, and the TV on in the living room. But the only noise I could hear was the dogs' claws as they padded around on the wooden floors. Everything around her reflected her mood. A massive vase of drooping flowers in the hallway, piles of ironing on one of the armchairs, dirty dishes in the sink. But it wasn't just the appearance of the house which was usually cleaned and tidied to within an inch of its life, it was her own. Her hair didn't look as if it had been washed for days, and she was wearing a stained pair of tracksuit bottoms and a baggy T-shirt. Her nails, usually manicured and painted, were bitten, and her skin had broken out into spots.

'Helen, what's wrong? You look...'

'Shit. I look shit. No wonder he doesn't want me anymore.'

'What's happened?' I said, leading her by the hand like a child to sit down at the kitchen table. There was no point in me sharing my woes. Hers were obviously a lot more serious. But at least she'd let me in.

Her eyes, usually so blue, looked grey with pain. 'He's definitely sleeping with her. He's admitted it now. I've seen the texts he sends her, the same as he used to send to me.'

'Come here,' I said, holding out my arms. She folded her own tightly in front of her. 'It's me. I pushed him away. I was always too tired for everything. What am I going to do?' Maybe take a few lessons from Daniel's wife, I thought. She definitely wasn't finished with me yet. And who could blame her? Like Slutty Susie I'd stolen her husband right from under her nose. My only defence being that I thought the marriage was over.

Giant tears ran down Helen's face. 'I didn't realise how much I loved him until now.'

By the time the children had arrived home from school, I'd tidied up the house while Helen showered and washed her hair, and arrived downstairs looking more like her old self. I rooted around in the fridge and found ingredients for dinner and soon we were all sitting round the table tucking into a spaghetti bolognaise and garlic bread.

When Ben's key turned in the lock, Helen visibly jumped.

'He said he was going to be late,' she said as he strode into the room registering a vague look of surprise as he spotted me.

'Well if it isn't the famous Lottie Gilbert,' he said, his voice slurred. 'To what do we owe the pleasure?' he added, pouring himself a large glass of red before he'd even taken off his coat. One by one, the children excused themselves, and disappeared off to their rooms or to watch TV.

'Do you want me to stay?' I asked Helen when Ben took himself off to answer a phone call.

'No, it's okay. He's been like this a few times. He'll fall asleep in front of the telly. Lottie,' she said, taking hold of my arm as I was about to leave. 'Sorry I've been such a shit friend. Do you forgive me?' I always forgave Helen, whatever she did. None of us is perfect, least of all me. Especially now. In her eyes I was probably was no better than Slutty Susie. I was the one who needed forgiveness.

Mark was waiting outside with the engine running. And I'd barely pulled shut the passenger door when he sped off.

'It's okay you can slow down now, we're not being chased,' I laughed.

'Oh yeh,' he smiled. 'I feel a bit like your minder at the

moment.'

'You are,' I said, feeling strangely warm towards him. He'd obviously made an effort to change into his best black roll neck and smart jeans, and he'd styled his hair with gel.

'What's happening with Tara?'

'Ah well that's where I'm going after I've dropped you off. Will you be okay?'

'Of course. Do you think you'll stay?'

'If I get lucky,' he said, smiling to himself. I had no right to feel such a surge of disappointment, but I did. A couple of times recently it had felt like the old days with Mark and his banter back in the house. Plus he'd been there for me when I needed him. After three or four glasses of red wine at Helen's, and the fact that he was looking especially tasty and not at all like a younger brother, I might have been tempted to...

'Oh lookie here, there's always one,' said Mark as we pulled up outside the house. A lone car was parked over the road with what looked like a lens poking out of a gap in the window.

'Perhaps we should have a snog. That would throw the cat amongst the pigeons,' he said, chortling to himself. Much as I rather fancied the idea, I gave him a peck on the cheek, and hurried inside as he sped off into the night.

After checking the back garden in case Colin was lurking in the bushes, I took myself to bed. There was a missed call and a message from Kevan who said to be ready at seven a.m. as Chas was picking me up to meet Daniel for breakfast. Breakfast? That was an odd one. But then I suppose when your life is scheduled for you by the minute, it might be your only free time.

By four in the morning I still hadn't been to sleep. The last thing I wanted was to meet Daniel looking like death. Finally I dozed off about an hour before the alarm went. And then I couldn't wake up, wandering around the house as if in a trance.

The plan was similar to yesterday. Chas would pull up with the engine running and I'd run into his car, hopefully avoiding any early risers from the tabloids.

It worked. The couple of bleary-eyed photographers lurking

outside weren't even ready with their cameras as he screeched into the road. Chas was silent most of the way to our destination, apart from his announcement he was taking me to a small cottage in the Cotswolds, owned by Daniel's mother. He had the keys to use it when she wasn't in residence. Beth, he said, had no knowledge of the place, neither did the press. Unlike his London apartment where paparazzi had been spotted several times over the past few days.

'Is Beth still at Morton Manor?'

'Can't rightly say Miss,' he said, before turning up Radio 4 so that I wouldn't be tempted to ask any more questions. I noticed a copy of *The Daily News* on his passenger seat, and asked to see it. Colin had now become a tabloid star looking very handsome, his picture on page five, with one of me pleading for readers to help find him.

COLIN...THE OTHER LOVE IN LOTTIE'S LIFE

Soon motorways morphed into green fields, and now that the winds of yesterday had dispersed the clouds, the sun had a chance to break through.

We pulled up outside a thatched cottage that looked like something out of Beatrix Potter. In the summer I imagined there would be roses around the door and a garden bursting with wild flowers. Its stone walls were almost suffocated with ivy, and there was even a brown picket fence and a gate with the name Bluebell Cottage on a brass plaque. Bluebells, it would be bluebells, my favourite wild flower. This was my fantasy cottage. And one day it would belong to Daniel, which was a horrible thing to think because that meant killing off his parents.

As Chas returned to the car, the front door opened and Daniel stood there in jeans and a dark blue sweater, his hair still wet from the shower. Not a word was said. I just fell into his arms.

The inside of the cottage was as picturesque as the outside. Wooden doors with black wrought iron handles leading to cosy rooms and pine beds under patchwork quilts. In the living room Daniel had to duck to avoid the dark beams which criss-crossed the ceiling. Wood crackled as it burnt in the small brass grate in the kitchen. There was the smell of fresh coffee and toast.

I would have been quite happy to miss breakfast and snuggle up under one of the patchwork quilts. But even the kissing was put on hold until after we'd eaten. I didn't care that his scrambled eggs were so rubbery they could have bounced off the ceiling or that he burnt the bacon. All I cared about was that something remained of us. The us that I longed for. The us that had nothing to do with fame or fortune but two lost souls who had found each other. I could see it in his eyes, the uncertainty. And when I tried to kiss him, he put his hand gently over my mouth.

'I have something to tell you,' he said, brushing that annoying piece of hair out of my face and tucking it behind my ear. It was over, I knew it. He was just trying to sugar coat it by bringing me here rather than texting, or me reading about it in the papers.

'Lottie Gilbert, I love you,' he said, looking deeply into my eyes.

'Say that again.'

'I love you. I didn't realise how much until now. But I can't be with you. Just yet.'

He looked confused and embarrassed, running his hand through his hair, ruffling it up in frustration.

'What's wrong? Is it Beth?'

He nodded. 'She's pregnant.'

26

I am not a drama queen, never have been, but for a moment I was incensed that he'd invited me over to declare his love, and then dropped this bombshell. So I did a fair amount of flouncing about, grabbing my coat to storm out of the door, although God knows where I was going to flounce to. I had no idea where we were. And I was lost enough as it was, without being physically lost.

When Daniel tried to hold me, I stiffened up. But finally agreed to sit and listen, which is quite difficult for someone like me who has a compulsion to interrupt every five seconds.

Admittedly I needed answers, like how is it possible to get pregnant by Skype which is the only way I thought Daniel had been in touch with his wife for months.

'Not entirely. I flew over to LA about three months ago to see Beth because we needed to talk. We agreed pretty much that the marriage wasn't working. And, well we got drunk to celebrate the end of a terrible marriage.'

He dropped his head into his hands. 'This is a mess Lottie, and I don't want you to be part of it. I have to let you go. Just for now.'

This all seemed a bit convenient, Beth being pregnant the minute she finds someone else is on the scene.

'Does she want the baby?'

'She talked about nothing else at the start of our relationship. But when things started to go wrong between us, we decided it wasn't the right time. Trouble is she's so emotional at the moment – hormones she says – that she's threatening to have a termination if I end the marriage.'

'Even though she seemed happy to end the marriage before?'

'You never know with Beth. That's always been the problem. I never did get to *know* her. We met and married so quickly. And half of that time she was in LA. On the surface she seems happy and confident. But underneath she is so messed up and insecure, I don't have a clue who she really is.'

I followed him out to the kitchen while he made more coffee. 'When we first got together, she didn't have that much going for her on the work front. It's as if I filled that gap in her life. But when she got a break on *School Daze*, she was euphoric. Filming over in the States, it was as though she didn't need me anymore. She had everything she wanted. New friends she made on the show, and her family are over there too of course. So whenever we met up all we did was argue about where to live.'

It was time to interrupt. 'But I thought she loved England, the history of it all, and being in Morton Manor.'

'Oh she did, for five minutes, until the novelty wore off and she realised how cold it was in the winter, especially in creaky old houses, and how homesick she felt seeing her friends on FaceTime lapping up the Californian sunshine. Finally after three years of falling in and out with each other we'd sort of decided she should stay in the States, me over here and gradually go our separate ways. That's when I met you.'

'But hang on, what about your birthday party? She was meant to come.'

He looked a bit sheepish. 'Yeh, that was a last ditch attempt to see if there was anything between us. Then her filming got in the way.'

'And now? What happens with us now? Are we staying in touch?'

'I'm sorry Lottie.' He shook his head, and I felt this pain that I'd never had before. Like someone had taken a hammer and smashed my heart, and then stomped all over my hopes and dreams. It hurt too much to cry. I needed to get away from here. I didn't belong. This wasn't my story. It was as though I'd just stumbled into someone else's life which was nothing to do with me. As for this idea of Daniel letting me go "just for now". What did that mean? That he was going to divorce Beth after she'd had the baby? There is no way he would do that, or that I would let him. You can't bring a child into the world and then say, I'm out of here. Bye!

First thing tomorrow I was going back to The Loft to beg Marsha for my job back, press or no press. I'd just have to keep making them chocolate brownies to keep them sweet. Or learn how to ride a motor bike so I could escape from them. Plus I needed to be around for Helen, helping her through her drama, and find myself a new boyfriend who I could snog without appearing in every national newspaper in the UK.

We said goodbye like strangers. The only way I could cope was to somehow pretend this was all a dream, so that I could wake up to my old life.

27

By the time Chas dropped me off I was exhausted and it was only lunch time. I'd spent all the way back giving myself a talking to. What made me even think there could be something between us? He was Daniel French for fuck's sake. Get a grip Gilbert. For a while I'd believed it was real. It was the stuff of fairytales, and maybe he did have feelings for me. But like a wonky piece of jigsaw, I didn't fit into his life. And I never would, even if Beth hadn't come back holding the pregnancy card.

I waved to a couple of photographers lurking outside who gave me the thumbs up when I promised to get the kettle on. But before I could make any hot drinks, there was a ring at the doorbell. I did my normal trick of peering through the blinds and could see a middle-aged woman wearing a fur coat which had seen better days. She had her back to the door, probably looking at the photographers, but when she turned I could see she was holding Colin.

Within seconds I'd flung open the front door and taken him from her. 'Thank you so much for finding him.'

'Oh, not me kid. I didn't find him. He just wandered up to the house and plonked his arse down at the front door,' she said, in a thick Liverpudlian accent, pushing her glasses up onto her head. Her face had a well-worn look to it, and judging by her brittle blonde hair, it seemed unlikely that she had been to a good hairdresser for years. Her make-up was badly applied, especially her scarlet lipstick which bled into smoker's lines fanning out from her mouth. I guessed she was in her late fifties and when she looked at me with bloodshot blue eyes, I shuddered as if someone had walked over my grave.

'Mum?'

Mum. A word I seldom said. It even felt odd saying it. Mum, mummy, mother, Tina? What do I call her? As if life couldn't get any stranger. The weird thing was that even though I hadn't seen her since I was three-years-old, I knew her straight away.

'What the hell are you doing here?'

'Well, that's a nice welcome. I've come to see my daughter. Thought you'd be made up,' she said as she waltzed into the house as if she owned the place. I'd rehearsed a million times the questions I'd ask if I ever saw her again. Where had she been all these years, what had she been doing? Had she even given me a thought? I could have been dead for all she knew. Like Ron, her husband. Did she even know he'd died?

But now that she was here, all I felt was rage. Pure unadulterated anger. Taking a pack of cigarettes out of a large black synthetic leather tote bag she spoke. 'Mind if I...?' I snatched the packet from her and threw them onto the table. 'Yes I do mind. What do you want?'

'I saw you in the papers. I couldn't believe it was you, kid. My little Charlotte. Not that I would have seen you if it wasn't for the nice newspaper lady.'

'What nice newspaper lady?'

'Jean something or other from *The Daily News*. She gave us a call out of the blue and to start with I thought she was from the council or something, but then she asked if I was your mum. She tracked me down, fancy that, and drove up to show me the stories of you in the papers.

She did an interview and asked me if I wanted them to help with a reunion. And I thought, why not? Maybe my daughter would want her mum back in her life now that I've changed.' She smiled revealing yellowing teeth and I noticed she had the same gap between them at the front as I did.

I studied her as she spoke. Tina Gilbert, my mother. Making herself at home, she'd slipped off the fake fur coat, to reveal a red fluffy jumper with shoulder pads and black trousers with scuffed high-heeled boots. She waved her wrinkled hands around a lot as she talked, her voice deep and throaty, and on thin bony fingers she wore a thin gold wedding ring. She was on the skinny side, with gaunt cheeks. Probably attractive when she was younger, but now she looked scraggy and old before her time.

'Must be a bit of a shock for you, all this, kid.' I wished she would stop calling me kid. And yes everything was a shock. Meeting Daniel, being stalked by the press and Twitter trolls, Beth's pregnancy and now my estranged mother crawling out of the woodwork. What next?

'So are you being paid to be here? Is there a tape recorder in your bag?'

'How would I know how to work one of those things you daft bugger? They brought me down in a car, and are paying for me to stay at the Red Lion. Bit grotty, but it's local.' It was also her local when she lived here, so nan told me. The pub where she worked for a while as a bar maid, drinking her life away.

'Look I'm not sure quite what you're expecting. But this isn't one of those gushy TV shows where I'm going to throw my arms around you, sob and say it's fine, I forgive you. In fact, I want you to leave. Now, Tina.' I wanted to call her mum but the word stuck in my throat.

'But I've only just got here,' she moved towards me as though she was about to give me a hug. I stiffened and held her at bay with my hand.

'That is my point. You've had thirty-five years to get here. Have you any idea what you did? Nan took me round to your flat one day and you'd gone. Vanished. What type of mother leaves their three-year-old daughter and disappears?'

She paused and gave me a world-weary smile. 'An alcoholic one. I don't blame you for being angry Charlotte. It might look like I was a terrible mother. But I was trying to be a good one by getting out of your life. I would have ruined it, the way I ruined mine,' she said, big fat tears rolling like rivulets through her wrinkles. 'But things are different now. *I'm* different.'

She took a tissue out of her bag and blew her nose very loudly. 'Just give me a chance to explain and then I'll leave you to your life. Promise.'

'You had enough chances to explain. Bit of a coincidence you decide to reappear in my life after you see me in the papers with Daniel French who happens to be a multi-millionaire. Is that it? Or are you being paid by a newspaper for your exclusive inside story? Either way Tina, you can get out.' She pulled a face like a belligerent teenager who is about to say 'whatevs'.

'Don't be like that Charlotte. I don't want to stay in that grotty pub with sticky carpets. Why can't I stay here?' She registered the disbelief on my face. 'Okay, maybe that's a bit too much to hope for.'

'How you can hope for anything is beyond me. I'll call you a taxi.'

'Is that it then? You don't want to hear my side of the story.'

'There is only one story. You fucked off out of my life,'

'Put like that, I know when I'm not wanted.' She took her purse out of her bag.

'I'm the one who wasn't wanted mum.'

'Well that's not quite the way it was, kid.'

'I am not your bloody kid. I need you to go.'

'Even brought you a pressie,' she said opening her bag as if to get something out.

'Whatever it is, I'm not interested. Just go.' She looked deflated, but nodded as she picked up her coat.

'Can't blame you. I've only got a couple of quid, can you....?

Being the softie I am, I made sure she had enough money for the cab and for something to eat at the pub. As I opened the door to let her out I told her: 'Walk quickly to the cab and say nothing to the reporters.'

'Nothing! I'm saying nothing!' she shouted as they flocked

around her pushing cameras in her face and firing questions.

Opening the taxi door for her I snapped: 'I didn't mean *say* nothing, I just meant keep your mouth shut. Oh forget it.'

'If you change your mind kid.'

'I won't.'

Back inside the house I slammed the front door, sank to the floor and leaned against the wall holding my knees as Colin brushed against me. I picked him up and he lay perfectly still while I buried my head in his fur. God knows what I'd read in the papers tomorrow. Some headline about throwing my own mother out onto the streets no doubt, followed by more death threats on Twitter. I was almost getting used to the hatred now. But there was one troll in particular who bothered me. She, I assumed it was a she, seemed to know a bit too much about me. One of her tweets was her wish that I'd crash my Mini and die. How the hell did she know what car I drove? Maybe I should go to the police. But what could they do?

From where I was slumped I could see into the living room. What was that under the coffee table? Curiosity forced me to get up and find out. It was a faded red leather purse. My mother's purse. Somehow it had ended up on the floor. Probably Colin, he was always knocking things off tables.

I should probably get it to her. There might be things in it she needed. Inside the zipped section there were a handful of pound coins. I opened the wallet section which contained a bus pass, a couple of supermarket loyalty cards, and a prescription. Just about to close it I noticed something white peeping out of another section. Slowly I pulled it out. It was a faded black and white photo of me. I must have been about three-years-old and I was smiling.

28

When I walked into the bar of the Red Lion, she was sitting alone at the table with a half empty bottle of red wine and a glass.

'It's just the one,' she said looking down sheepishly at her drink. 'I was upset.'

'Nice try, Tina, leaving the photo,' I said, handing her the purse, followed by the photograph. She shrugged. 'Give us a break kid. It was the only one I had. I used to look at it every night before I went to sleep, and that's God's truth. I'd try to imagine how you turned out. You're quite a looker, I'll say that. You were such a funny little thing. All those freckles. Got my hair too.'

'You have red hair?'

'Used to. Dyed it so much that even my hair thought it was blonde.'

'What about my real dad? I always thought it must be him who had the red hair.'

She shook her head. 'God knows what colour his hair was, I can't remember.' I could feel my face drop with disappointment. The one thing I'd hoped was that if we ever met, she would have some snippets about my real father.

'Sorry kid. I can't tell you much. He was a one-night stand. I met him at Cinderella's night club soon after we moved down from Liverpool to Luton. Can't even remember his name. Might have been Dave. Or then again it could have been Dennis. I think it began with a D. Donald, Don, that might have been it, or it could have been Dickhead for all I remember!'

'Mum!'

'What do you know? She called me Mum. That touches my heart that does Charlotte. You have no idea. Would you mind if I...?'she said taking my hand in hers which was wrinkled, dry and cold. And for a moment I let her hold it.

She took a deep breath. 'I was eighteen when I had you, Charlotte. A kid. Moved down from Toxteth when I was seventeen with me mam and dad. Had to leave all my friends behind. I was so livid, I didn't speak to my parents for weeks.'

She shook her head, and stared helplessly at me 'The reason we left Liverpool was so me dad could take up a job at the car plant round here. But two months later he was dead. Car hit his motorbike. And mam went out of her mind with grief. They'd been together since they were sixteen. She loved me, but he was her world. Two months later she was dead too. Bottle of whiskey and sleeping tablets.'

Her bloodshot blue eyes glazed over with tears. Either she was a very good actress, or the pain of losing her parents in quick succession had never left her.

'When me mam died, I was already pregnant with you and didn't even know it, by that Dave fella. Or it could have been Dean. That sounds more like it.' At this point I firmly removed my hand from her grasp.

'Please just get on with it.'

'Oh yes, sorry. I'm a terrible one for remembering names. Any rate, I was five months gone before someone said, hey Tina, you look like you're up the duff. We were so naïve in those days. I thought it was too many chip butties.

'So when the bloke next door, Ron and his mum offered to take me in, and look after me and you, I said yes. Ron was a nice fella. And he brought in a bit of money from his little caff. But I never loved him. Not sure he really loved me, but he bloody idolised you the minute you came screaming into the world.

And in those days it was hard being a single teenage mum, so I married him.'

She told me how she'd always hoped to go to art college and make something of her life. But when her parents died, something in her died too. She took a photo from her bag and handed it to me. It was a picture of her with her mum and dad sitting in a row of deckchairs and eating ice creams. They were all laughing. She must have been about ten.

'I was an only child, but they didn't spoil me. Far from it, they taught me that I had to make my own way in life. It was like they knew somehow that they wouldn't be in it for long. If only I'd listened to them more, instead of letting Ron and his controlling mare of a mother run it for me.' I couldn't believe what I was hearing about my dear old nan. Maybe she wasn't quite such a dear as I'd thought.

There was bitterness in Tina's voice as she spoke about my dad Ron and nan. But nothing she said was going to make me think differently about them, especially dad. He'd been more of a father to me than if he'd been my biological dad. And I wouldn't hear a bad word said against him. But Tina wasn't finished.

'Ron was a mammy's boy. Always. Not saying he wasn't a great da to you. But he was under the thumb of his mam. She was a strong woman. One day after a sherry she told me that she always wanted a girl, and now she had you. It was as though she thought you were hers and I was just an inconvenience. She encouraged me to go out and enjoy myself, and I didn't need telling. I was a teenage girl, and I wanted to party.'

'What about dad, Ron? There must have been something between you.'

She roared with laughter. 'Not if I could help it. Like I said, he was a good bloke. But he was ten years older than me and he looked it too. No fashion sense. He dressed like a middle-aged man. It was like sleeping with my dad. I hated it. So he left me alone and on the sly he took up with the waitress in his caff, Babs. She was more his age. Nothing came of it. But I think when he shut the caff of an evening, they'd pop upstairs and indulge in a bit of hanky panky.'

I certainly remembered Babs, who had a wallflower personality somehow at odds with the tight skirts and her red kitten heels which she loaned me once for dressing up. But she always had a good word for everyone, even my absent mother. She was probably a much better match for dad. When eventually a customer at the café snapped up Babs to be his wife, he was heartbroken.

'He should never have married me, Ron. We never got divorced, do you know that?'

By the time I'd filled her in about her husband's death, she'd worked her way through a bottle of wine and excused herself while she went outside for a cigarette. I ordered a large glass of white, for me. While she was gone, I tried to imagine her, an eighteen-year-old girl with red hair, missing her life in Liverpool, and orphaned while she was pregnant.

'But surely it must have helped having me. At least I was family,' I said as soon as she sat back down.

'You were a baby. A baby I didn't know how to look after. I was a child myself. A hopeless mother. All I wanted to do was go out and get drunk to numb all the pain of what happened. So I got a job here, behind that very bar. And see that bit over there,' she said pointing to a dance floor area. 'There was a small stage where the band played. And that's the first time I saw Jamie,' she said.

An hour and another bottle of wine later and I knew that Jamie was a fellow Scouser who sang in a band called The Waystars.

'As soon as I saw him, I knew. It was like he had a spell over me. So when he asked me to move in with him, I did. It was only round the corner from where you were. So your nan would bring you round to see me every now and then. Don't look at me like that,' she said, unable to look me in the eyes. ' I was still only twenty and married with a husband I didn't love and a baby...'

'...you didn't want!'

'...that I couldn't look after. Let's have a look,' she said gently pulling up the sleeve of my sweater. 'Oh God,' she said as soon as she saw the badly scarred flesh on my upper arm.

'That happened on the one night your nan left you with me because she was ill and Ron was working late. You must have dragged a stool over to the stove and climbed up to see what I'd left cooking. Always such a curious little thing you were.' She paused and there was a choke in her voice. 'You pulled over a pan of boiling water onto your arm.'

'Where were you?'

'Asleep. Drunk. It was six o'clock. I must have put it on to boil some veg. Your screams woke me, and Jamie arrived home in time to take us to the hospital. It was bad, Charlotte. Really bad. That was it, then. I knew I couldn't trust myself to look after you. And Ron and his mother made sure I never got near you again.'

'You could have tried. What about on my birthday? Did you ever think about me then?'

'Course I did, and I did try to see you. Well, once, anyway. Jamie and I went back to live in Liverpool. And on what would have been your fifth birthday, I bought a present and took the train down to see you. But your nan wouldn't let me. After that I didn't try again. Decided you were better off without me,' she said and sat there looking at me, as if waiting for forgiveness.

So she did come to see me. I tried to think back to my fifth birthday and what I was doing. God, I couldn't forget that one. Dad had arranged a party for me at the café. I remember, because it fell on the same day as another girl from my class, and hardly anyone came to mine.

'What was the present?'

'How the hell do you expect to remember what I got you all those years ago?' she said, smiling. 'But as it happens, I do. Because I kept it, hoping I'd see you one day to give it to you.' She opened a tatty plastic carrier bag. Inside was a faded pink bear with a rainbow across his white tummy.

Slowly I took the toy from her hand. 'A Care Bear! I always wanted one of those.'

29

'Have you got any hot chocolate?' asked my mother from the doorway of the spare bedroom. Instead of the thin nylon nightdress she'd brought with her, I loaned her a cosy pair of my pyjamas. Her hair brushed and face scrubbed of make-up she looked younger and more innocent. Without the black eyeliner, the hardness had gone from her eyes.

I stood at the bottom of the stairs looking up at this woman who had re-appeared back into my life like a character from a bad TV soap.

'I'll bring one up.'

'No, you're alright. I'll come down,' she said, smiling. 'Thanks for bringing us home. You're a star.'

'No I'm not. I just didn't want that journalist woman getting at you. She's probably already got enough to run something on us.'

She followed me downstairs and into the kitchen where she took over making the hot chocolate.

'Maybe, but she's got nothing much. And for once in my life I'm keeping my gob shut. Anything you tell me about your famous bloke and you is between us, and that's a promise,' she said, as we made our way to the sofa. It was so odd having her beside me.

There was still so much I didn't know. Was she still with Jamie? How did she earn a living? And where did we go from here? The anger was beginning to dissolve, but I still felt uneasy about having her in my life and in my home. We were strangers. But at the same time, even if she hadn't been my mother, I imagined she was a good strong ballsy woman to have on my side during these difficult times. She wouldn't take any stick from the press, or from the trolls. Despite some of her sob stories about what a hard life she'd had, there was a toughness about her. Put it this way, I wouldn't want to mess with her.

And so we talked, and I learned that Jamie had finally gone off with a younger woman several years ago, leaving Tina alone and lonely in a one-bedroom flat in Liverpool. She paid the bills by working as a barmaid in the local tavern and, she admitted, was partial to a bit of shop-lifting from department stores.

'That adrenalin. It was the only exciting thing in my life,' she said, revealing that she'd been caught once or twice, but had escaped prosecution by claiming she was suffering from menopausal confusion.

'You don't still do it, do you?' I asked, making a mental note to hide my jewellery somewhere safe.

'No, you're alright. I wouldn't steal off my own daughter. Who do you think I am?' I had no idea who she was. But part of me wanted to find out.

There was gentle snoring coming from the spare room. Not loud like Mark, but persistent. I crept in to have a look at my mother asleep in bed. My *mother.* I'd lived most of my life without one, so it felt like such an odd concept. Her hair was spread in thin wisps across the pillow and there was a gentle smile on her lips. I couldn't stop looking at her to compare the likenesses. Her lips were like mine, not full but nicely bow shaped. Her eyebrows had all but disappeared, and her complexion was pale as though she rarely saw the sun. But around her nose she had a scattering of freckles, like me. She stopped snoring for a minute and half-opened one eye.

'Go back to bed kid,' she said. And so I did as I was told.

Next morning my picture was back in *The Daily News*. A long distance shot of me on the doorstep talking to Tina, and a half-page story about the mother I'd never known. But it was what was on the front page that bothered me most. A picture of

Daniel helping Beth into a car, his hand on the small of her back. She was looking happy which I could understand. But the annoying thing is so was he! So much for him saying he loved me. That was about the last contact I'd had with him. There had been a text last night asking how I was, to which I answered "fine", but with no kiss. Strangely I didn't want to share the news about my mother arriving out of the blue. It was too big to be thrown away in a text message.

'So he's back with his missus is he?' asked my mother sitting down on the bed with a mug of tea.

'Looks like it,' I said handing her the paper. 'He hasn't got a choice. She's pregnant.'

'Oh is she? Wouldn't be the first wronged wife I know to try that one.'

'Really, you think...?'

'Well what would you do to get your hubby back? It's worked hasn't it?'

'Yes, but she could be. He says they slept together three months ago which fits.'

'So who says it's his?' she said, slurping her tea. 'I think we ought to pay madam a little visit.'

'Why would we want to do that?'

'To find out what's going on. Whether she really is pregnant.'

'Even if she's there, how are we going to know?'

'Oh, I'll know, don't you worry. Bit of a witch, me.'

'I don't doubt that, but what excuse are we going to use to pay a call?'

'I'm sure you'll come up with something,' she said, winking at me.

The answer came sooner than expected when I was getting dressed. Still going through my mind was the picture that my mother had painted of my dad Ron and my nan, and the way they'd pushed her out of my life. I looked in my dressing table drawer for the locket dad gave me just before my twenty-first. Perhaps I should wear it to reconnect with him. It wasn't there. It had to be. Where else could it be? In my mother's handbag, that's where. Oh my God. How could I be so stupid as to let a self-confessed thief into my house? I needed to be careful how I approached this.

I waited until I could hear her downstairs in the kitchen boiling the kettle, and crept into the spare room which she had obviously made an effort to leave tidy, apart from a bunch of screwed up tissues on the bedside table. Her bag must be downstairs.

There was a smell of bacon coming from the kitchen where my mother had insisted on cooking me one of her fry-ups.

I crept downstairs into the living room, hunting for her bag. But there was no getting anything past my mother. She'd obviously heard me.

'One egg or two?'

'Two please. And put that cigarette out,' I shouted back.

'Sorry,' she said and laughed with an awful witchy cackle. 'You hear that Colin? Your mistress is having a pop at me,' she said. 'Hey that's a point, the bloke I slept with, your dad, his name could have been been Colin, like your cat.'

'If you say so,' I called back, still searching through her bag. I couldn't feel anything. But maybe she'd hidden it somewhere else. Her coat pocket perhaps.

'You won't find much in there kid,' she said as I turned to see her standing in the doorway.

'I'm...'

'What, you think I've nicked something? Well that's bloody nice that is, I must say,' she said walking over and tipping the contents of her bag all over the sofa. 'What am I supposed to have taken?'

'The locket dad gave me. It's gone,' I said, racking my brain to think where else it might be.

'More than he ever gave me. Any rate, hate to disappoint you, but I haven't got it. When did you last wear it?'

Good question. Let me think. It was with Daniel, over at Morton Manor. I remembered exactly the night. He commented on it, and we talked about my dad and how lost I was when he died.

'I must have left it at Daniel's house. I remember now. I'm so sorry.'

'So you should be. Well, there's your excuse.'

'To go back to the house? Supposing Daniel's there?'

'Can't you track him on your phone. You know, that app that lets you see where your mates are?'

'No. We never did that.'

'Then we drive over there, and if he's at home, you pick up your locket and we think of something else.'

This was already beginning to feel like a bad idea.

30

Thankfully I still had a note of the code to open the gate and as we approached the front door I hoped and prayed that Meg wouldn't be there. It might be harder getting past her than the security gate.

I doubted the wisdom of bringing my mother, but on the other hand it might be helpful to have an observer. First of all I had to remember where I'd left the locket. Probably in the guest bedroom where I'd slept after my fall.

The doorbell echoed through the house. There was no sound of Oscar barking. Maybe he was out for a walk with Daniel. As we stood there like Jehovah's Witnesses on the doorstep, the wind whipped up and the pale watery sun ran and hid behind the forbidding clouds.

'There's someone in, I can hear a radio,' said my mother, keeping her finger on the doorbell.

'Mum, don't!'

'You called me Mum again,' she said her face lighting up.

'That was a mistake,' I said, trying not to laugh. Much as I was quaking with nerves at the thought of confronting Beth or even worse, Beth and Meg, I couldn't help but be pleased I had my mad mother by my side. The sound of a chain being put on, alerted us to someone opening the door.

'Who is it? ' asked Beth, her bright eyes widening as she saw us.

'It's me, Lottie. Listen, I know it's a bit of a cheek, but I've left a locket behind. Is it possible to get it?' I asked.

'A what?'

'A locket. A necklace. Silver. It's important to me. My dad bought it for me.'

'You are joking. Like I'm going to let you and that...who is she?'

'My mother.'

She stared at Tina who I must admit looked a sight with her badly applied make-up and unkempt windswept hair. 'She looks more like a scarecrow than you do.'

'Why you cheeky mare. Who do you think you are?' said my mother, pushing the door against the chain.'

'Mum please, leave it. I'm sorry Beth, I'm so sorry for everything that's happened. I wish I could rewind the clock. I've brought you something.'

I held up a tin. One of my prettiest with a large cartoon sun over a field of wild flowers. 'I made you a cake as a sort of peace offering.'

'You expect me to forgive you because you made me a fucking cake?'

'No of course not,' I eased up the lid to reveal the freshly cooked lemon drizzle cake. She looked tempted. 'I don't eat junk food.'

My mother chipped in: 'You don't know what you're missing. All that lovely lemony sponge full of vitamin C. It's delicious and very good for babies, Please, we've driven all this way to get the necklace. She needs it to pawn now that she's run out of money.'

I'm not sure who looked more horrified, me or Beth.

'Is she really your mother?' asked Beth, taking the chain off the door to let us in, and taking the tin from me.

'Unfortunately yes,' I muttered under my breath.

'Okay, tell me where your precious necklace is and I'll get it for you,' she said leading us towards the kitchen. As we stood waiting for her to disappear upstairs, my mother nodded at the kitchen table on which stood what looked like a glass of water.

As soon as Beth had gone she sipped it. A look of glee passed over her face.

'Vodka,' she said.

'Are you sure?'

'You're asking an alcoholic?

'Surely she wouldn't be drinking if she was...'

'Here look,' said my mother. Under a pile of magazines was the corner of an iPhone. As if by sleight of hand, it disappeared into her pocket.

'What are you doing?'

'Oh don't worry, she'll get it back, once we have looked at her text messages.'

'So it's not there,' said Beth from behind us. 'You must have made a mistake.'

'Okay. Sorry to waste your time. Enjoy the cake. And once again, I'm sorry. I would never have...'

'You know he's done this before don't you?'

'Done what?'

'Had an affair.'

'Who with?'

'His ex-girlfriend Naomi Lincoln. And he still came back to me.'

31

My mother insisted we pull into a pub car park while she trawled through the phone.

'She's probably calling the police,' I said, horrified by what we'd done.

'Maybe,' she said, 'so we need to get into this phone fast. I've tried 1, 2, 3, 4 and that doesn't work.'

'Be careful. I think we can only have a few tries before the phone locks.'

'Well look some stuff up on Google. Year of birth. It's what I use on my phone.'

'1980. Is it four or six digits?'

'Four,' She keyed in the year. 'Nope, not that.'

'How the hell are we going to get the phone back to her?' I said, not quite believing that I was going along with my mother's crazy plan.

She nudged me. 'Let me deal with that. What's her birthday?'

'July 18,' I said scrolling through Beth's website.

'So, hang on, that would be 1807. Nope that's not it.'

'Don't try any more mum. Let's think this through.'

'Don't the Americans do something a bit funny with dates?'

'What do you mean?'

'Back to front or upside down or something?'

'That's right. They put the month first, then the date. Try 0718.'

My mother's face lit up. 'Bingo! We're in. Here you look through the text messages,' she said, passing me the phone 'I'm going in for a drink.'

The White Horse was empty for a lunch time. What if the police set out to look for us? They'd soon find the car, I thought, scrolling through the messages. A few from Daniel, mainly letting his wife know times he would be home, and plans for eating. I got the impression that Beth didn't cook. And there was a whole thread of texts from Beth to someone called Gracie.

As we stood waiting at the bar, I read them out. 'What do you make of this? From Beth: "I'm going to lose it. He won't dump me then," and Gracie says: "you're that desp to keep him? What about me bitch?" And Beth says: "But I need him," And then Gracie says. "You need his money hun." Who is Gracie I wondered as I looked up Beth online, and then I worked it out. Lenny Grace, an actor who starred with her in *School Daze*. He had to be Gracie.

'There's your evidence. She's made out she's expecting, then she's planning to have a "miscarriage",' said mum, doing that quote mark thing with her fingers.

'But how do we know she's talking about the baby? I'm going to lose "it".'

'She's not talking about her bloody virginity is she? I'm going to lose "it" means I'm going to lose the baby. What an evil woman. Can you take pictures of messages?'

'Of course,' I said taking screenshots of the incriminating words and sending them to my phone.

When Beth's mobile rang loudly from a withheld number, we both jumped out of our skins. Maybe I should disguise my voice.

'Here,' said my mother, holding her hand out for the phone. I passed it to her. She put it on loudspeaker.

'Hello, who's that?' said Beth's voice, sounding sharp.

'Lottie's mother, and before you ask, petal, I borrowed

your phone, and we've got copies of your text messages to your mate Gracie which prove you're not pregnant. So if you want to call the police go ahead kid. On the other hand if you want us to keep quiet and not let on to Daniel and the press about the messages and your made up pregnancy, I'll leave your phone behind the bar of…where are we?'

'White Lion, Morton.'

'The White Lion, Morton, for you to collect when you need another voddy. In the meantime I'd find that locket if I was you and get it back to my Charlotte. Bye kid.' And she hung up, just like that. I stared at her.

She looked at me as though butter wouldn't melt. 'What?'

Before she handed the phone to the barman, my mother wiped it clean of prints and told him that we'd found it at the table.

'The owner rang it to see where she'd left it. She'll be in later,' she said, winking at me as we made our way out into the car park. The winter skies were grey and heavy with rainclouds , and as we drove home, I barely spoke. Surely the thing to do was show the texts to Daniel, and once he knew she was faking the baby, he'd finish with her and he and I would have a chance together.

On the other hand, explaining how I happened to have screenshots of his wife's text messages wasn't likely to endear me to him. Then again, if Beth was telling the truth, there was the revelation that he'd been unfaithful with Naomi. If we ever did get back together how would I trust him not to do it again?

'So he's been at it before with someone else. And his wife's a liar. Sounds to me like they deserve each other,' said my mother as we parked outside the house. The number of reporters had doubled, probably all hoping to get a quote after this morning's picture of Daniel and Beth. The last thing I wanted to do was to fight my way through them to the front door. So I stayed put to carry on our conversation. 'It's not that simple. He says he loves me.'

'If I had a pound for every bloke who's ever said that to me…' she said, looking scornful.

'And I think I love him too.'

'You think? Along with all of his millions of fans who love him? I'd have been pretty chuffed if Tom Jones had ever caught my frilly knickers and taken me backstage I can tell you. But that's not love.'

'It's not like that.'

'You sure?' she said as we climbed out of the car into a wall of cameras. I physically had to drag my mother to the front door to stop her waving at everyone.

'Mum, for God's sake.'

Upstairs on my bed, I re-read the stolen text messages. These could ruin Beth's career as well as her marriage. But on the other hand, didn't I owe it to Daniel to let him know she was with him under false pretences? My phone rang, it was Helen in tears. 'Ben's left me.'

That night my mother and I drove over to her house where somehow my broken friend managed to keep the tears at bay until her children went to bed. But once the coast was clear, there was no stopping her. She kept telling me how much she loved him now that he'd gone.

'I should have been a better wife,' she told my mother as they worked their way through a second bottle of wine.

'We can all be better at things. I could have been a much better mother.'

'You could have been a mother,' I said under my breath.

'I heard that,' she said. 'The thing is Helen, if you really love him then fight for him.'

'How?'

'Well, you won't get far looking like a tramp,' she said pulling a face at Helen's baggy jeans which were falling off her. 'Tart yourself up, and start making a plan to get him back. Invite him for dinner. No kids, lots of candles and seductive stuff, and make sure you look a million dollars. Then you behave like you're having a ball without him. Don't nag or criticise. Make a fuss of him, and laugh at his jokes. He'll soon be back.'

For the first time all evening Helen looked hopeful. 'You think so?'

'Yes because you've got all that history together and his kids. All she's got is novelty which soon wears thin.'

'Where are you getting all this wisdom from mother?'

'Agony aunt columns. I read them all, me,' she said, raising her glass and taking a giant slurp of her wine.

In bed that night I tossed and turned over my choices. Either, like Helen, I had to fight for Daniel or let him go. I was also wrestling with the new idea which had been planted by my mother, that my love for him would not survive outside his celebrity bubble. That somehow it wasn't real. The bottom line was that I could never live with myself or the trolls if his marriage stood a chance of surviving without me around. But the very thought of never seeing him again or lying in his arms made me ache with loss. The universe had a nasty sense of humour, setting me up with my soul mate and then whipping the magic rug from under my feet before I'd had a chance to fly on it with the most desirable man in the world.

'Magic carpets? Soul mates? No wonder you're so pissed off with life if you believe in that rubbish,' said my mother when I tried to explain. 'My Jamie and I didn't last because we fell out of love with each other, and he fancied another woman, younger and prettier than me. Life happens. There are always going to be other women throwing their G-strings at Daniel. You don't need it. The best thing you can do is be your own star.'

'Did you read that on a problem page as well?'

'You may laugh my girl, but it makes sense. The press knows who you are, so make the most of it. All this flipping fame, you might as well use it.'

Where was my mother all these years when I needed her advice? And now, it was coming thick and fast. But should I be listening to a woman whose only claim to fame was winning Miss Toxteth in 1977?

The next day I took my mother for breakfast at The Loft, shadowed by a couple of photographers and a reporter who had followed me there, and Helen who had already taken my mother's advice and dolled herself up.

As we arrived at the top of the stairs, I was met by Marsha.

'Charlotte,' she said, looking slightly awkward. From the kitchen I could hear unfamiliar laughter. And instantly I knew that I'd been replaced.

'Michelle was looking for a job, and she's working out so well covering for you that I thought...'

'...you'd sack me.'

'Not exactly,' she said, pulling me gently to one side as she threw a smile at our press entourage who were trying to listen. 'But you have to admit it's been a bit difficult.'

'For me, yes. But I was planning to come back.'

'That may be Charlotte, but with all this fuss and bother...' she nodded at the reporters who seemed to have set up their little press table in the corner, '...it's probably better, if you find something else. I can pay you a month's money and will give you a good...' before she could finish, Pat came running out of the kitchen.

'We've missed you,' she said, giving me hug.

'Sounds like it,' I said as more laughter rang out from the kitchen.

'You know Ryan's gone, don't you?'

'Gone where?'

'London. His friend Max has found him a job at his club, working behind the bar and doing some deejaying. After that he couldn't stay at home any more. His stepdad made it quite clear he didn't want 'his type' living there.' That would possibly explain the black eye I'd noticed last time I saw him.

While Helen and my mother found a table, I followed Pat into my old kingdom to meet the new queen. Michelle, a tall skinny blonde who delivered everything she said in a loud over-enthusiastic manner. And Ryan's replacement, Billy who could only have been just over five feet tall, but boasted a gym-toned physique and a cheeky-chappy demeanour.

He threw his tea towel over his shoulder and bounded over, but was beaten to it by Michelle who threw her arms around me as though we'd been besties for years.

'Here she is, the superstar chef. What's it like to be super famous? It must be super cool,' she said being super irritating.

'Super,' I said, wishing she would go away so that I could talk to Jess, who was already on Twitter to show me that my followers had more than doubled to 32,000.

'You ought to be tweeting,' she said, 'and you'd get even more.'

'And more trolls I expect,' I said, as a plan started to form in my mind.

32

'Who was that reporter you were dealing with on *the Daily News*?' I asked my mother once we'd arrived home.

'Jean something or other. I'm sure I've got it written down somewhere. Why?'

'For once, I'm going to do what you told me. Be my own star. If I've got to put up with all the hassle of being famous for the wrong reasons, then I might as well make it work for the right reasons.'

'Well I don't know what you're flipping going on about. But so long as it makes sense to you kid,' she said, flicking on the kettle.

By the end of the day, I'd arranged for reporter Jean Day to interview me and my mother.

I would call Kevan and ask him to warn Daniel that I would be in the papers, but tell him not to worry. It would be an apology to Beth, and a story about how being famous had brought my mother back into my life. And now that I'd left my job, I was planning to start a new career as a TV chef. Why not? What did I have to lose?'

'That's my girl,' said my mother.

'I'll help you make a video of you cooking and you can put it on YouTube,' said Jess almost exploding with excitement when I revealed my exciting plans.

'And I'll lend you some of my clothes and jewellery,' said Helen who offered to be my personal stylist when I broke the news. 'Think of the stuff people will send you to wear. So long as I can borrow it sometimes.' That's my Helen, I thought. All I needed now was an agent.

Stella. Why not? I still had a number for her somewhere from when she invited me for a drink.

But first I needed to contact Kevan.

'Mary mother of Jesus,' he said his voice sounding more animated than I'd ever heard it. 'I need to sit in on your interview.'

'No you don't. This is nothing to do with you or Daniel.'

'Well, it is if you're talking about him to the press. Okay, so here's the deal. I'll be there to make sure the reporter doesn't stitch you up. And I'll help you make this work.'

'How?'

'Promote you. Find you a TV slot on a daytime show perhaps. And once that is sorted, we need to organise a shoot in a magazine of you looking glamorous in your amazing kitchen ready to start cooking.'

'I'm not glamorous and I don't have an amazing kitchen.'

'You will be. And you don't need one. They'll find someone who has and shoot it there. Leave it with me.'

A fountain of excitement was beginning to well up in me, which washed away some of the pain. Hey, this fame malarkey might be fun.

Before agreeing to any photos, Kevan had insisted that the newspaper book a make-up artist and stylist.

On the morning of the shoot, my tiny living room was bursting at the seams with people. The photographer, his assistant, the stylist and her assistant, the make-up artist, and the reporter. My mother was so excited about her make-over that we had a job keeping her quiet.

'I've made a note exactly what she's done, that make-up lady, so I can do it at home. What do you think of your mam? Look great (which she always pronounced as 'crate') don't I?'

she said, staring at herself in the mirror.

Finally after a few quotes from my mother about how thrilled she was to find me, it was time for me to talk about my affair with Daniel. Whenever the reporter asked a leading question, Kevan helped me to word the answer so it didn't paint me as a scarlet woman. But more as a young woman who made a mistake falling for a married man who, at the time, was estranged from his wife.

The night before the article was due to appear I could hardly sleep and by six o'clock the next morning, I was dressed and hot-footing it to the corner shop to buy the newspaper, followed close behind by my mother in my old dressing gown.

'Well, who's going to look at me this time of day?' she reasoned.

And there it was...

FRENCH MISTRESS: MY REGRETS

Exclusive interview with sexy chef Lottie Gilbert

Ooh, I liked the 'sexy' bit. There was another smaller headline about how I'd found my mother after thirty-five years and only one sentence about me wanting to be a TV chef, but when Kevan called, he told me not to worry.

'The fact is that both you and Daniel have come out of this looking good. So let's get a move on.' And I did. Look good, that is, compared with the fuzzy snatched pictures which had been taken before. I told Kevan about my plan to put myself on YouTube, but he suggested we did, what he called a proper showreel.

'What does that mean?'

'That it won't be a wobbly video your mate has done for you.'

However excited I was, I couldn't stop thinking about Daniel. Had he found out yet that his wife wasn't really pregnant, or had she already 'lost' the baby? And what did he think about the idea of me using my new found 'fame' to follow my own dream?

'He's fine with it hun,' said Stella when we met at The Ivy in London. The Ivy. Me at the Ivy, star spotting. Maybe one day someone will be there spotting me, Lottie Gilbert, TV chef extraordinaire. Stella's voice broke the spell.

'Hey, where are you? Looks like you've drifted off somewhere.'

'Sorry, I was just...'

'I said that Daniel was fine with the feature. Anyway he owes you.'

'Why?'

'Because he dragged you into this shitty lonely dark world inhabited by trolls that we called celebrity.'

33

Two weeks later and Kevan had rented a studio in London complete with hair and make-up artist, a mini film crew and director. He had arranged for all the ingredients and cooking utensils I'd asked for, although I'd insisted on taking my own knives and lucky saucepan.

'So long as you don't wear it on your head,' he joked as I arrived to make the showreel. Daniel had insisted on paying for everything which was very generous, but apart from a couple of good luck texts, there had been no contact.

'And after that, it's down to you,' said Kevan, before he introduced me to the crew. 'If we have to get you on *Masterchef* first, then so be it. But let's hope we can fast track you, because of your celebrity, er, connections.'

By the time I'd been styled and made up with Minnie Mouse false eyelashes, I barely recognised myself as I walked onto the set. It had been dressed as a vintage kitchen, full of wonderful old polished copper pots and pans, mixed with state of the art equipment. It was decided that to fit in with the 'good enough to eat' look, as Stella put it, I should be dressed in a tight red low cut dress and high heels, with instructions not to be coy about my cleavage on camera. And that my curls should be free to cascade down onto my shoulders.

The menu was a Thai chicken curry followed by a winter

fruit pavlova which I'd practised so many times, I could have whipped them up in my sleep. Except I wasn't getting much of that. Every couple of hours I'd wake up with nightmares about messing up in front of the camera. I had one shot at this and it had to go well.

My mother had travelled home to Liverpool with a promise to return for a few days if I needed any help fending off the press. I couldn't believe how much I missed her, and kept thinking up reasons to ask her back. She'd even left me an answerphone message saying: 'Good luck kid. I'll be thinking of you. And remember. Just be yourself. Everybody else is taken. Oscar Wilde said that. Yeh he did. Right? Anyway I read it somewhere.'

The newspaper story had cooked up another flurry of comment, with my public apology to Beth doing nothing to appease the vitriol on Twitter. It seems I'd attracted an entire new army of trolls intent on tearing me to shreds. But I was determined not to let them spoil my day.

'How is Daniel?' I asked Kevan in a break before filming.

He threw me a hesitant look as if to say, oh here we go. Another round of *Twenty Questions*. 'He's doing okay.'

'Has he talked about me?'

'He said to give you his best wishes for today.'

'He did? What did he say?'

'Give Lottie my best wishes for today.'

'And Beth. How is she?'

He sighed deeply. 'You're getting nothing out of me. So stop trying. Nothing has changed since you last spoke to him.' And that was it. As much as I missed Daniel, or the excitement of him, it wasn't going to bring him back. The trick was not to think about him too much. But it was hard when every five minutes one of his songs was playing on the radio,

As the director gave us a five minute warning, Kevan whispered in my ear: 'What is it they say instead of good luck? Oh 'break a leg,' or maybe in your case it should be 'break an egg,' he said, making me laugh.

It was then that I felt a charge of energy. A thrill which ran through my whole body. This was almost better than sex. Almost, I said. But as soon as the director shouted: 'Action,' I caught sight of myself in the vast mirrored wall opposite and froze. The sexy Nigella look was startling, but it wasn't me. Not for cooking. And within the next hour this became evident when my hair fell over my face several times annoying the camera man. Next I knocked over a glass of red wine I was supposed to be sipping seductively. Oh, and the high-powered electric whisk splattered my cleavage with cream, all of which brought sniggers from my small audience. All the way through, I was aware how stilted I sounded, my voice wobbling with nerves. And worst of all, every time I glanced at her, Stella's eyes would roll up to heaven.

'Okay folks, I think we're done,' she said. 'Thanks everyone,' she said, shaking her head at Kevan.

If you've ever had a cheese soufflé fall flat, that was how I felt, multiplied by a million. I'd let them all down, especially Kevan, and Daniel who'd put his money behind me. What on earth made me think I could be a TV chef? Like the papers said, I was nothing but a small town girl who'd fallen for a big time star. And that's all I'd ever be.

'Sorry, it just wasn't me,' I said to Kevan as he came over to offer me an unexpected supportive hug.

'What is you then?' he said looking me in the eye as held me at arms length.

It was then that I remembered my mother's good luck message on my answerphone when I woke this morning.

'Just be yourself kid,' she said. That was it. That was the answer.

'I need one more chance,' I said looking around at the crew who were waiting for instructions to pack away.

'You've had your chance, hun,' said Stella, looking at her watch. 'These guys can't hang around. We'll have to pay them extra.'

'Please. All I need is a few minutes to get ready.'

As Kevan nodded his approval I raced off into the small dressing room to reinvent myself. Within ten minutes I'd ripped off the fake lashes, reapplied a light make-up, tied my curls up loosely in a bright rainbow scarf, letting a few tendrils escape. I replaced the dress with my tight blue jeans and white shirt and threw off the heels for ballet pumps. When I reappeared, with a huge smile, there was a murmur of approval.

Somehow it didn't matter if the naturally clumsy Lottie messed up this time as she cooked. I made a joke of it, and everyone laughed along with me. I could sense my confidence growing along with the atmosphere in the room. And when I'd finished, a cheer went up.

'You star,' said Kevan. 'If you want to, you can do this. There's a niche for someone like you. Slightly ditzy girl next door who makes mistakes, but still gets it right. What do you think?'

All I could think is that I wanted Daniel to have been there. But it was clear from a picture in the morning papers that he was very much back with his wife, at least publicly, with more smiley pictures of them together, her head nestling on his shoulder in the back of a car. I wanted to convince myself that he was just putting it on for the photographers and that he meant it when he said he loved me. But then I had to ask did he ever really love me? Or was it all an act like the rest of his life?

Back at my house, Kevan couldn't stop talking. 'So now the next step is to get you a try out on *The Today Show*. Or maybe the trendier one, *Brunch*. You need to think up a great dish to demonstrate your skills. And preferably not anything with whipped cream,' he laughed.

'Thanks for reminding me, I said throwing the tea cosy at him. I rather liked having a gay personal manager. It was like a cross between a big brother, and a best friend, but without all the aggro of a relationship.

'And remember what we said? Get tweeting about your new career as a TV chef.'

'It hasn't happened yet, so how can I?'

'I'll send you the showreel, so you can link to that. The more people who see it the better. You might get more offers. How many followers do you have now?'

I opened my Twitter page, 'Fifty thousand and rising,' I said scrolling through a few new tweets. At the sight of one of them my stomach lurched. There she was again. 'The knives are out for you. I'm coming.' A proper death threat, surely. I could feel the colour draining out of my face.

'Hey, what's up,' asked Kevan, passing me a mug of tea.

'Nothing. A troll.'

'Show me.'

'It's nothing.'

'Show me,' he said sternly. I handed him the phone.

'How many have you had like this?'

'A few but this is the worst.'

'No it isn't. I've seen far worse, but if it's worrying you, we'll take it further. I'll get Chas onto it,' he said making a few notes.

'Shouldn't I go to the police?'

'Chas has police contacts. He'll find out who's behind this.' He looked at his watch. 'I'd stop with you this evening to protect you from evil trolls, but it's Max's birthday and he's arranged some flashy restaurant or other.' He paused. 'You could come.'

I didn't want to be a gooseberry on Max's special night. Besides, I was so exhausted, all I fancied was beans on toast and an early night.

'I'll be fine. I've got Colin to protect me.'

'And I'm sure you'll do a great job won't you, fella?' he said tickling his ears. 'Okay you have my number,' he said, as he and another of his Nordic horror sweaters disappeared out into the darkness.

I stood in the doorway as his car lights disappeared into the distance and then vanished round the corner. It was then that the loneliness hit me like a punch in the stomach. I just stood there looking up at the sky. No moon, no stars, and even the lights from the houses opposite which usually provided some source of comfort were all out. It was as though everyone in my street was out having a fun life somewhere else.

The blackness around me filtered through into my mood. It was only seven o'clock but I was already counting down the minutes until I could go to bed and hide from the world under my duvet. Let's face it I was scared. Supposing this woman who was clearly crazy, and off her trolley so to speak, knew where I lived? Maybe I should go to the police. Kevan might forget to mention it to Chas.

I sat in silence with a glass of wine, the smallest sound sending me off on a search around the house until it was identified. I was just starting to relax, and make some food when there was a gentle knocking on the front door. Maybe it was a reporter. If I was quiet they might go away. But the knocking was persistent, growing louder.

I peered through the slats in the blind. All I could see in the gloom was a woman in a bobble hat. Did trolls wear bobble hats? Probably not. The next thing I know a familiar voice was calling through the letter box.

'Coo-eee it's me, Meg. I've got your locket for you. Are you there?' Oh for God's sake. Why couldn't she just drop it through the letter box?

'I'd drop it through the letter box, but if you're there I'm busting for a wee.'

'Hold on,' I said making sure that Colin was in the kitchen.

'So I was in the area, and I thought to my little self, I know, I'll drop Charlotte's locket into her,' she said as I let her in.

'Where was it?'

'Found it when I was cleaning. It had fallen down behind a bedside table. Oh I say what dinky little houselet,' she said taking off her hat. 'Have you lived here long?'

'Yes,' I said, not wanting to get into detail. 'Listen thank you so much for this. The loo is upstairs, on the left,' thinking perhaps I ought to follow her in case she went snooping.

She handed me her hat. 'Okey doke. Back in the shake of a little lamby's tail.'

Knowing every creaky floorboard in my house, I would know if she went into either of the bedrooms. She didn't and was back down stairs in a flash.

'Gosh your place is so cute. Can I see your kitchen?' she said, not waiting for an answer. She oohed and aahed at my state of the art food mixer, and opened a couple of cupboards. And then she spotted my pine knife rack. As if in slow motion she slid one of my knives out sending a chill up my spine as her face took on a weird expression. It was as if she was in a trance.

'What are you doing?' I snapped making her jump so that she dropped it.

'Nothing. I was only thinking we should have some better knives at Morton Manor. I'm sorry, I was only being nosey. Silly me.' She looked so genuinely apologetic that I immediately regretted my outburst.

'It's okay. It's me who should be sorry. I'm a bit on edge,' I said, forcing a smile.

'Are you alright Lottie?' she said rubbing my arm. 'It must have been so awful for you, all this. Seeing Daniel and his wife in the papers looking so cosy.'

'So they're definitely back together?'

'Well it certainly sounds like it when I walk past their...' she stopped and gasped. 'Oh my giddy aunt. I didn't quite mean it like that. Anyway it's not like I stand outside listening,' she laughed. 'What I meant was, I think so. Sometimes it does a marriage good when someone else comes along to shake it up a bit. So you probably did them a favour.' Maybe she was right. Maybe that's what happened when he had an affair with Naomi Lincoln. It spiced up their marriage.

'Gorgeous news about the baby though, isn't it?' she added, a smirky smile spreading across her face. I was dying to say, what baby? But I just nodded.

'They're out tonight having a romantic meal together,' she said, with a dreamy look in her eyes. It was as though she had no filter between her brain and what came out of her small pinched mouth.

'Meg, you'll have to excuse me but I'm waiting for a friend to arrive,' I said, hoping a white lie would speed up her departure.

'Of course. Sorry. I'll get out of your hair. Oh, lest I forget,' she said, feeling in her coat pocket and pulling out the locket which she laid gently in my hand.

'Take care,' she said as she opened the front door to let herself out.

It was 2:15 a.m. when the phone rang. It was Daniel.

'Hey I'm outside. Can I come in?' What? How was it that the inhabitants of Morton Manor were somehow gravitating towards my little house? Next Beth Blackshaw would be rocking up for a chat.

From the window I could see a car, and Daniel in his baseball cap hovering outside the front door. I grabbed my dressing gown, ran downstairs and took a deep breath before I unlocked the door. Sheepishly he stepped into the hall. It was if he was waiting for my reaction.

'I'm so sorry, I didn't know where else to come,' he said as I led him through to the living room. His face was pale and his eyes were bloodshot as though he'd been crying.

He looked more like a small boy than a giant popstar. I wanted to hold him, but I could feel an invisible barrier in the way.

'Beth. She's lost the baby. She told me tonight over dinner. But she says she wants us to stay together so we can try again.'

'I'm so sorry,' I said, bursting to tell him the truth. But how could I? It would totally destroy anything they could possibly have together?

'So what are you going to do?'

'God knows,' he said shaking his head.

'How is she?'

'Out cold after two bottles of wine when I left her to come here. Now she hasn't got a baby to worry about, she's gone back to her old habits.'

If only you knew, I thought as we sat side by side on the sofa staring at the empty fireplace. It was probably best to say nothing. But my tongue has a life of its own, and before I had time to think about what I was saying, it was too late.

'How do you feel about losing the baby? Do you think it would have worked if she'd had it?' What on earth was I talking about? There was no baby.

'Gutted. Mainly for Beth. I know how much she wanted it.'

'But you told me you wanted children as well.'

'Well, yes, I do. I didn't want her to lose it. But things with Beth...' he took my face in his hands. 'It doesn't seem right to be with her when I can't get you out of my mind.'

God how I wanted to hear those words, but somehow they didn't mean as much when they were bound up in someone else's pain. No matter what I thought about Beth and the lengths she had gone to in order to keep Daniel, I didn't really know her reasons. Maybe she wanted to stay in the marriage for the money, or maybe she really loved him but had a funny way of showing it.

'She must be in a terrible state Daniel. Now is not the time to be thinking of us.'

'I don't know what to think anymore,'

I went into the kitchen to make a brew. What the hell was I going to do? While he believed her lie that there was a baby, he would feel guilty and tied to her. Surely he should know the truth, then he could decide on a plan of action. I carried in the steaming mugs of tea and handed him one. But I stayed standing.

'Supposing there was no baby?'

He stood slowly up and moved towards me. 'What do you mean?'

'Supposing she'd made it up to keep you.'

'She'd do a lot of things but not that.'

'But supposing she did? Pretend there was a baby because she didn't want to lose you?'

He stared at me looking puzzled. 'You're talking like you know something.'

By this time I'd picked up my phone and opened the photos. There it was, her message: "I'm going to lose it. He won't dump me then."

'What's this?'

'A message on Beth's phone.'

'How did you get it?'

'Long story.'

He carried on reading. '"You're that desp to keep him?

What about me bitch?" Gracie? That must be Lenny Grace. He's gay, or that's what she tells me. So how did you get these?'

'We went to pick up my locket from your house, and Beth was there. Drinking vodka.' By this time Daniel was pacing the room, still staring at my phone.

'Not when she's pregnant.'

'My mother tasted it when Beth left the room. It's what made us wonder if she really was having a baby. And to find more evidence, my mother took her phone. Well, borrowed it. She's got it back.'

He looked at me as if I'd just admitted murdering someone. 'You stole my wife's phone?'

'Technically it was my mum who took it, but yes,' This clearly wasn't going too well. There was a look of disbelief in his eyes.

'I don't know what to think. You stole my wife's phone?'

He re-read the messages.

'She says she's going to lose "it". It doesn't say anything about a baby.'

'Well, what's "it" if it's not the baby?'

'I don't know. What else could she lose? Her mind? Her memory?' He just stared at me and then spoke quietly. 'Lottie, I can't believe you've done this.' Nor could I. Apart from the vodka we had no actual proof that Beth had done anything wrong, or that she was referring to a fake miscarriage.

In my defence I reminded him about the other part of the message. 'There was the bit about her needing your money.'

'Probably a joke. It's always been a joke that she married me for my money. I can't believe what I'm hearing. That you went to my house, and stole my wife's phone and then invaded her privacy by doing screen grabs of her messages. What in the world were you thinking?'

I don't know. I don't know what we were thinking. This was a nightmare. Why did I listen to my mad mother?

'But supposing it's all true? Beth pretending to be pregnant?'

For a minute he thought about it. 'Then you're as bad as

each other,' he said, grabbing his coat. However upset I was about Daniel's reaction, I couldn't quite bring myself to be angry with my mother. And she was probably right. Beth had invented a baby either to keep Daniel or his money or both. But I should never have gone along with the idea of looking at her messages. Or even worse, showing them to Daniel. By this time it was hardly worth going back to sleep. I'd ruined any chance of a future with the man of my dreams, I was fast running out of money and I was a thief. Not a good day in the life of Charlotte Emily Gilbert.

For the next two days I tried to keep myself busy by practising dishes that would be easy to cook on TV, and pretending to talk to a camera by chatting to myself in front of the mirror. But all I could think about was how I'd hurt Daniel and possibly destroyed his marriage for good.

'You could have waited 'til I met him before getting dumped,' said Helen when she called round on her way to yoga.

'Sorry, I'll remember that next time.'

I still wasn't entirely sure what had happened. Had I already been dumped by Daniel that day in Bluebell Cottage? In which case this time I'd been double-dumped if there is such a word. But the one person I wasn't going to discuss it with in detail was Helen who only wanted to talk about herself.

She was still buzzing after Ben had asked if he could stay the night the last time he called round to see the children.

'I followed your mum's advice. Dressed to kill, cooked his favourite meal, and even hinted that I'd been asked out by a guy from the gym. And you ought to have seen his face. I don't think it's going to last long with the she-devil.'

'And you'd take him back?'

'Not sure,' she said, parading herself in front of the mirror. 'Quite fancy this guy at the gym.'

'So he's real?'

'Of course he's real. Think about it. Childhood sweethearts are so old school. I've been with Ben forever. He's been my only real lover, apart from a couple of spotty oiks in the sixth form and a lecturer at uni when we'd broken up for a while. I want to know what I'm missing.'

'And what about the kids? Don't they count?'

'Of course they do. But nearly everyone in their class has parents who've split up. Until now they've been the odd ones out. And they keep hearing how easy it is to play one parent off against the other and get double the presents and treats. So they're not too bothered.'

'Helen, that's awful.'

'No it's not. It's life.'

By the time she left, all I wanted to do was curl up under a blanket, eat chocolate and watch rubbish telly. I convinced myself that the only person who would really understand was my mother.

'You've got five minutes. I'm in the pub. Working,' she said, As expected my description of Daniel's visit was interrupted by her regular expletives.

'For fuck's sake Lottie, why are you giving yourself such a hard time?'

'Because of the damage we've done.'

'What damage? His wife is the one who lied about being pregnant.'

'But supposing she really was pregnant, and we misinterpreted the text.'

'Then it's a bit convenient that she loses the baby the very next day.'

'But coincidences happen.'

'Yeh on the telly. Let's look at this kid. When you met Daniel frigging French, he wasn't living with his wife and they were discussing divorce. Then the minute she hears about you, she's back like a shot pretending to be pregnant. And he's angry with you? What are you supposed to have done?'

'Stolen his wife's phone?'

'That was me.'

'Shown him the texts?'

'Shown him what she was like, a lush and a liar? Listen, you have nothing to apologise about. How do you know he didn't use you to get her back? There have you thought about that?

He could have planned the whole thing, including those pizzeria blokes snapping you in Manchester.'

'Paparazzi mum.'

'Whatever they're flaming called.'

'But mum he hates me now.'

'He probably hates himself for being taken for a ride.'

'Supposing he calls the police?'

'He doesn't want this getting out any more than she does.' She was always full of common sense my mother.

'So you don't think we did anything wrong?'

'Course we bloody did. We nicked the phone of a Hollywood film star,'she said, doing her witchy cackle, and hung up.

That night I wrote in my journal everything that had happened to see if it made any more sense. It didn't. But the one thing I didn't believe was that Daniel had used me in some sort of game to get his wife back. We met each other, and had fallen in love. End of.

34

Strange how when life gets busy, you stop thinking about lost love quite so much. After a screen test on the *The Today Show* which went well, apart from me calling the presenter Lucy instead of Lacey, I'd landed a trial on their Friday show, live from the City Studios. Live TV. Me in front of millions of viewers with no chance to say 'cut' if things went wrong.

When Friday came, Stella was on hand to deliver some of her words of wisdom as I sat in make-up. 'This is your big break hun. You crack this today and it could lead to all sorts. Your own cook book. How about Menus from a Mistress?'

'She's only joking,' said Kevan who had wandered in to see how I was getting on.

'No I'm not,' said Stella who was jotting it down.

'I'm not a mistress anymore,' I said, trying not to squirm with embarrassment in front of the make-up girl.

'Lottie's Love Affair with Food,' she said, completely ignoring me.

'Like that one better,' said Kevan, nodding at her.

Earlier Gary and Lacey had popped their heads round the door to wish me luck.

'You look great,' said Lacey. And I felt great, well as great as you can feel when you've only had about five minutes sleep. I'd decided to wear the same outfit which the producer had approved during the run through. Jeans, a bright pink shirt, and my signature scarf keeping my curls under control.

Before I knew it I was in the studio kitchen with a fixed smile on my face, waiting for Gary and Lacey to announce my presence and wander over.

First Lacey: 'And here she is, the new chef on the block, Lottie Gilbert whose food seems to have tempted many, including superstar Daniel French.'

I glanced over at Kevan who, standing behind a camera, shook his head and looked displeased. It had been agreed beforehand that Daniel's name wouldn't be mentioned. I could feel the heat of my nerve rash travelling up my neck at a rate of knots.

'...as well as many other customers in The Loft vintage café where she is renowned for her home cooking.' That shouldn't have been mentioned either, since I'd been sacked weeks earlier. I could see Stella checking her mobile phone and looking worried before she whispered something in Kevan's ear.

'So Lottie, welcome to *The Today Show*. What are you cooking for us this morning?'

It had been decided that as this was my first time I should stick to something simple like my perfect pasta sauce. All went well until Lacey – probably because I got her name wrong in the screen test – starting asking awkward questions relating to Daniel.

'We have to ask what is his favourite dish?' she asked, her face the picture of innocence.

'Her probably,' said Gary.

'Actually it's shepherd's pie,' I said deciding to go along with the joke.

'Well we'll definitely have to have you back to show us how to satisfy a superstar,' said Lacey, winking at the camera.

I was determined not to let her get the better of me. 'I'm sure I can certainly teach you a few things,' I said, directing my gaze at Gary.

'All getting a bit hot under the collar here,' he laughed as the suggestive pair tucked into my pasta sauce, making orgasmic noises. It was about this time that I sensed all was not well in the studio. Even Lacey looked serious as she listened to something being fed through into her ear.

As we went into a commercial break, they thanked me for joining in the fun and not taking offence at their mischief, but said I should be aware that there was breaking news.

Kevan marched across the studio and grabbed me by the hand.

'We need to get you out of here,' he said under his breath.

35

Kevan literally dragged me along a rabbit warren of corridors as one of the producers let us out of an emergency exit at the back of the building. He ignored my pleas to ask what was going on, until I was strapped into his car and we were driving away from the reporters already flocking like vultures outside the TV studios.

'For God's sake, what's happened? Is it Daniel? Is he alright?'

'He's alright. Beth's not. She's in hospital,' he said, as we sat in a queue of traffic. I could see what looked like a member of the paparazzi snaking through the cars on a motor bike.

'Hold on tight,' said Kevan, as he swerved left without indicating, and started weaving through the back streets, losing our tail.

Within minutes I heard the whole sorry tale. How Daniel had spent the night in the guest room after an evening of arguing with his very drunk wife. Over dinner, it appeared, she had admitted everything. An affair with Lenny Grace, her bi-sexual co-star from the TV show *School Daze*; a jealous rage once she found out about me, and a fake pregnancy as emotional blackmail to keep her husband.

'When he took her coffee early this morning, he found her out of it in their bed, an empty packet of sleeping pills next to her.'

A rush of adrenaline coursed through my body and my mind went into panic mode.

'Is she...will she?'

'She's going to be okay. It appears she hadn't taken as many as first thought. It's not the first time.'

My stomach churned with anxiety at the thought of playing yet another part in the breakdown of a fragile woman.

'But if I hadn't shown Daniel those texts, it would never have happened.'

'Not so sure about that,' said Kevan, keeping his eyes on the rear-view mirror as another couple of motor bikes caught up with us.

'Hang on,' he said, as he screeched to a halt and did a super fast U-turn on the spot like something out of a chase movie, careering off down a one-way street the wrong way.

'Yes it was a crazy thing for your mother to do, taking the phone, I agree. And maybe not a great idea showing him the texts. But it turns out he'd been checking her phone anyway as he suspected she'd been cheating on him, and that it might not have been his baby. If there had been a baby.'

This wasn't making me feel any better. If I hadn't interfered, they might have been able to sort it out. Stopping at the lights, Kevan sighed. It must be quite an exhausting job managing the dramas in other people's lives.

'Is she really going to be okay?'

'Yes her mother is coming over from the States to take care of her. As for you young lady...'

'Is my career as a TV chef over?' I asked as I envisaged my appearance this morning attracting the nasty comments it probably deserved. I could imagine them now. "Look at her the smug-faced bitch mistress, while his wife was fighting for her life."

'For the time being,' he said, squeezing my hand as he drove. 'This is going to be all over the papers. Which is why it's best to get you out of here.'

To be honest I wouldn't care if I never saw another TV camera ever again. If this was fame you could keep it. I was beginning to feel like a naïve pawn in a very complicated game of celebrity chess.

As we fought through the press pack outside my house, Helen was on her way over. She had agreed to stay until my mother arrived on the train from Liverpool so that she could hand over the key and feeding instructions for Colin. Mark was back in the blissed-out land of love again with Tara, so he wasn't around to help. I'd have to hope to God that my mother didn't burn the place down while I was away, or get caught shoplifting, or...best not to think about it.

When Kevan let Helen in, she was buzzing with excitement.

'All those photographers. They were snapping away when I came in. Probably wondering who I was. Will I be in the papers?'

'Yes, as Lottie's new lesbian lover,' said Kevan with a straight face.

'You're not serious?' said Helen looking worried before she got the joke. Although, let's face it, nothing the papers printed would surprise me.

She followed me upstairs: 'Where are you going?'

'I wish I knew. He won't tell me,' I said while I packed my case. There was a text from Jess asking what was going on and warning me not to check my Twitter account, which of course I did immediately. In amongst the other foul comments, I saw another tweet from 'her'. 'Silly you. Now you're asking for it'. Silly you. Silly me, that's the way that Meg spoke. Could it be her? I wondered if there was a way for Chas to check it out. The thought of her being in my kitchen and picking up that knife. Surely not. Was she really mad enough to hurt me?

When Kevan arrived upstairs to carry my case down, Helen nudged me.

'He's quite cute in a kind of Irish way, apart from his sweater,' she cooed.

'He's also cute in a kind of gay way with a very cool partner called Max who owns an equally cool night club. Remember I told you that our kitchen porter Ryan had left The Loft for a job with Max.'

'I don't listen to half of what you tell me,' said Helen hugging me goodbye. 'And don't worry, I'll make sure Colin and your mum are okay.'

As we opened the front door, an army of press literally surged towards us. Kevan had instructed me to walk with my head up, to say nothing, and not to smile. That wasn't difficult. There wasn't anything to smile about.

36

I woke up in the most comfortable bed I'd ever slept in to the sounds of dogs barking, sheep baa-ing and the distant lament of seagulls.

Running my hands over the bedspread which was made up of embroidered hearts in different colours sewn together I looked around. For the first time in days I felt a sense of calm.

The evening before as we flew into Cork airport it was already dark, and after a ninety minute drive to Ballylock Farm, I could barely keep my eyes open. With a pitch-black backdrop apart from the farmhouse lights, it was difficult to tell much about where I was.

'Sure you must be exhausted,' said a softly spoken woman with the most beautiful silver grey hair I'd ever seen pulled back in a clip. She must have been about seventy, but with an amazing figure in dark blue jeans, sheepskin boots and a long grey cardigan.

'This is my mother Mary, and my dad Tommy,' said Kevan as a ruddy-faced man with similar white hair and a twinkle in his eye strolled into the farmhouse kitchen followed by a border collie who almost licked me to death, and a jet black kitten.

As Kevan excused himself to take his luggage to an adjoining cottage, his parents made an overwhelming fuss of me. 'Welcome to our mad house Lottie,' said Tommy, shaking my hand so hard I thought he'd crush it. 'It's a pleasure to have a beautiful young girl here for a change.'

Mary gave him a playful dig and helped me off with my coat.

'Kevan has his own place here on the farm, but it's always such a mess. We thought you'd be more comfortable in the guest room. It's on the ground floor, so you're near to the kitchen if you get hungry in the night,' she said leading me towards a small room at the back of the house with an en-suite bathroom. I already loved everything about this house, from its heavy pine doors and dark wooden beams to the homely rugs, red cushions and cream throws over the large brown sofas which I could sink in forever.

'This used to be Kevan's room when he was a teenager which was great, because if he got home after a late night out, he didn't wake us,' she said, plumping up the pillows on the bed.

'Make yourself at home. There are clean towels in the bathroom, and when you're ready I'll feed you. Our son tells me you're a chef, so I'm a little nervous.'

'Kevan says you're a marvellous cook, and I'm looking forward to finding out more about Irish food,' I said,

'Oh that you will,' she said, as she left me to freshen up and get my bearings. As we sat down to dinner round an enormous oak kitchen table, I could see where Kevan got his dry humour from. His dad. The two men bantered back and forth speaking so quickly it was hard to pick up what they were saying. Kevan's accent had definitely broadened since we arrived. I spoke mostly to his mum who was a joy. A glass-half-full woman, who despite a hard life on the farm had kept a sense of style and beauty. She dished up the best Irish stew I'd ever eaten with dumplings and home-baked bread, while Tommy made sure my glass was full of his delicious homemade wine. Conversation flowed, mainly about me and my life before Daniel. They were not people given to talking much about themselves.

I was fascinated to ask about Daniel and how he'd been as

a little boy when he stayed with them in the boarding school holidays.

'A little angel, so long as he got his own way which he almost always did. And even at a young age he was very gifted. We had an old piano at the time, and he'd spend ages playing it, while Kevan was outside getting himself filthy dirty on the farm,' said Mary, her velvety-brown eyes smiling with the memories. 'Isn't that right Kevan?'

Kevan's Irish eyes were most definitely not smiling. 'He wasn't such a cherub you know. I could tell you some stories, so I could.'

His mother tut-tutted. 'I won't hear anything bad about our Daniel. He's like a son to us. Still comes over a couple of times a year to get some peace and quiet for writing songs. Brings his own keyboard, so he does. And when he's here we have a grand time. Our own private performance, isn't that right Tommy?'

'Does he ever bring his wife?'

'She's in America when he comes over. Only ever met her at the wedding. Seemed nice enough,' said Mary. 'Although I did hear something on the news about her not being at all well.'

At that stage Kevan managed to change the subject. He told me later that his parents weren't the sort to keep up with showbiz news or gossip. They possessed one mobile phone between them which was only used for calls, and were unlikely to have read about my affair with Daniel. As he saw me to the bedroom door, he asked if there was anything I needed. A cuddle. A cuddle was what I needed. And forgiveness for this whole sorry mess I'd got myself and everyone else into.

Midnight, and even though I'd been tired earlier, I was now wide awake. So I searched through the bookcase for something to help me drift off. And there it was. A Winnie-the-Pooh book. Perfect. Wait until I saw Kevan tomorrow. Something different to tease him about apart from his sweaters. Finally I dropped off until a noise woke me.

When I looked at my phone it was only half past midnight. But there was someone in the kitchen. I could hear sounds of cupboards opening, and a quiet male voice probably talking to the dog.

It had to be Kevan, I thought, as I put on the soft grey woollen dressing gown which Mary had kindly left on the back of the door.

Quietly I opened the door and walked out. The only light in the kitchen came from a small lamp over the oven. I could see a figure in the corner of the room making himself a sandwich.

As he spun round, it took a while to realise who it was.

'For fuck's sake I thought you were a ghost,' said Max Diamond, looking like one himself, his bleached blonde hair standing on end. Or was that his hairstyle?

'I'm so sorry if I made you jump. I'm Lottie. I was the chef at Daniel's birthday party.'

'I've heard about all about you,' he said, patting a chair for me to join him at the table. 'I just flew in tonight without time to eat, so I'm bloody starving. Ryan's passed out in bed. So I've left him to it.'

Ryan? Ryan was here with him?

'Ryan? Who used to work at The Loft with me?'

'The very same. He'll be surprised. He didn't know you'd be here. Nor did I,' he said, tucking into his sandwich.

'How is he?'

'Yeh he's cool man. You'll see him tomorrow. Keep forgetting you two worked together.'

'Yeh man,' I said, trying but failing miserably to be as cool as Max.

'Have you seen Kevan yet?' I asked trying to make conversation.

'No. But you're okay. We won't let onto to the press about you being here,' he laughed.

'Thank you,' I said, feeling awkward. There was silence for a few seconds.

'So do you come over here a lot?' I asked, wondering how Kevan's parents felt about him making himself at home in their kitchen.

'Course. Grandma's cool about it.'

'Grandma?' I know it was the middle of the night, but my brain was going into overdrive trying to figure this one out.

'Grandma?'

'My grandparents. Dad's brought me here ever since I was a baby.'

'Dad?'

'My dad,' said Max looking quizzically at me.

'Your dad? Kevan is your dad?' I said, the penny beginning to drop big time.

It was odd, but pleasantly reassuring to see Ryan at the breakfast table the next morning. It was weeks since I'd seen him and his hair had dramatically been cut short emphasising his large soulful eyes, high cheekbones and full lips. There was a moment when everyone else was engaged in conversation when we turned to each other and exchanged looks. As if to say, how on earth did we both end up here? One minute he's peeling spuds at The Loft and I'm cooking fry-ups for hungry shoppers. The next he's in Ireland as the new boyfriend of a gay millionaire club owner, and I'm the ex-mistress of a global superstar.

Thankfully Max didn't divulge our meeting in the middle of the night. Although he'd probably already told his father who was giving me strange looks over the toast.

'So you thought I was gay?' said Kevan as we wandered down towards a row of garages where he kept his car.

'Ever since I saw you kissing Max at Daniel's party.'

'As I recall that was a fatherly kiss, not a full-on snog,' he said.

'And his age. Max must be in his mid-twenties, and you're only ....'

'Forty two. That's on account of I fathered him when I was seventeen and still in the sixth form at boarding school. Christine, a vicar's daughter from the nearby village was trying to make Daniel jealous by sleeping with me. It didn't work, but she got pregnant, and her parents didn't believe in abortions.

Which is just as well or I wouldn't have my boy,' he said with a look of pride. 'We had him christened Conor O'Brien, but when he got into his twenties, he decided he wanted a much cooler name, so he changed it to Max Diamond and bleached his beautiful chestnut hair.'

'What happened to his Irish accent?'

'Oh, you know, kids. He thought it was much cooler to talk with a 'mockney' accent.'

'And now he's with Ryan?'

'Looks that way. Nice kid too.'

'Yes he seems a lot happier now he's come out.'

Kevan nodded knowingly. 'Max never made a secret of what he was all about. His mother went on to marry and have four more children. And he's still in touch with her, but he spent most of his childhood with me here on the farm with his grandparents.'

'Oh I see,' I said, barely listening. Something about Kevan and Max was bugging me. When I'd spoken to Daniel about them as a gay couple, he hadn't corrected me. Why would that have been, I asked him.

'Typical Dan. He was just going along with it probably to put you off finding me attractive in any way. Not that you would,' he added quickly. 'It was a pain in the arse having a best mate like him, I can tell you. He always got the girls I fancied, even if he didn't fancy them back. I didn't stand a chance.'

Oh I don't know, I thought sneaking a look at him. That dark curly hair and his expressive blue eyes which could change like the weather. I loved his voice as well, the Irish lilt and the laid back way that he never panicked when things went wrong. Even his monstrous taste in sweaters was rather endearing.

We were in the car with Buddy the sheepdog on our way to the beach for a walk which Kevan thought would do me good. I wasn't so sure. Not even the fierce biting cold wind was capable of blowing away the dark clouds which had been gathering over my head since the news about Beth hit me. I tried to concentrate on the scenery. The brightly painted cottages which lined the lanes, and local butchers and bakers and sweet looking pubs. As we walked briskly, the wind in our face, he didn't try to make conversation, which was just as well as we might have been drowned out by sound of the Atlantic surf. But all I could think of was the shame which I felt over being outed online and in the tabloids as the woman who had wrecked Daniel's marriage. Kevan had made me promise not to check my Twitter account under any circumstances.

'You need to take a break from all of this,' he said as we arrived at the beach, almost deserted apart from a man and his dog.

'Here you hold him,' he said, handing me Buddy's lead, while he wrapped his woollen scarf around my neck. 'You are going to need that,' he added as we headed towards the giant boulders which led onto the sand. After a few minutes he took back Buddy's lead so that I could power on alone. I headed towards a cluster of rocks and chose one to sit on while I waited for Kevan and Buddy to catch up. He'd stopped to talk to another dog walker and I relished the time alone for my thoughts.

If Kevan hadn't insisted that he and Daniel stopped off at The Loft for some home-cooked food that day, none of this would happened. I'd never have fallen for Daniel, and been drawn into his showbiz web where I was trapped by pictures of us taken together. Without me on the scene Beth might not have flown over to the UK. My mother wouldn't have turned up in my life, stolen her phone and I wouldn't have cast doubts in Daniel's mind which possibly led to the massive argument and her suicide attempt. As for me, I'd still have a job with my kitchen family at The Loft and wouldn't have become the notorious mistress who had to run away from press, death threats and trolls.

I wanted my old life back so I could walk from the bus stop without being hounded by reporters camped outside my house. I wanted to cuddle up with Colin and bemoan the fact that I only had fourteen Twitter followers. I wanted to believe that I was a good person who would one day meet a man who loved me for me. I wanted to get rid of the flutters in my heart when I thought about those first few days with Daniel. And the dread which now lived permanently inside me. What had I done? I'd made a mess of my life, that's what. The enormity of what had happened closed in on me, and the next thing my body was wracked with great sobs which made me breathless with sorrow.

The next thing I knew Buddy's head was in my lap, and I cuddled up to him using his fur to dry my tears as I used to with Colin. Kevan made me budge over so he could fit on my rock, and he put his arms around me.

'Hey Lottie, it's okay. You're a good person,' he said as though he had read my thoughts. 'You've always done what you thought was right. I know that. Showing Daniel the text messages might not have been the smartest thing in the world to do. But if you hadn't, none of this would have come out about her affair. Or her fairy story about losing a baby. Think about it. He could have carried on living a lie with her, until the truth came out which it would have done.'

'You think?'

'I know. She needs help with her alcohol problem. And maybe now this has happened she might get it. Her mother is taking her home to rehab.'

'And is the marriage over?'

'It was already over,' he said holding me tight.

The next three days I lived in a cocoon of laughter and love, much of it experienced around the kitchen table over the evening meal. One night Ryan helped me prep and cook them all a steak and kidney pudding followed by apple pie which went down a treat.

'I can't have you stay here too often I'll put on too much weight,' said Mary who I decided I wanted to adopt as my mother, okay my other mother. The one who did things that mothers were supposed to do like make me delicious mugs of hot chocolate to chase away the winter blues, not steal phones and get me into trouble. 'I think this ring is going to have to come off. It's far too tight,' she said struggling to pull off the antique-looking diamond ring she wore on her right hand. Then there was Kevan's lovely dad Tommy who taught me Irish songs and accompanied my bad singing with his piano accordion. Max who was like the naughty little brother I never had, forever teasing me; and Ryan who it turns out had a wicked sense of humour and could talk for England or even Ireland in the right company. And of course Kevan who joined in the musical showing-off by playing his guitar and singing us an Irish song in Gaelic. Who knew?

One night around the table, Max got his selfie stick and took a photo of us all raising our glasses. It was the scene I'd often imagined, but had never happened. The family I'd always wanted to be part of.

37

'Meet Amber,' said Kevan as the head of a glossy chestnut horse appeared over the stable door upon hearing his voice. 'This is my mother's horse, and she's as gentle as they come,' he said, feeding her some apple.

'This fella on the other hand is the opposite. A real scallywag called Victor,' he laughed as the most handsome white animal I'd ever seen snorted at me.

As one of the stable hands saddled the horses, Kevan suggested we take them for a walk. Nothing else, not yet. I'd somehow convinced him I could ride. A bit. That I'd been on Helen's ponies when I was young, so of course I could trot and even a canter on a good day. Who was I kidding? So there I was in my jeans and boots, a roll neck jumper, gloves, and warm jacket on loan from Kevan's mother feeling quite the country girl. That is, until he produced the riding hat which made me look like one of the priggish girls from those pony club books Helen used to read.

Hauling myself up into the saddle needed a lot more strength than I remembered. Possibly because Helen's ponies were barely bigger than large dogs. Somehow, don't ask, Kevan managed to push my bottom up and onto the saddle, at which point I remembered I suffered from vertigo and wanted to get down. But he wouldn't let me.

'What? After all this effort of getting you up there? You're staying put,' he said, leaping onto Victor with the speed and skill of a stunt rider. It was the oddest feeling being on such a powerful animal who could obviously sense my fear and was probably thinking: 'Oh we're going to have some fun with this idiot.' To start with I kept wanting to lean forward and throw my arms around Amber's neck every time she moved. But after a few minutes of strolling towards what looked like a wood in the distance, I started to relax, even though my hands were fast turning into blocks of ice. Hey, I could do this.

'There you see, it's not so bad, you're doing well,' said Kevan, adjusting my grip on the reins. How on earth were you supposed to control such a large animal with these silly bits of leather, I thought as we began to pick up speed.

'Could we slow down please?' I said, wondering when we could turn round and go back.

'We're only going about the speed of a tortoise right now, so there's no need to worry,' he said, pulling a funny face which was presumably meant to be me. God did I really look like that? I tried to smile, but it froze along with my breath as it met the air.

After about fifteen minutes I was looking at my watch, and I think he sensed that not only was I cold, but I was cold *and* miserable and totally out of my comfort zone. While he on the other hand looked like a cowboy on his white horse. Not for him some silly hat I noticed.

In the distance I started to imagine I could hear the engine of a helicopter.

'What the…?' he said as the sound grew nearer, and Amber started to trot sideways in a rather worrying manner. It really was a helicopter which, judging by the noise, appeared to be preparing to land nearby.

'Hold tight,' shouted Kevan, attempting to grab my reins, but Amber had no intention of being grabbed, and as the engine noise grew louder she reared up on her hind legs. Don't ask me how, but somehow my instinct took over and I held onto her mane as she broke into a gallop with enough speed to win the

Grand National. As we headed towards the trees, all I could hear was Kevan's voice. But I couldn't make out what he was saying. The strap on the stupid riding hat had loosened so that it slipped sideways on my head, and I knew that if I was to prevent myself from being decapitated, I would have to start ducking under the branches which were looming ahead.

To my credit I didn't scream, but started wondering what the odds were of me staying on the horse or being hurled to my death. Oh the press would love that. I could see the headlines now. **THAT'S LOTTIE'S LOT.**

Behind me I could hear thundering hooves and Kevan shouting at me to hang on. What the hell did he think I was doing? After what seemed like an age, Victor caught up and Kevan was beside me, taking control of Amber and speaking to her in what I assumed to be Gaelic, until she slowed down and eventually stopped.

He jumped off Victor, who wandered off as though nothing much had just happened, and held Amber as he told me to bring my other leg around so that I could slide off forwards and into his arms. For a moment I felt safe. But Kevan's body was taut with rage.

'I'll bloody kill him,' he said as he tied the horses to a tree.

'Who? Who is it?' I asked, as he marched towards the helicopter. He didn't answer, so I ran behind him until I saw a familiar figure in tight black jeans, a black polo neck and brown flying jacket walking towards us. It was Daniel.

38

'What's he doing here?' I asked as Daniel waved.

'Bringing you some chocolates if you're lucky,' he said, still sounding angry. I laughed. Fresh from his helicopter and looking supercool in black he did look, for all the world, like the Cadbury's Milk Tray man in the TV advert.

'Don't say a word, but it was announced yesterday that his TV series isn't being re-commissioned, so he's gutted,' said Kevan as Daniel speeded up towards us.

'Is that why he's here?'

'And to see you.'

'And you couldn't tell me because?'

'He made me swear not to.'

'And you do everything he says?'

'While he's paying me, yes,' he said, under his breath.

Daniel was full of apologies for failing to let Kevan know he'd booked an earlier flight and was taking a helicopter from the airport. And to me for frightening the horses.

Kevan left us in his cottage to talk while he went back to the farmhouse to inform his parents that they might have an extra guest tonight. Although Daniel had booked in at a local hotel under the name of Paddy McGinty, Kevan insisted he stayed at the farm. Ryan and Max were still asleep in the cottage guest room, so as long as we didn't shout at each other, we'd be fine he added. Although how they hadn't been woken up by the helicopter, which had now taken off back to Cork, was a bit of a mystery.

After four days with Kevan constantly at my side, it felt so odd to be without him for reassurance. At one point after he left, Daniel had made a move to kiss me, but I turned my head sideways so it landed on my cheek.

'I don't blame you being angry with me,' he said as we sat stiffly either side of the kitchen table.

'What for being nearly thrown to my death from a horse? It's nothing,' I said, trying to make a joke of it. He didn't laugh.

'For everything. You were right to show me Beth's texts.'

'No I wasn't.'

'Yes you were,' he said, taking my hand. 'I know things didn't end well, but at least it made us face facts about our marriage and she will get the help she needs. And we're managing the story about the overdose, saying it was accidental due to stress. In a few weeks, we'll announce that she's decided to live in the States for her career, and that we're separating amicably.'

That sounded all very neat and tidy but I wasn't quite sure what this had to do with me. Over here in Ireland I felt so far removed from his life. I was looking down at my hands, thinking how bitten my nails looked, when I realised he was staring intently at me. My heart did that little skip thing it did when I first met him. He looked so sad, with bags under his eyes as though he hadn't been sleeping.

Almost in a whisper he said: 'Come back with me.'

'What?'

'I meant what I said about loving you Lottie. You are the only sensible part of all this madness. I need you in my life. And soon, when all this has died down, we can be together. Start afresh. Be a proper couple. Please.'

'What about all the bad stuff that's out there about me as the mistress breaking up your marriage?'

'Stella will set up a couple of interviews and photoshoots where you and I will spin that around, and maybe even a TV interview.'

'Without making Beth look bad?'

'Without making any of us look bad.'

I couldn't believe what I was hearing. 'Really? You want me as your proper girlfriend?' I said trying to make light of what was fast becoming a very serious proposal.

'Yep, my proper girlfriend. Think about it. We'd never have to be apart. You could travel the world with me. Stay in the best hotels. Life would be first-class all the way. You'd have everything you ever wanted. Jewellery, cars. And we'd get you the best stylists, make up artists, hairdressers. You underestimate yourself Lottie. I want the world to see how beautiful you are.'

'She looks fit enough to me,' said Ryan who wandered into the kitchen in his pyjama bottoms and a white T-shirt rubbing his eyes. 'Sorry mate, didn't mean to interrupt,' he added, grinning at me.

Ryan, Ryan, how you've changed. You'd have never have spoken like that to a superstar a couple of months ago. As soon as he wandered out again we managed a kiss to seal our renewed relationship. God that man could kiss. I couldn't believe what had just happened. He loved me, Daniel French loved me. Me, me, me. He was desperate for us to spend the night together in his bed, but out of courtesy to our hosts I insisted that I stayed put in my current room.

While Kevan and Daniel sat down over lunch at the cottage to discuss business, I went back to the farmhouse to shower and change. We'd decided to stay the night and travel by helicopter to the airport the next morning. From there I'd go home and start planning our future together. He agreed with me that rather than move into what had been his marital home, he would put that on the market and we could go house hunting for something maybe more modern, in grounds, of course, with tennis courts and a gym.

'Could I have a walk-in closet?'

'Anything you like.'

'And a swimming pool?'

'Of course. A home cinema, that would be a must, and a

state of the art kitchen for you.' While all this was going on, I'd stay at home, and when I eventually moved out, Daniel was quite happy to carry on paying the rent so that, if she chose, mum could relocate from Liverpool to look after Colin in case he didn't hit it off with Oscar the dog.

Standing in the shower, the unhappiness of the past few weeks just washed off me. And I felt a new lease of life and happiness, with excitement mounting by the minute every time I thought of something else I'd like in our new house. I started to dream about dinner parties I'd give with Helen there and his rich and famous friends. And who knows maybe my mum could come if she promised to behave. Perhaps we could give Mark some painting and decorating work. Maybe Naomi Lincoln could become my new best friend, so long as I managed to conquer the jealous streak in me about them having an affair three years ago. It was all falling into place beautifully. Except for Meg. I hoped I could persuade him to get rid of her. She gave me the heebie jeebies. Even if I was mistaken about her being a Twitter troll.

As I helped Mary plan for tonight's meal I wondered if Daniel had revealed our plans to Kevan yet. And what his reaction would be.

Getting ready for dinner, there was a firm knock on the door. I was all prepared for it to be Daniel, but it was Kevan.

'So the happy couple fly off into the sunset,' he said, sitting on the end of the bed. 'Are you sure about all of this?'

'Me and Daniel? Yes. Why? Shouldn't I be?'

'Of course you should, if you're in love with him.'

'My God, who wouldn't be?'

'Exactly, there are millions of women out there who would cut off their right arms to be you.'

'And why is that wrong?'

'Because they're in love with Daniel French the singer. Daniel French the sex symbol. Daniel French the superstar whose image has been created by the media and fed into by his hideous hangers-on. Over the years I've seen countless women fall in love with him or think they are because being with someone so famous makes them feel so special.'

'That's exactly how he makes me feel.'

'You're already special Lottie,' he said, with a look in his eyes I hadn't seen before. It was as though he could see through all the rubbish I talked, and down to the truth.

'What about Beth? She wasn't just someone who fell in love with him because he was famous.'

'Sure, her ego was nearly as big as his and the two of them collided. But she wasn't worth anything near as much as he is, and money meant everything to her. So him being rich helped.'

'I'd love Daniel even if he was a nobody.'

'No you wouldn't.'

'Being famous doesn't make him any different.'

'You don't think it makes him different living his life in public with thousands of strangers commenting on the minutiae of his life on Twitter? Invading his every minute on earth in some way with their demands to own him?'

'God that's very profound.'

'He lives his life under the spotlight which you'll be sharing, putting on an act for the crowds. I don't think even he knows who he is anymore.'

'He says he loves me.'

'I'm sure he probably does in his way. He hasn't experienced a lot of real love, and he sees in you someone who is cute and funny and loyal who would fit into his life and make it better.'

'What's so wrong with that?'

'Nothing as long as you're happy sacrificing yours. And that you understand that the real turn-on for him is the adoration he gets from being Daniel French. It's doubtful you'll ever get to know the real Danny. The kid that I knew before fame sprinkled her poison on him and turned him into someone else.'

There speaks a man who is jealous, I thought to myself as I finished getting ready for our goodbye dinner. The man who has always lived his life in the shadow of his best friend and can't bear to see him happy. Any doubts I had quickly disappeared around the dinner table where Daniel held court by announcing our plans. It was as though I was living on some sort of pink cloud where dreams came true and everything in life was perfect, or maybe it was the champagne which was being topped up by Tommy every time I took a sip.

'My goodness that was quick,' said Mary, as we drank a toast. 'All a bit of a whirlwind, like a movie. Do I need to buy a hat?'

'You've got time love, he's not divorced yet,' said Tommy, who like Kevan, appeared to be not so caught up in our excitement.

'There's no rush,' said Daniel. 'We want to do things right. I'll make sure that Beth is looked after. Anyway I've got a world tour starting February.'

'Will you be going on that?' asked Ryan, who up until now had stayed silent.

'Er, I don't know. Maybe,' I said, wondering how long I'd be away from home.

Daniel slid his arm around my shoulder. 'Of course she will. We'll be away for a good couple of months. The States, and Australia, and then back for a while before we do Hong Kong and China.'

'How exciting,' said Mary, 'I've always wanted to go to China. We'd never be able to though. Our Tommy isn't keen on the food.'

'If you need a roadie, I'll come,' said Ryan, 'furthest I've been is Bournemouth.'

Furthest I'd been was a couple of Greek islands with Mark. As someone who has to be virtually tranquilised before I fly, I wasn't sure whether to feel thrilled or terrified by the prospect of all this air travel.

'I've got my house over in Florida, so we'll probably hang out there for a couple of weeks, you'll love it Lottie,' said Daniel, just as I was working out how I was going to fit in visits to Colin and my mother between all this jet-setting around the world. As I looked round the table at all the happy faces joining in the banter, the only serious face belonged to Kevan.

No wonder he was trying to put Daniel down. He'd probably spent his whole life wishing he'd been the one who got the girls and made it to the top, instead of just his manager.

When he left the table to pick up some bottles of wine from his fridge in the cottage, I made my excuses and tailed along with him.

'To what do I owe this honour?' he said as we followed the large torch beam up the lane to his front door.

'I need to speak to you.'

'You are.'

'Okay yes. So I need to ask you why you're being so mean about me and Daniel?'

'I see it as trying to warn you before you get sucked too far into this fairytale romance.'

'So what? What's wrong with fairytales? Makes a change from all the doom and gloom. Once upon a time I was going to be married to a painter and decorator whose idea of a romantic night out was chicken and chips at the local Harvester. Now look at me.'

'I am,' said Kevan, and he pulled me roughly towards him and kissed me. Just like that. He kissed me. On the lips. And it was a shock. A nice shock, but still a shock. It wasn't like kissing Daniel. Daniel's kiss was all soft and sensual. This was harder, more passionate. When I pulled away from him, he shrugged.

'You kissed me.'

'Is that what I was doing?'

'You bastard, how could you do that to your best friend. Are you jealous of him?'

'No because I know I won't end up a lonely old sod having to do reality shows and end of the pier gigs just to kid myself I'm still a celebrity.'

'That's a horrible thing to say,' I was rapidly going off Kevan.

'Yes it is. I take it back. Anyway that's never likely to happen to Daniel. He's far too smart. I'm sorry,' he said, although he didn't sound it. 'And yes you're right I am jealous.'

'Of his money? His career?'

'Because he has you,' he said, and that was the last time he spoke to me that evening.

39

Unlike the black kitten with no name who was asleep like a little purring coiled spring on my pillow, I couldn't be more awake if I tried. When it got to three in the morning, I got up and went to the kitchen. I wasn't the only one. Ryan was there, his head in his hands at the table.

'What's wrong? Can't you sleep?' I said giving him a hug.

'Max and I had a dreadful row.'

'What about?'

'You and Daniel.'

'What about us?'

'Do you love him Lottie?'

'What's not to love about a gorgeous man who has flown all the way here to declare his undying love and take me home? And he happens to be a superstar. How lucky am I? What was the row about?'

'Max thinks you're star struck.'

'He's been listening to his dad.'

'I stood up for you. I mean I never thought I'd have a boyfriend like Max. Why shouldn't you? You deserve it.'

I'd never seen Ryan looking so happy. I wanted to hug him. 'We both deserve it. I'm sure you and Max will make it. And when we've got our house, I'll make sure you come round.'

'To help?'

'No, with Max. As our guests,' He smiled wearily and put on his hoodie to make his way back to the cottage.

After he'd gone, I spent the rest of the night back in bed staring at the patterns on the ceiling made by the moonlight filtering through the trees. I decided to flick through Kevan's Winnie-the-Pooh book. I'd forgotten to tease him about still having it on his book shelves, but when I opened the cover it was dedicated to his son on his seventh birthday.

"To my wonderful son. Make sure you put your Big Boots on," he'd written, referring to Pooh's observation that every time Christopher Robin put on his big boots an adventure was going to happen. I must make sure I remember that when I put on my boots tomorrow I thought. I had a feeling that when I left here, I would be breaking the bond I had with Kevan. I was sure to see him, but it wouldn't be the same. Things between us could be awkward. I really liked Kevan too. Maybe even more than liked. I would miss him. I'd miss them all, my new Irish family. Mary and Tommy and Max, Buddy and the black cat with no name, even Amber if she ever forgave me for riding her so badly.

The next morning was a quiet affair around the breakfast table. Daniel kept asking me if I was okay, and I really wasn't sure how I felt. Instead of being beyond excited, my feelings were muted and mixed.

Before I left, Mary plonked the little black kitten in my lap.

'She'll always be yours when you come back,' she said, 'So I think you ought to name her.' The kitten sleepily opened her green eyes and then shut them again.

'Emerald like the Emerald Isle and her eyes. Emmy,' I said, as she started to paddy paw in my lap.

'Emmy it is,' said Mary with a smile. 'And you're her mammy. Don't forget that. You'll need to come back and visit.'

Daniel was on the phone most of the morning to Stella discussing up and coming meetings with another TV production company for a new show to replace *The French Connection.*

'Sorry I can't talk honey. There will be plenty of time later,' he said apologetically when I took him some coffee. I guess this is what my life would be from now on. Fitting in with his busy schedule, but then that was okay. There was plenty I could do.

We heard the helicopter before we saw it hovering in the grey skies which looked laden with rain. Everyone wrapped up and was planning to see us off, except for Kevan who excused himself to make a phone call. We'd already said our rather terse goodbyes earlier with Daniel looking on.

'Take care of yourself Lottie. You know where I am,' he said, as I kissed him on the cheek.

'Oh, and I noticed this on your bed. Take it with you,' he said handing me his son's old Winnie-the-Pooh book.

'Won't Max want this?'

'He doesn't need it,' he said, and gave me a sad smile.

Outside as the helicopter approached, I checked my bag to make sure I had my passport to hand. It had wedged itself inside the Winnie-the-Pooh book. As I pulled it out, the book fell open at the page where Kevan had written to his son. In black ink was a new message: ***"Enjoy your Big Adventure Lottie. And don't get too big for your boots! Oh, and forgive this Irishman of Very Little Brain!"*** signed K with a kiss.

I stuffed the book back in my bag. I needed to find Kevan, just to tell me him that everything was okay and that we could still be friends. He would be in his cottage. But it was too late. Daniel had finished his phone call to some American producer or other, and was walking over to join me. As we waited to board, I looked over at my new little family who all waved simultaneously.

'This is it Lottie, a whole new world,' said Daniel, as a smartly uniformed pilot came over to greet us.

'Oh hang on a minute,' he said as his phone rang. 'Brad hey buddy. I'm all yours. Great to hear from you. What? Oh nothing special,' he added, glancing at me and holding up his hand to silence me.

'I think I prefer my old world,' said a voice, which I realised to my horror was mine. Daniel held his phone away from his ear.

'I'm sorry?' he said looking at me as though I'd let lose a string of swear words. 'Hey Brad, let me call you back.'

'I rather like the world I've already got,' I said again grabbing hold of my suitcase handle before the co-pilot could take it.

'Lottie, come here,' said Daniel, leading me to one side so we wouldn't be overheard.

'What the hell are you going on about? I thought we'd talked about all this, about the fact that sometimes I'd be busy.'

'Yes we did, but I didn't realise then.'

'Realise what?'

'That I was in love with you for the wrong reasons.'

'What? For my fame and fortune? Okay, so what's wrong with that? We can have the most fantastic time with it. It's who I am.'

'It's not who I am though.'

'Sir, we're ready when you are,' said the pilot calling over and looking at his watch.

'Sorry, I'm not,' I said, watching Daniel's perma-smile vanish.

'Not what?'

'Ready. I'm not ready to give up my life and all my hopes and dreams to fit into yours.'

'You wouldn't be. We'd be a team. I'd let you do anything you wanted. Be who you want to be.'

'You'd let me? Oh that's generous. Actually I'm already who I want to be, but thank you Daniel.'

'Everything alright Lottie,' said Kevan, from behind me, his voice melting away any fears that I had.

'It is now.'

Two months later

If you'd told me a couple of months ago that I would have an affair with the mega rich superstar Daniel French, and then dump him when he offered me the world, I'd have said you were crazy. When actually you'd probably be thinking it's me who's crazy. And I must admit as the helicopter became a dot in the distance with its famous cargo, I started to think the same. But when Kevan took my hand on the walk back to the farmhouse, it felt like I was coming home.

We didn't rush into anything, which made it even more of an event when we finally slept together back at his London house. It wasn't bells and rockets and fireworks as it had been that first time with Daniel. That thrill of being with someone so famous. It was just down to earth and real. There were no nerves, just a calm feeling of contentment and the certainty that nothing was going to come between us.

The more I knew him, the more I grew to love him. Waking up to his untidy curls, and his blue eyes looking sleepily into mine. His deep sexy Irish accent which never failed to charm me even when he was being Mr Grumpy. His dry sharp humour, mixed with a boyish mischief. His incredible knowledge of the world, his strength, and logic. His confidence and faith that all of life's problems were 'figure-outable.' His family who had virtually adopted me. The fact that he was such a great dad.

That in his own quiet way he loved someone like me, just for me. And that he was the most genuine person I'd ever met. What you saw was what you got.

On Valentine's Day, Kevan took me to a curry house called The Indian Ocean to celebrate my fortieth birthday. A place where the food more than made up for the slightly tacky décor. And surprise! There they all were. The people I loved. Mary and Tommy who had flown over from Cork. Helen who was giving Ben another chance, Jess, Pat and her husband Frank, Max and Ryan, Stella who was trying to talk me into writing my 'mistress' memoir, and Marsha whose cough was notably worse. And my mum of course who was now happily ensconced in my old house with Colin. 'You kept this quiet mum.'

'Oh you know me kid, I can't resist a Korma. And it gives me the chance to give you a birthday card for once in your life,' she said handing me an envelope.

It was such a wonderful shock seeing everyone together. And as I sat and listened for a minute to the chatter around me, I realised that the cliché about life beginning at forty couldn't be more true.

Half way through the meal Kevan turned to me and said quietly: 'Lottie will you marry me?' As if the rest of the table knew telepathically what was going on they all stopped talking.

'It's okay, I asked your mum,' he added.

'And what did she say?'

'That I can have you so long as she can keep Colin,' he said smiling at my mother who was obviously in on all of this.

'I thought you didn't approve of whirlwind relationships? We've only known each other five minutes.'

'Is that right? It feels like forever to me,' he said at which point I playfully punched his arm. Looking around at the red flock wallpaper and tacky decor it wasn't exactly the most romantic setting for a proposal.

'So why here?'

'Because then I could say I proposed in the middle of The Indian Ocean which would be great in a bridegroom speech.'

'Only if you go down on one knee.'

'You're a hard woman to please. And you'll probably get cross because I haven't a ring yet,' he said getting out of his chair and down on one knee.

'Yes you have,' said Mary, taking off her grandmother's diamond ring she'd shown me back in Ireland and handing it to her son.

'Okay, so Charlotte Emily Gilbert, will you do me the honour of being my wife?' he asked, holding out the ring. Nothing fake about this diamond.

'Yes,' I said laughing and crying simultaneously which you would know is quite hard if you've ever tried it.

In between glasses of champagne, Marsha called me over. 'I should never have let you go and taken on that dreadful girl. Can you ever find it in your heart to forgive a silly old fool like me?'

'Of course,' I said giving her a hug. Under the wool of her brown dress she felt much thinner than I remembered. And her cough was worse.

'That night we talked at the restaurant and I told you all about my affair? I was trying to kid myself that I wouldn't have it any other way. That he was the love of my life. But that's not the truth,' said Marsha.

'What do you mean?'

'He loved me, but not enough. At the end of the day I was always the other woman. The mistress. I would have given anything to have what you have with Kevan. A man all to myself. Not a man I had to share. You'd always have to have shared Daniel. You know that.'

'I know,' I said as I walked her back to our table. Two days later I had a call from her godson to say that she'd been taken into hospital. And the next day she died.

A few weeks later came word that her godson would now be running Pandora's Box, but that she had left The Loft to me.

Four months later

Mark was the first to arrive at the launch party of Lottie's Loft to admire his decorating handiwork. We'd done a complete make-over, buying antique pine tables and chairs, painting the walls white and introducing an old Welsh dresser decorated with china I'd chosen from the antique store downstairs. I'd also found a couple of beautiful old lamps to light up the corners and invested in a stunning Art Deco jukebox.

Tara had long since been out of Mark's life and he'd been renting a room back in my old house with my mum. It took me a while to realise that since he'd been in the café every day decorating, he'd been flirting with Jess, who had given up the idea of being a WAG, and that the two of them were now dating. I was paying her to manage my Twitter account for me, in the hope we could use it to promote my new cookery book. And she was happy to report that the troll I thought might be Meg had closed her account.

Kevan had put his house on the market and we were looking for somewhere locally so I could be near my new restaurant.

Pat was in charge of the party buffet, and couldn't stop talking about her new role entertaining our evening customers twice a week singing old cover songs from the Fifties and Sixties.

Stella was ever present in our lives, mainly I discovered, because she had always had a crush on Kevan.

'To think that two carat diamond could have been mine. You bitch,' she whispered in my ear as she admired my engagement ring.

Kevan had parted ways with Daniel and was launching his own talent management company. While Daniel, it was rumoured, was back dating Naomi Lincoln who had split from her husband and never did become my new best friend.

'At long last the truth might come out about her daughter,' said Stella, as she held out her champagne glass for Billy our kitchen boy to top it up.

'What do you mean?'

'Oh come on darling. She and Danny Boy had an affair nearly four years ago and she has a three-year-old. Work it out.'

'But that was with her husband.'

'What that drunken old sod? I don't think he could get it up if he tried, which is why she probably had the affair,' she said.

'So why didn't she ever have a paternity test?'

'Probably because at the time she was married, Daniel was married, and then you came along. Bet she hated you.'

'But she seemed really nice to me.'

'Lottie, when will you ever learn?' she said, with what looked like a genuine expression of pity.

It was then out of the corner of my eye I saw her standing in the doorway with her familiar brown bob, deep red lips, ultra high heels and tight black dress. She spotted me and walked over, clapping her hands with glee as she spotted my ring.

'So it's true. You and Kevan. How marvellous.'

'Meg what are you doing here? This is a private party.'

'I came to say sorry. About being so beastly to you, right from the start. You know when you made that lovely cake for Daniel's birthday and I spoiled it all by ordering a better one. I'm good at spoiling things.'

This was beginning to sound weird. I tried to catch Kevan's eye but he was busy talking to some of our guests.

'What do you mean Meg?'

She took me to one side and spoke in a whisper. 'I could spoil things for you by telling the press that you stole Beth's phone and photographed the text messages which broke up their marriage and caused the suicide attempt. They might still be together if it hadn't been for you.'

I should have known Meg had been feeding Beth every piece of information she'd been able to hear by listening at doors and probably checking Daniel's emails and texts. It occurred to me, with the copy-cat outfits, that maybe it was Beth she had a thing for, not Daniel. After all there had never been a sign of a real boyfriend. Up until now, I'd been willing to ask Kevan to escort her out of the party as politely as possible. What ruined her chances was the silly little giggle she gave me, as if to say, guess what I can do to you.

Grabbing her by the arm, I marched her towards the top of the stairs. 'Better still, how about I call the police and tell them you've admitted to stalking me on Twitter and that you came to my house and threatened me with a knife in my kitchen. Do you think your darling Daniel will keep you on then?'

'But I didn't threaten you with a knife.'

'No, and I didn't break up Beth's marriage. She managed that all by herself. And since you haven't denied the death tweets, I think I can take that as an admission. It should be easy enough for the police to find out if it was you threatening me on Twitter. So I suggest you get the hell out of here you nasty little troll, and stay out of my life.'

If looks could kill I think I would already be dead.

'What the hell was she doing here?' asked Kevan just as Meg disappeared down the stairs.

'You don't want to know.'

'Looks like you handled it.'

'Yeh, I did, didn't I?'

He took my hand and walked me back into the party. 'But then I didn't have any doubts you would. Someone like you.'

The End

About Pam

Pam Francis has been a journalist since she was 18, interviewing some of the biggest names in showbusiness over the past 30 years. She still writes for national magazines and newspapers.
She has two grown-up children, a granddaughter and lives with her partner Mike and cat Saffy in Bedfordshire.

Twitter:@pammiefrancis

Message From Pam

If you enjoyed the book, please let me know, and leave a review on Amazon.
I'd love to hear from you, so do contact me on my website www. pamfrancis.co.uk.

33084625R00162

Printed in Great Britain
by Amazon